HOUSE OF FIRE

PARALLEL MAGIC: BOOK TWO

EMMA L. ADAMS

The first enemy I made as the Death King's official Fire Element was a zombie horse named Neddie.

The skeletal beast hissed and snapped its sharp teeth at me when I tried to climb onto its back. Its polished forehead reflected the weak sunlight from the overcast sky above, while a shadowy figure floated up to my side, laughing under her breath as I tried to mount the stubborn horse.

"What's the problem?" I said to Neddie.

"Probably scared you'll set him on fire," commented Harper.

I withdrew my hand before I lost a finger. "Good chance of it if he keeps biting me."

Harper was a lich, a reanimated ghost of sorts whose soul was bound to an amulet in exchange for immortality. Nothing out of the ordinary for a castle full of similar shadowy beings without any visible features and reanimated skeletal wights that far outnumbered any living people. The zombie horses, though, I hadn't expected.

Neddie snorted again and snapped his teeth inches from my hand. I gave him a glare. "Have it your way, then. I'll find another steed."

"Why do you need a horse, anyway?" asked Harper.

"I'm sick of getting mud on my boots," I responded. "We can't all wear nothing but a semi-transparent cloak and defy gravity. Besides, I like to know there's an easy way out if I'm being chased."

My first rule for living in the Parallel: always be ready to run. Or ride, as the case may be. If my steed cooperated, that is. The swamp was hard to traverse on foot, even wearing the new heavy black boots the Death King had given me. He'd also given me matching dark trousers and shirt, laced with armoured material which offered protection while being lightweight enough not to slow me down. I also wore a cloak lined with fiery crimson and embossed with the Death King's symbol of four elemental symbols surrounded a skull. Kind of overkill, pun intended, but I looked actually intimidating for once in my life. It didn't hurt that my dark brown hair was positively glossy after having access to adequate showering facilities for the first time in forever, while a disguise charm I wore around my neck hid my pointed ears and elven features. I hadn't quite got used to showing my real face—old habits died hard—but it was nice to command a little respect for once.

Footsteps sounded and two people wearing armour like mine, a tall black woman and a tall Asian guy, walked into view. Felicity, the Water Element, gave Neddie the horse a confused look. "What are you doing, trying to tame him?"

"He doesn't like fire mages," said Cal, the Earth Element.

"Told you so," said Harper.

Neither of them appeared bothered at talking to a floating cloak without a face, but they'd lived here in the castle for years. Felicity had been nice to me so far, unlike the other Elemental Soldiers, but I knew better than to expect it last. I had secrets up to my eyeballs and a family which made the Death King's denizens look like cuddly bunny rabbits.

My second rule for living in the Parallel: adapt to survive. And taking on the job from the Death King had been necessary for my survival, so I'd deal with the consequences.

I went looking for another horse, but Neddie didn't like that. He cantered into my path and would have head-butted me across the swamp, had I not pivoted away at the last second. "What did I ever do to him?"

"Perhaps he senses nefarious intentions," said Ryan, joining their fellow Elemental Soldiers outside the castle. The Air Element looked more intimidating than the rest of us put together, with a shaved head and broad shoulders under their armour.

"I haven't got nefarious intentions," I protested. "I'm risking my neck for His Lordship's sake, you know."

"You should have more respect for our master," said the Air Element.

A small humanoid fiery figure floated past and snorted loudly. "I have no respect for anyone, and His Deathly Highness still lets me guard his hall of souls."

I felt an unexpected rush of gratitude towards Dex, which vanished when Neddie lunged out and knocked me flat on my arse, causing the fire sprite to burst into laughter.

"The Death King wants you, by the way," Dex said between snickers.

I lifted my head. "Did he mention why?"

"I assume he has a mission for you," Felicity said. "I wouldn't dawdle."

I tried to get to my feet, only for Neddie to knock me backwards again. Harper burst out laughing. Her voice was colder and higher as a lich than it'd been as a human, which made a frankly disturbing backdrop as I climbed upright and ran towards the castle before the zombie horse could hit me again.

I entered via the back door and walked past the Elemental Soldiers' quarters, which now included my new room. The Death King's official Fire Element got some pretty swanky perks, and until recently, I'd never have believed I'd go from living in a hovel to an honest-to-god *castle*, even if it did belong to the King of the Dead. Not that I'd had much chance to enjoy the accommodations yet, because I'd spent most of the time waiting for the other shoe to drop. Or zombie horse, as the case may be.

After walking down the wide stone corridor, I pushed open the oak doors to the main hall and approached the wooden dais on which the Death King stood. Tall and cloaked in armour the colour of the night and with his face hidden by a dark mask, his very aura radiated menace. His voice was cold and echoing when he spoke.

"I need someone to go to the House of Fire," he said, without preamble.

My heart missed a beat. "You want *me* to go to the House of Fire?"

"I was under the impression that you had contacts there," he said.

"They also want me dead," I said. "If I set foot in there, I'll be deader than one of your liches. Several times over."

He gave me a cold stare as though he didn't appreciate the joke. It was kind of impressive how someone without a visible face could pull off any sort of expression, but he managed to. "This is your job. You signed up for it."

Not really. I'd signed up to work as the Death King's soldier, not his spy, especially where the House of Fire was concerned. Let's just say we had an unpleasant history, the least of which was that they'd recently jailed Tay, my best friend. I'd felt that was the best outcome for her after she'd betrayed me, but it still hurt to know she'd put her own needs ahead of our friendship and my survival. She was probably safer behind bars than walking free, but that didn't mean my presence there wouldn't elevate the risk for both of us.

More to the point, this job was the first stable employment I'd ever had in my life and going back to the House of Fire might land me right back where I'd started. Admittedly, I'd fallen into the position by accident, but my third rule for living in the Parallel was to adapt to my surroundings. I hadn't expected to be removed from the castle so soon.

"It's my belief that the inferno cantrips used by the saboteurs during my Fire Element contest may have been developed by someone connected to the House of Fire," the Death King added. "I can trust you to ask a few questions, can't I?"

From the warning note underlaying his tone, I suspected that if I didn't, I'd find myself envying Tay's fate. "I have no idea whether anyone in the House of Fire might have been involved in creating those cantrips. Nobody I know there will tell me anything either way."

"Then you'd better find a way to get through to them," he said.

This dude made a soul-sucking phantom look reasonable. "I really don't think this is going to work."

"Then endeavour to speak to them and bring me a report on your progress, regardless of whether you're successful or not," he said. "Take your lich friend with you, if you like."

I doubted Harper wanted to set foot near the Houses either, but I wouldn't be able to argue further without risking drawing his ire and getting myself fired or worse. They said the Death King conscripted anyone who crossed him into his army of liches, and while he'd offered me this coveted job, the last person to wear the Fire Element's armour had ended up turning traitor and having his soul ripped out as a punishment.

"I will, but don't blame me if this goes wrong." I turned to leave, and almost collided with a small humanoid fiery person on the way out. "Dex, want to come with me?"

"Where?" said the fire sprite.

"The House of Fire."

"I have to join Liv to help with her D&D game," he said. "The House of Fire? That sounds like fun. What is it, a contest to see who can start the biggest bonfire?"

"D&D?" I said. "Oh, your Dungeons & Dragons game. How can you play? I mean, you don't have hands."

He made a sharp noise of indignation. "I'm going to pretend I didn't hear you say that."

"Didn't mean to hurt your feelings," I said. "The House of Fire, though, it's hardly a party." *Especially if they* did *create those inferno cantrips.*

They hadn't, though. I already knew the culprit, and it was someone who made a night in the House of Fire's cells seem like a relaxing day at the beach.

Dex flew off, pouting, so I left the fire sprite and made my way out of the castle. I found Harper and Felicity beside Neddie, who seemed quite serene now I wasn't trying to tame him.

"See?" said Felicity, petting him. "He's harmless when you're nice to him."

"I was being nice," I objected. "Nicer than the liches, I reckon. Anyway, I'm not gonna need a ride where I'm going."

Even a transporter spell wouldn't get me out of the House of Fire's cells if they decided that I'd be better off joining Tay behind bars.

"What did the Death King want?" asked Harper, as Felicity vaulted onto the horse's back and cantered away across the swampland.

"He needs someone to go to the House of Fire," I said. "I know. He's got it into his head that the people at the House know the origins of those inferno cantrips."

"Ugh," she said. "Count me out."

"I wasn't gonna ask you to come with me," I said. "I know you hate that place."

Not that I was keen on a trip down memory lane

myself, but while I had an inkling I knew precisely who'd made those inferno cantrips, their location remained a mystery to me. On the other hand, the Houses were unlikely to know where they were hiding, either. After all, the people in question were the last prisoners known to have escaped the Houses' strongholds, years after my own escape.

"You haven't heard from the Spirit Agents?" she asked.

"Not yet, but I doubt they want to get involved in House drama," I said.

The Spirit Agents were independent mages allied to the Death King, since there were only Houses for the other four elements and not the spirit mages. I was pretty sure they'd want to know about the Death King sending me to the House of Fire, but I hadn't lied when I'd said it was a waste of time. I'd go there, they'd shut the door in my face, and then I'd find something else to do instead after risking my dignity and my new job—not to mention the safety that came with it. As safe as it was possible to be in a castle of the dead, anyway.

As there was no sense in delaying, I checked I had enough cantrips on me and claimed a sword from the castle armoury. Then I walked out of the gates in front of the castle and headed for the gleaming node which stood alone in the swampland like a geyser of pure white light. when I stepped into the midst of the current of energy, the light soared above my head and blanketed the castle in a pale glow. In my mind's eye, I fixed an image of the city of Elysium, my former home, and the location of both the Spirit Agents and the Houses of the Elements.

The swamp vanished in a flash of light, and I reappeared in a narrow alleyway. As the largest city in the part of the Parallel which overlapped with the UK, Elysium had been hit hard by the war thirty-odd years ago, and large parts of it had been destroyed and rebuilt. The four Houses were placed at intervals at each corner of a square in the very heart of the city, facing outwards as though the people who'd built them had intentionally wanted to avoid anyone having to look directly at the former Citadel of the Elements. I kept one eye on the towering obsidian shape as I made my way around the warren of streets until I found the right building.

The House of Fire stood on the southwest corner of the square, its bricks scorched with burn marks from escaped prisoners. A formidable structure several storeys high, it held several underground dungeons in addition to the floors above the surface. On the other side of the nodes dividing the two realms, London had a robust underground transport system. What did Elysium get? High-security prisons for mages who stepped out of line or otherwise ticked off the authorities. I'd done more than step out of line, though. I'd danced over the line a thousand times and even then, prison had been safer than where I'd grown up. That was partly why I'd stayed here in Elysium after walking free, and why I felt little fear that I'd find myself caged again. My old haunts had been miles north of here, and besides, nobody would be able to legally arrest me now I worked for the Court of the Dead.

Didn't stop apprehension from locking around my chest as I walked up to the crimson door of the House of Fire and knocked. My heart hammered against my ribcage, old instincts urging me to get away, and I found myself wishing I'd persuaded Harper to come with me. As a lich, the guards would never have recognised her unless she spoke. But me? Everyone in this building knew my name.

Sure enough, the man who answered the door narrowed his eyes in recognition. "I know you. I never forget a face."

I hadn't forgotten his, either. Harris, security guard for the House of Fire and royal pain in the arse. Squat, flat-faced and with enough grease in his hair to put on a barbecue, he regarded me as though he'd happened upon a giant spider he wanted to crush beneath the heel of his boot.

"Good for you," I said. "The Death King sent me. I'm here as his official Fire Element."

"And I'm a vampire lord."

Ha ha. I showed him the skull symbol imprinted on my crimson-lined cloak. "See that? It's his logo."

"What poor sap did you steal that from?"

"Wasn't the former Fire Element once an inmate here before the Death King hired him?" I queried. "Is it hard to believe I followed in his path?"

The last Fire Element, Davies, had been saved from imprisonment in the House of Fire by the Death King, and had then thrown it back in his master's face and betrayed him. For all I knew, maybe this was a kind of test to ensure I wouldn't do the same.

"You're not even a proper mage," he said. "You're a freak."

Anger stirred, but I met his stare. "I wanted to talk to someone inside the House of Fire about a matter of importance to the Death King."

"It better be bloody important, then," he said. "Someone was murdered today. Nobody is allowed in."

"Murdered?" I echoed. "Who?"

Not an inmate, surely. They didn't exactly value their prisoners highly, especially people like me.

He tilted his head. "Weren't you friends with that Tay girl? The one with the exploding magic?"

I tensed. "What of it?"

He gave a cold laugh. "She's the one that done it."

My blood turned to ice. "What? Tay didn't do anything."

"I beg to differ." He leaned on the door frame, a leer twisting his mouth. "She's the main suspect. She was found at the scene of the crime."

"There has to be a mistake." I took a step towards the door. "Can you let me in? I'll talk to the man in charge. Maybe—"

"The man in charge is the one who died," he said. "Chief jailor."

"What?" No. He had to be lying. "You mean Zade?"

"The one and only." His leer twisted into an expression that contained more anger than humour. "Your friend is doomed, Bria."

Shit. His tone was dead serious. The former jailor of the House of Fire, who'd tormented me throughout my imprisonment, was dead.

2

I passed the sneering guard and walked into the hallway. Every inch of the place was seared into my memory from my inprisonment here, and it was easy for me to navigate my way through the whitewashed corridors to the source of the murmuring voices coming from behind a wooden door.

The jailor's body had been laid out on a low wooden table inside the room, and several other guards glanced at each other and muttered when I walked in. Ignoring their stares, I looked down at the body, at the face I'd seen from the other side of a barred door more times than I'd could count. He'd taken great pleasure in pushing the boundaries as to what the House was allowed to get away with in how they treated their prisoners, be it taunting me through the bars or 'forgetting' to feed me for days at a time. Yet lying there on the table, he looked unexpectedly pathetic, from the dishevelment of his usually neatly combed grey hair to the reddened blisters fanning across his papery skin which made him look like he'd been stung by a flock of angry hornets. The red-and-black uniform all the guards wore did not help that impression.

I wrenched my gaze away from Zade's face. "How did he die?"

"His body shut down, seemingly of its own accord," Harris said dispassionately. "We found a cantrip at the scene, but it was blank. Convenient."

"Where—" I broke off, seeing a blank cantrip lying on the edge of the table, face-down. Even blank, I recognised the signature on the back of the golden coin.

The Family. The Family had created the cantrip. I wouldn't lie, part of me had always wondered if someone in here hadn't contributed to their escape. They were supposed to be incarcerated in the Houses' most secure prison, not walking free.

Not using their cantrips to kill people.

"What's she doing in here?" said one of the other guards. "Isn't she... wait, isn't that the *Death King's* symbol?"

"Got it in one." I flashed the scarlet interior of my cloak at them. "Where did this cantrip come from?"

"As if you don't know," said Harris.

I frowned at him. "I had nothing to do with this. I've been in the Court of the Dead ever since the trials for the next Fire Element came to an end. Ask the Death King to back me up if you don't believe me."

"Bold claim, that," said one of the other guards.

"Sure you want to risk pissing him off?" I said. "He sent me to negotiate with you about a new agreement between the Court of the Dead and the Houses of the Elements."

"A likely story," said Harris. "You're a former inmate.

Why would the King of the Dead give a job to the likes of you?"

"It's true," I told the guards. "Turns out I have the skills he wanted for his personal Fire Element, so he gave me the position. I take it you're declining the Death King's offer?"

I hadn't exactly expected the House to fall over themselves to team up with the Court of the Dead, but the fact that they outright refused to believe I worked for the Death King pissed me off to no end.

"Tell your boss," said Harris, "that we have our own business to deal with at this moment in time. Feel free to also tell him his new Fire Element's best friend is a murdering liar."

"You mean you really think Tay's the one who killed Zade?" I said. "Where would she have got hold of a cantrip? I assume you had the sense to confiscate everything she brought in with her."

I'd thought his comment about Tay was a taunt, but had she really been out of her cell when Zade had died? She wasn't good at following orders at the best of times, but she must have known better than to murder the chief jailor and get herself caught at the scene of the crime. Besides, she couldn't have got hold of a cantrip from behind bars. Right?

"You tell me," said Harris. "Your friend Tay was out of her cell when he died. Facts are facts."

"She couldn't have got her hands on anything," I said. "Not if she never left the place and was under constant guard. If there *is* a chance she might've got hold of a cantrip and sneaked out of her cell, then blame your own security for not keeping a close enough eye on her."

Harris scowled. "She's a sneaky bitch. She has magic."

"She can't walk through walls," I said. "If someone managed to break in here and spoke to her, you might want to have another look at that, not focus all your attention on Tay."

Like me, Tay's magic was different than the norm. Her ability to control and channel electric energy was previously unheard of, in fact, but the very walls of the dungeon cell would have muted her power. Not even spirit mages could use their astral projecting abilities to get into the lower levels of the building. So if someone had given her the means of killing a guard, they'd have had to walk in through the doors in person. Either the guards were admitting their security held more holes than my old shoes did, or they were too convinced that both Tay and I were lying to consider there might be issues with their assumptions.

Harris walked up to me and waved the cantrip in my face. "You know where this cantrip came from?"

"No." It wasn't a lie. The Family didn't have the same resources as they had before. Or I thought they didn't. "Don't look at me like that. I have nothing to do with the Family and I have no idea where they're hiding. I thought *you* were the ones who were supposed to keep them incarcerated. Have standards slipped that much?"

Harris loomed closer, so close that I could smell the smoke on his breath. "You want to be locked up, too, is that it?"

"You're welcome to try," I said. "And see if your security can keep out the Death King himself."

"Don't lock her up," said one of the other guards.

"Look, she's definitely wearing his gear. She can't have taken it from Davies. We removed his body."

Harris shot him a glare. "Then she stole it from the castle. The Death King is losing control of his army, the rumours say."

"Not me." I folded my arms. "You know, it'll go a lot easier for all of us if you believed me. Do you want me to tell the Death King that you have no interest in accepting his offer to work with him?"

"Not as long as your friend refuses to admit to any wrongdoing," said Harris. "As long as there's a killer loose in here, we're not wasting our time by sending our people to negotiate with the Court of the Dead."

"Why don't I talk to her myself?" I asked.

I didn't expect him to say yes, but another guard spoke up first. "Why not? Maybe the Death King's Fire Element can help loosen her tongue. Better than waiting for her to decide to speak to us herself. Unless she responds better to force."

"If you hurt her," I began heatedly, "I'll bring a pack of liches in here with or without the Death King's permission."

"The Death King doesn't give a shit about the mages," said Harris. "He doesn't care about your friend."

Unfortunately, he might be right on that one, but that didn't mean I'd let them get away with tormenting Tay. While they didn't often use torture on their prisoners, it wasn't illegal here in the Parallel, not when the Houses themselves had written the very laws governing the city of Elysium.

The prisoners were organised by floor, with the least dangerous on the upper floors and the highest risk prisoners on the lower levels. Tay's danger level had her on the lowest possible floor, and during our imprisonment, we'd been in cells opposite one another on the same corridor. Ironically, behind bars was the best place I could have been the first time Zade had hauled me in here. At least until I'd been certain my so-called family weren't going to be able to escape their own secure cells. More than five years had passed since then, yet the sight of the narrow staircase leading down into the depths of the prison brought all those old memories roaring to the surface.

It'd been pure chance that'd seen Tay and I imprisoned close together. The House's guards might not know all the details of my past, but they knew who'd raised me, who'd been responsible for my magical talent, and they hadn't taken any chances. What they'd overlooked was that while Tay hadn't been raised by the Family herself, their cantrips had gifted her with magic which was volatile and hard to control, and we'd bonded over that while plotting to escape. Eventually, we'd walked free and built a life together. Now that life lay in ashes, thanks to her decision to throw her lot in with a group of rogue spirit mages in the hopes of getting her magic under control and being on the winning side in a new elemental war.

She'd paid the price for her choice. I felt it when I walked down the stairs to the lowest level—a pressure emanating from the row of cells that would have cut off my fire magic as effectively as dunking a bucket of water over my head. The cells were formed of thin bars made of an unbreakable metal, laced with the same material as the walls and ceiling of the dungeon which muted any magic that came into contact with it.

Inside her cell, Tay was doing sit-ups on the hard floor. It couldn't possibly be comfortable, but she'd never been good at dealing with being cooped up. The higher security prisoners weren't allowed out of their cells at all, for any reason. No privileges. No escape. Unless you were resourceful like us, that is.

Harris stood back to watch me as I approached the cell. "Tay?"

She lifted her head, then she moved into a sitting position against the wall. "They got you, too?"

"No."

Her gaze landed on the uniform I wore, and her eyes narrowed to slits. "I see how it is."

"Do you?" Defensiveness rose inside me. "I took the job working for the Death King because it's that or let the Family hunt me down. The Family you *helped when you turned against me.*"

"I'm not the one who encouraged them to come after you," she countered. "You're working for a murderer. You know how many people the Death King has had killed or turned into liches to join his army?"

"Look, I was originally going to take the job to keep both of us safe," I said. "Besides, you chose to turn your back on me. What was I supposed to do, go back to working for Striker? The authorities caught him, too."

"I know they did," she said. "You couldn't have picked anyone else to work for? The Court of the Dead is going to be one of the first places to fall apart when the war kicks off."

"I thought the war was on hold after most of the conspirators ended up jailed." Including Shawn and the surviving spirit mages who'd betrayed the Spirit Agents.

Most of the fire mages who'd tried to infiltrate the Death King's castle had ended up dead or jailed, too.

Okay, I understood why the guards wouldn't believe in Tay's innocence of the jailor's death. Considering her allies had killed people and she'd let it slide, I wasn't sure *I* did, either.

"Not at all," she said. "You haven't seen the half of it yet."

"See, this is what I mean," I said, trying to suppress a shiver of dread at her words. "You accuse me of working for a murderer, but I know what Adair and the Family did. I saw it for myself. Yet you worked with someone who was responsible for everything that went wrong in both our lives."

She ducked her head, not before I spotted a shimmer of guilt in her eyes. "The Family will be on the winning side in the war, I guarantee it. They'll be ready to pick up the pieces."

I didn't doubt they would. The Family didn't start wars, for the most part. They just cleaned up the aftermath. Yet there was nothing they could gain from another conflict which they didn't already have.

Except me, a voice whispered in the back of my mind. I'd left Adair behind, left him for dead, and while he was as tightly locked up as Tay was, I couldn't help wondering how he'd got out the first time around. Admittedly, there's not much you can do to keep a half-elf, half-human semi-immortal with unpredictable magic under lock and key. Adair had the additional advantage of being able to use his own magic to persuade anyone to obey him, and I wasn't sure even the magical protection on the dungeon would be able to keep it contained. If he was given the slightest leeway, he'd walk free once again, and I'd prefer not to end up taking the blame if he did. Though chance would be a fine thing if the Death King kept sending me to *talk* to these people. At least my alibi was solid and there was no denying I wore the symbol of the Court of the Dead.

"Why did you come here, anyway?" asked Tay.

"Why else? The head jailor was found dead and you're the main suspect." I sucked in a breath. "You know what they'll do if you're found guilty. I couldn't walk away after that."

"Do *you* think I did it?"

"You tell me," I said.

She gave a shrug. "Guess you wouldn't believe me either way."

That stung, but I brushed it off. "You haven't seen Adair since they brought you in? Or heard from him?"

"How would I? He's miles away on the other side of this floor."

That's not an answer. Adair's mind-controlling abilities might have easily convinced her to kill the jailor if he'd managed to make eye contact with her during her brief escape from her cell. She wouldn't have needed a cantrip to kill if she'd had access to her magic, but she didn't. Adair, on the other hand? The verdict was out on that one.

"Then why were you out of your cell?" I asked.

Her eyes narrowed. "None of your business."

I threw up my hands in exasperation. "Tay, I'm trying to save your life."

"I don't need your help," she said. "I'll speak for myself."

"You want to be executed for a crime you claim not to have committed?" I said. "Can't you put aside our personal issues and focus on the big picture here? I'll gladly leave you be if you just tell me what you want."

"I don't want to die." She spoke to her hands, not looking at me in the eyes. "But they've already decided I'm guilty. And I'm not willing to provide evidence otherwise."

"There you have it," Harris said from behind me. "Sure your Death King master will come to the aid of a dead woman?"

Tay's head snapped up, disbelief colouring her voice. "That's what you said? You told the guards the Death King would help save me?"

Heat seared my neck. "Actually, that isn't what I said. I did say that I'd bring a group of liches here to stop your execution if necessary, whether the Death King gave permission or not, but I'm thinking of retracting that promise."

"You think a bunch of dead people can help me?" she said.

"I reckon the liches can give it a shot." I turned to Harris. "I know you want a straight answer from her, but if I were you, I'd keep an eye on Adair. The guy can use persuasive magic. He might have ordered her not to answer any questions."

"Don't tell me what to do," said Harris.

"I bet Adair's hard to keep contained," I added, ignoring his petulant tone. "Does his magic still work in here? Because that's one hell of a gamble to take, unless you keep him blindfolded."

"Like you could do any better."

I lifted my head. "You know liches are immune to his persuasive magic, don't you? If you ask me, he'd be more secure in the Death King's jail than here. I'd like to see him try to convince *them* he had nothing to do with the jailor's death."

"What?" He cocked a brow at me. "Nobody told me that before."

"I thought you knew." Admittedly, most people didn't consider immortal lich lords when designing their jail cells. "Does that make you think differently about the Death King's offer of cooperation with the House of Fire?"

Tay made a sceptical noise. "He could gain the cooperation of all the Houses and it'd make no difference. The war will bring this place crashing down. It's only a matter of time."

"You want me to make you take back those words?" said Harris.

"Okay, that's enough," I said. "Tay, if you aren't going to help me, then good luck. I'm outta here."

In truth, I was worried she'd provoke the guards into inflicting a worse punishment on her, and I had nothing more to say to convince her to admit the truth. Not as long as Adair held her in his grip. So I stepped away from her cell and followed Harris back upstairs, my mind ticking over the possibilities. Would the Death King dismiss my idea of taking Adair into custody outright, even if the House of Fire somehow agreed to the transfer?

"Bitch deserves to die," said Harris.

Anger clenched inside me, even if I knew Tay hadn't exactly made herself look the picture of innocence. "Look, I'm ninety percent sure Adair hit her with a full blast of his magic. It wouldn't surprise me if he convinced her to kill the jailor before he was even imprisoned."

"Even if he did, she broke out of her cage by herself." He tilted his head. "You want to visit *him* next?"

"No thanks." I suppressed a shudder, well aware that some of the guards believed I would take Adair's side, given the chance. At least my new job gave me some measure of protection—once they stopped denying that I was telling the truth about being the new Fire Element, that is. Which might take a face-to-face meeting with the Death King himself.

Unfortunately, I was going to have to go back to him and explain that the House of Fire refused to commit to any kind of deal for the time being, at least until he was able to give them an offer they might accept. If he did offer to take Adair off their hands, it would solve a lot of problems for them, and as a bonus, it would solve my worry that he'd give them the slip at the first opportunity.

On the other hand, the idea of Adair being imprisoned next door to my place of employment didn't exactly fill me with confidence either. Yet if he refused to confess to being behind the jailor's death, then Tay would pay the price for it.

Harris reached the top of the stairs. "She'll have one trial. One chance to explain herself. That's all."

"Are you sure you shouldn't be focusing on Adair instead?" I pressed. "Unlike Tay, he definitely has the ability to influence people to do his bidding, and I'm not sure even the defences on this place can dampen it completely. How did he and the others get out last time?"

"Did you think I'd tell you?" He gave me a contemptuous stare. "You're lucky you didn't get arrested for aiding in their escape."

"I didn't know they escaped at all until Adair tried to kill me," I pointed out. "*When* did it happen? Come on, you might as well tell me. They're already at large."

He scowled. "Less than a month ago. What does that have to do with anything?"

If they were involved with the jailor's murder? A lot, possibly. Especially as the Family seemed to be making contingency plans for a war in which I wasn't even sure who the major players were. I couldn't think why the Family would murder the lead jailor, though, unless they'd intended to have revenge on the Houses for imprisoning them. But that didn't work either. It hadn't been the House of Fire's jailor who'd been in charge of their incarceration after they'd been dug out of the wreckage of their house. They'd been locked up in a different facility north of the city, as far as I was aware.

"Because they used to make a living selling illegal cantrips." I walked down the corridor to the room which contained Zade's body, where I lifted the cantrip from the table, displaying the symbol on its surface. "That's their signature. I thought their factories shut down five years ago."

Or more accurately, burned down. I'd set the entire estate ablaze during my escape.

"You think your family made that cantrip?" Harris said from behind me. "Am I supposed to believe you weren't involved?"

"Can I take this with me?" I said, ignoring his taunts. "Maybe the Death King knows where it came from."

Unlikely, but I could ask Miles or his friends if he

didn't. If it'd been obtained somewhere local, the Spirit Agents would be more likely to know, since they were based here in Elysium. As the cantrip itself was blank, it wasn't like I could use it against anyone, as the guards ought to know well.

"Go ahead," said Harris. "And don't come back here again unless you have something useful to say."

I slipped the cantrip into my pocket. Whether Tay had been the killer or not, it wouldn't hurt to figure out how the murderer had taken the guard's life without leaving more than a rash on his face.

"I'll inform the Death King you have no desire for an alliance with him," I said to him, reaching the door. "Or should I mention that you might be open to transferring a certain prisoner to the Court of the Dead?"

A muscle ticked in his jaw. "Is it true? He can't use his powers on the dead?"

"Yes, it's true." I didn't expect him to take my word for it, but the Death King would gladly confirm anything I said. "It's also true that he's more likely to start talking if the Death King is the one running the interrogation."

Harris studied me. "I'll ask. If it turns out you're bull-shitting, we'll move up your friend's trial."

My hands clenched at my sides, over the cantrip in my hand. "If you even think about hurting Tay without first considering the Death King's offer, then I'll insert this cantrip somewhere you won't forget in a hurry."

And with that, I left the House of Fire and walked out into the street. The citadel towered over the rooftops, an obsidian structure gleaming against the overcast sky. While a node gleamed nearby, it wasn't too far a walk to the Spirit Agents' home from here. While I hadn't heard from any of them since my first day working for the Death King, they'd want to know about the strange murder in the heart of the House of Fire.

Not that any of them were fans of Tay, either… but despite it all, I didn't want her to die.

3

It took me close to an hour of walking in circles through the confusing warren of streets around Elysium's centre before I reached the house where the Spirit Agents made their home. It was a pretty nice house by the Parallel's standards, with whitewashed walls and a wide garden with neatly trimmed lawns. Someone among the Spirit Agents must be a keen gardener, because it wasn't exactly common to hire services to mow one's lawn here in the Parallel, where having a roof over your head was in no way guaranteed.

I entered via the gate and knocked on the red-painted door. I hoped Miles might answer, but Tate, a guy of around my age with dark skin and hair shaved to stubble, looked me up and down and said in disinterested tones, "Oh, it's you."

"Nice to see you, too," I said. "Is Miles in?"

"Sure." He called over his shoulder, "Miles?"

Miles appeared at the door a few seconds later, his straw-coloured hair rumpled as though he'd neglected to cut it recently. Together with his casual clothes and lean and unassuming figure, he looked nothing like he could rip the soul out of a person with his fingertips if he wanted to. The Death King might have the intimidation factor mastered, but the understated threat of the average spirit mage meant that few would look at the group of close-knit twenty-somethings and teenagers who lived here and believe they could give the Houses of the Elements a run for their money.

"Hey, Bria." Miles's mouth quirked in surprise at the sight of me on the doorstep. "Did the Death King send you to reprimand me for not checking in with him?"

"Nah, I was in the area and thought I'd drop by to talk." I added the unspoken word *alone*. While the other Spirit Agents were his closest friends, I'd prefer that they didn't find out about the jailor's death *or* that my ex-best friend was suspected of his murder, even if Zade had been a total wanker whose fate I'd hardly shed tears over.

"We can talk out here," he said, indicating the garden.

"Sure." The two of us walked across the path winding through the lawn. Several vampire chickens were still roaming around, and I watched them peck at the ground for a moment while I gathered my thoughts. "Who set up this place? I didn't know Spirit Agents were keen gardeners."

"Tate and Shelley," he responded. "This is possibly the best-tended garden in the entire Parallel. The house used to belong to a vampire, you know, so we take good care of it."

"Seriously?" I looked up at the house, trying to picture a shadowy vampire roaming its bright corridors. "Why would anyone abandon a house like this?"

"The house's owner left Elysium to join the vampires' council in Arcadia," he said. "Lord Blackbourne let us have the property. He's the leading vampire lord."

"I think I've seen him before," I responded. "He's a friend of the Death King's, right?"

"Sure," he said. "Speaking of whom, how's living in the castle working out for you? The job isn't too strenuous, right?"

"It wasn't, at least until he sent me to the House of Fire to negotiate with them," I said. "Which went off the rails when it turned out someone was murdered in their jail."

"Eventful week, then?" he said. "Who died?"

"The chief jailor," I said. "Not someone I particularly liked. The slight problem is that everyone is trying to blame Tay for it. She somehow got out of her cage at the time of his death and is refusing to admit why."

"You think she's innocent?" He lowered his voice, his jaw tensed. "You know what she did to you. To all of us."

I knew, all right. Her betrayal had nearly got us killed. Several of the Spirit Agents *had* died in the battle, which meant their distrust of me wasn't without reason. They were the ones who'd got me into the Death King's contest to begin with, but I gathered that nobody here had expected me to win. I pretended not to see the faces watching us from the windows, turning my head away and dropping my voice.

"I don't know why she'd bother lying," I murmured. "I *think* she went to speak to Adair when she was out of her cage, so he might have used his mind-control on her, but I don't know where she would have got the cantrip which killed the guard. Pretty sure they took all her weapons off her when they brought her in."

"Then she got it from one of his allies," said Miles. "She's resourceful, isn't she? If she won't tell you she's innocent, she's got something to hide."

I should have known Miles wouldn't believe she was innocent, though I wasn't certain why I did, either. Old naivety, perhaps. Or the nagging sense that the rest of the Family had been awfully quiet about Adair ending up in jail again. I would have expected them to at least make a move to get their beloved son out of the House of Fire, but I hadn't heard a word from them yet. They must know about my new position at the Death King's side, too, and their ongoing silence made me edgy, to say the least.

I pulled the blank cantrip I'd taken from the House of Fire out of my pocket and showed it to Miles. "I know it's blank now, but this is the cantrip that was used to kill the jailor. Check out the mark on the back. Have you seen it before?"

He examined the gleaming gold surface. "There've been a lot of those blank cantrips around lately. They aren't local, but I've never seen that mark on any of them before."

"It's the Family's signature," I told him. "It used to be on every cantrip they manufactured. When they were jailed, everything they owned was destroyed. Or I thought it was."

His brows rose. "Manufactured?"

"The Family's house was like a giant factory for experimental magic," I explained. "They mostly did it via creating new cantrips. There weren't many cases where they used actual people to experiment on."

Like my brother and me. Mostly they sold cantrips to

anyone willing to take the risk to earn some quick cash and then monitored the results from a distance. I'd assumed Tay would have an aversion to anything they'd touched, cantrips included, but she'd gone as far as to take the Family's side during the recent conflict. Before, I'd never have seen her as a cold-blooded killer, whatever the Houses might have said about her. They'd said the same about me, after all. Yet given what she'd done, had I truly known her at all?

"The Family escaped jail, right?" Miles said. "You think they went back to their home?"

"Couldn't have," I said. "I burnt it down. Razed the whole property when I escaped and left them for dead, destroying all their cantrips for good measure."

My chest tightened with each word, as though part of me expected a bad reaction. Miles had accepted what I'd told him so far, but he hadn't seen the Family's depravity with his own eyes. Not yet.

"They must have found somewhere new to hide out, then," he said. "How'd the jailor die? What did the cantrip do to him?"

"His body shut down, they said," I said. "His face was covered in these odd blisters. That's all I saw. The guards might not necessarily have known it was a cantrip that did it if they hadn't found one next to the body."

"Yeah, doesn't sound familiar to me," he said. "I can check with the others, if that'll help. Maybe someone knows."

"I was going to take it to the Death King," I said. "Not that cantrips are his area of expertise either, but he tends to be in the know about everything going on in the Parallel."

Judging by the way he'd known half the contenders competing to become the next Fire Element had turned out to be working against him, the guy played a long game. But he didn't know the Family, not the way I did. Adair might be back in custody, but the others weren't, and even I didn't know their current whereabouts. The House of Fire had avoided making the information about their escape public, which perhaps wasn't a surprise. Telling the population of Elysium that there was a group of magically gifted mass murderers on the loose went against their policy of pretending to be completely in control of the city.

As for the Death King? He had little to do with the Houses. In fact, *I* was supposed to be the person who ferried information between the Houses and him, but I hadn't reckoned on them being so hostile to the notion of allying with him purely based on their hatred of me. I might have been a notorious criminal, but I'd also handed the Family to them in the first place. It'd taken all four of the Houses' combined strength to get the three of them behind bars, and only because I'd significantly weakened them. The odds of me pulling off the same stunt again were low, but it'd be nice if the House of Fire's guards wouldn't automatically jump to the conclusion that I was the one in the wrong. If they'd told me where the Family had fled to after their escape, I might even be able to track them down. With or without Tay's help.

"Yeah, the Death King will know," Miles said. "Why'd he send you to the House of Fire, anyway?"

"To see if they'd be willing to work with him." I shook my head. "He refused to listen when I told him they hate my guts, but I didn't expect to find them dealing with a murder. They won't even consider speaking to him until that's cleared up, but if he offers to take a certain prisoner off their hands, they might change their minds."

His eyes widened a little. "Your brother?"

"Not my brother, but yes." I grimaced. "Honestly, he'd probably be more secure with the Death King, but it wouldn't surprise me if he tried to make an escape while they were moving him to the castle. He already gave them the slip once."

"Yeah, they need to be careful," he said. "I'm surprised they didn't lock him up in one of their more secure facilities, like the one at the north of the city."

"I think that's where the whole Family was locked up until a month ago," I said. "The guards wouldn't tell me the details, but it's the most secure of their prisons and the Family still managed to break out of there. I reckon that's why the House of Fire took Adair in instead, so the others wouldn't have the same knowledge of the layout. Once they've broken out of a place once, they'd be able to do the same again."

I was kind of surprised they hadn't tried to come and get him anyway, but it was beyond me to figure out the motives of the two people who'd raised me. For all we knew, they'd left Adair there as a punishment for getting himself caught.

"Yeah, the House of Fire likes to keep everything quiet," Miles said. "They barely acknowledge we exist, which works in our favour."

"Shawn thought they were going to take all the city's mages under their control," I said. "Including spirit mages."

His jaw tightened. "Shawn thought that turning on the

rest of us would be justified if it meant he could get revenge on behalf of the spirit mages who died in the war."

"I'm sorry," I said, wishing I hadn't brought up the subject. Shawn had been one of Miles's friends as well as a fellow Spirit Agent, and his betrayal hadn't helped their distrusting attitude towards me—or mine towards them.

"Don't worry about it," he said. "The others are having a hard time dealing with the fallout, but I'm just glad we found out before we started working closer with the Death King again."

"Be glad he revealed his true colours. He's an arsehole." I looked up at the sound of footsteps around the corner and saw the silhouette of someone outside the gate. "I think you have a visitor."

"Maybe they're here to pick up the vampire chickens," he commented.

"I thought you were keeping them."

"Nah, sooner or later someone will notice and tell tales on us to the authorities." He walked around to the front of the house and halted dead in his tracks.

Harris, the security guard from the House of Fire, stood on the doorstep. Had he followed me here? Maybe I ought to have watched my back more carefully, but I had assumed the guards would have been glad to be rid of me. Two more guards joined him, all of them wearing the same red-and-black uniform. My body tensed at the sight of them, automatically falling into a defensive stance.

"You again," said Harris. "I thought you were going back to the Death King. Your... employer." His tone dripped with scepticism.

"I dropped by here first to catch up with a friend," I said. "What're you doing here?"

"We have a directive from the upper echelons of the four Houses of the Elements, aimed at all independent mages in the city," he said. "The new rules will ensure that the city of Elysium remains a safe place for mages and non-mages."

"What rules?" said Miles. "Who even are you?"

"Harris," he said. "Representative of the House of Fire."

"Meaning he does the grunt work nobody else wants too," I interjected. "What's got the Houses all agitated, then? Aside from the obvious?"

The Family? Perhaps the Houses weren't as indifferent to their escape as they seemed. The other guards scowled at me from behind Harris, cracking their knuckles.

"The amount of crimes committed by mages has been on the increase over the last few weeks," he said. "Especially mages who aren't registered with the Houses. How many people live here in this property?"

"None of your business," said Miles. "We aren't part of the Houses because we're spirit mages, and our own House was shafted after the war, in case you've forgotten. But I guess you were a kid back then."

I hadn't even known there'd ever been a House of Spirit at all. Not that I'd met many spirit mages before I'd had my first run-in with the Spirit Agents, because to my knowledge, they'd been virtually wiped out in the war thirty years prior.

The guard cleared his throat. "I'm going to have to carry out a house inspection."

"A what?" Miles said blankly. "Inspection? What are you now, our landlord?"

"The Houses of the Elements own all the properties in this city," said Harris. "Step aside. If you have nothing to hide, this will go quickly."

Miles looked as baffled as I felt. "You should let me tell the others first, otherwise they'll think we're under attack."

He pushed open the front door and walked in. I heard him exchange words with one of the other mages, and then he stuck his head out again. "Come on in. Don't touch anything if you want to keep your fingers."

I walked into the house behind Harris, more to keep an eye on him than anything else. The other spirit mages had gathered downstairs, watching the intruders with a mixture of wariness and confusion as their group split up to search the upper and lower floors. The war's impact on the Parallel's population of spirit mages explained why none of their group was older than their late twenties. They hadn't been born when their predecessors had met their tragic fates, yet like everyone here in the Parallel, they'd lived under the shadow of the war their whole lives.

As the guards continued rampaging through the house, I ended up awkwardly standing next to Shelley, Miles's second in command, who'd replaced Shawn after his betrayal. She was Tate's brother, as I'd learned recently, and they shared the same dark skin and broad features. Where Tate's hair was shaved to stubble, Shelley's contained a vibrant pink streak. While she was friendly enough to the others, she wasn't my biggest fan. For good reasons... like the ones who'd followed me here.

"I swear, if they trample the lawns..." Her mutters trailed off as one of the uniformed guards marched past and into the kitchen. "Don't you even think about stealing our food supplies."

"Not sure that's what they're after." I shifted uncomfortably as a couple of the other mages shot me accusing gazes. Both were teenage girls, already bearing the scars and distrustful air of people who'd long since resigned themselves to being treated as pariahs by the magical community at large. Damn if I didn't relate.

There has to be a better way than this. The Houses' original purpose was to protect the public, not paint mages as a dangerous menace and ignore the real problems. The intruders showed no fear of the spirit mages in their presence as they continued their search of the house, and Harris returned to the sitting room carrying a box of cantrips. "Just what are these for?"

"The cantrips?" said Miles. "For protection, what else?"

"Acquired legally?"

My heart sank a little. Was this part of the Houses' long-neglected promise to start cracking down on illegal cantrips? You'd think they'd be more concerned with the one which had killed the jailor, but this might be a test to learn if the Spirit Agents had been involved in his death.

"Yes," Tate told him. "We have a supplier."

Harris insisted on examining each cantrip individually, while his mates finished inspecting the rest of the house. Then he handed the box back to Miles. "We allow you to stay in this city with the understanding that you obey certain laws. If it turns out you have anyone or anything in this house which falls outside of those laws, we will punish everyone who lives under this roof equally."

"I don't recall breaking any laws," said Miles. "We were just minding our own business over here."

"Then you have nothing to fear from us," said Harris. "As for *you*, Bria Kent, if I find out you're lying, you know where you'll end up."

Behind bars. Yeah. I'd figured as much.

The three guards left the house without so much as an apology for the intrusion. Once they were gone, Miles went to the door and firmly closed it behind them. "Show's over, folks. Go back to whatever you were doing."

The spirit mages dispersed, with the exception of Shelley and Tate, whose shared look of suspicion wasn't lost on me. The former then went to the window to watch them leave, as though she didn't trust them not to set the garden on fire on their way out. Which wasn't that far out of the realm of possibility for a fire mage.

"They overlooked the vampire chickens altogether," I remarked. "What were they looking for, then?"

I suspected I knew what… or who. Harris thought the *Spirit Agents* had been sheltering the escaped Family members. That, or he'd been more worried about the cantrip which had killed Zade than he'd let on.

Miles shrugged. "Anything that might undermine their rule in the city, I imagine."

"That, or he wants to seize our property," said Shelley. "Wouldn't be the first time the Houses have decided the vampires' old houses are theirs for the taking. Luckily, we have the paperwork to send them packing."

"Damn right we do," Miles said. "It's not like we're encroaching on their territory. Unless you count the incident with the wyrm."

"Or the time we accidentally sent those phantoms inside the House of Water," Tate added from behind him.

"You did?" I said.

"Miles's fault, as per usual," said Shelley, with an eye-roll. "Really, it's amazing the Houses haven't taken him into custody by now."

"How long have you been here in this house?" I asked curiously. "I assume you didn't grow up here."

"We didn't," Miles said. "Not all of us did, anyway."

"You and Grey were already living here with some of the others when you were, like, fourteen," Shelley pointed out. "Tate and I came along later. We moved out of our parents' house when it became clear they viewed having two spirit mages in the family as a double dose of bad luck."

"Sorry," I said. "I know about family issues."

Miles shot me a look of sympathy, then glanced out the window. "They're retreating. Don't come back here, fuckers."

"Were you telling the truth about having a cantrip supplier?" I asked him.

"Yes," he said. "Why?"

"I think Harris might have been looking for the source of the cantrip which killed the jailor," I said. "That or he thought the Family might be here, but it makes no sense for them to assume you were hiding them in the attic or something."

"Unless they know about Shawn," he added.

"Good point." It was either that or they assumed I'd dragged the Spirit Agents into my nefarious plans, but Harris plainly hadn't expected to find me here. "Maybe they do, but Shawn was jailed long before Zade's murder."

"Help me out here." Shelley looked between us. "You're saying someone was murdered at the House of Fire. Did they follow you here and assume we were in on it?"

"No," I said hastily. "The guy was murdered before I even came to Elysium today. The Death King sent me to talk to the House of Fire, and I didn't know anything about the jailor's death until I got there."

Shelley made a noise of distaste. "Right. The Death King wants an alliance with the Houses?"

"Yeah," I said. "Have the Spirit Agents ever cooperated with the Houses before? You mentioned the House of Spirit…"

"The Court of the Dead *is* the House of Spirit," said Miles.

"Wait, it is?" I said, disarmed.

"I thought you knew," he said. "All the surviving members of the House of Spirit got turned into liches after the war. We're what's left of the next generation of spirit mages who managed to escape the cull, mostly because we were born into non-spirit mage families. That's why we're not given the same authority as the Houses or recognised as a House in our own right."

This was news to me. "I know the other Houses ended up turning into prisons for mages after the war, but I didn't know there was ever a House for spirit mages. I assumed you did your own thing."

"We do," he said. "But any spirit mage who's related to anyone in the House of Spirit always ends up as a lich. Nothing we can do about it."

"You're not going to turn, are you?" I asked.

"Nah," he said. "I'm safe. No spirit mages in my family except for me."

"Good." I looked from him to Shelley and Tate, thinking of what she'd said earlier about him living here since he was a teenager. "So… you moved here when you were fourteen?"

"Not alone," he said. "There were half a dozen of us back then. Grey was the oldest… he became Death King at eighteen or thereabouts."

"Grey?" I echoed. "The Death King has a name?"

"Most people do," he said, amusement glittering in his eyes. "As for me… well, my parents are safely and happily incarcerated in the Houses' facility in the north of Elysium. They couldn't really take care of me after that."

His words knocked the breath from me. "They… they were arrested? For what?"

What had they done to get themselves locked up in the highest security prison for magical criminals in the city? The same place my family had been locked up in, no less, before they'd escaped? It seemed I was mistaken in thinking I was the only one of the pair of us sitting on some major secrets.

His mouth pressed into a line. "My parents are mages, but not spirit mages. They were House members, until they did something the Houses didn't like, and that was the result."

"Damn," I said. "I'm sorry."

"It was a long time ago," he said. "Those guys who came here to search the place didn't taunt me about it, so they might not know who I am."

"I guess they were more interested in looking for the Family," I said. "Or your cantrips."

Shelley gave me an appraising look. "Or the murderer?"

"Hey, don't look at me," I said. "They're the ones who decided to imprison Adair in their basement. The dude has mind-control powers which might be able to circumvent their magic-suppressing security. He might've convinced anyone to commit murder on his behalf."

"Isn't your friend in there, too?" said Tate.

Dammit. I should have guessed the others wouldn't forget so easily. "Yes. She claims she didn't do it. Even if she did, though, Adair's power gives him total control over the other person. I guarantee he'd have given her no choice."

"Like when she betrayed us?" said Shelley.

I shook my head. "I know you don't like Tay. I don't trust her either. But if she's found guilty, she dies, and the real killer gets away with it. Besides, someone smuggled that cantrip into jail in order to commit murder, and I'd like to know who was responsible. And where they got it."

Tay's own magic had been cut off and she'd been thoroughly searched when they'd taken her in, which meant there was another party involved in this, and they'd got the cantrip from somewhere outside of the jail. Somewhere which traded in reusable cantrips marked with the Family's seal.

"I'll check with our supplier," said Miles. "He might know where the latest reusable cantrips in the city are coming from."

"Thanks," I said. "Um—any word on Shawn? I know he isn't locked up in one of the Houses, but I didn't hear where he ended up."

"The vampires in Arcadia imprisoned him," he said. "Lord Blackbourne saw to it."

"Oh yeah, you're allies." A detail I'd forgotten, considering everything else that'd happened lately.

"Yes, we are, though Lord Blackbourne makes no secret of the fact that he prefers not to get involved in human affairs," he said. "It would be nice to know he has our back."

"Especially if the Houses keep sending people to search the place," I added. "You'd think they'd have more important things to worry about."

Like the murder, the Family… and the rogue spirit mages scheming behind the scenes. I knew they couldn't all be dead or jailed like Shawn was.

"Like your brother?" said Shelley. "If he has mind-control powers, what's to stop him from walking out of there?"

Precisely what worries me. I had zero desire to see him again, but I might have to, if the Death King agreed to take on custody of the House of Fire's prisoner in exchange for their help.

"What's to stop him?" I echoed. "The Death King, I hope. Anyway, I need to report to him before he thinks the House of Fire locked me in a cell."

"Good call," said Miles. "I might drop by the castle later. The Death King asked us to look around the citadels to see if we can figure out if Shawn and his friends left clues behind about how they turned on the spirit mages' old technology. We haven't yet, but we're keeping an eye out in case Shawn's allies decide to come back."

"I hope not." Dealing with my brother again would be bad enough, but I couldn't delay any longer. It was time to head back to the Death King and see what he thought of taking custody of a new prisoner.

4

———————————

I walked back to the Court of the Dead alone, this time watching my back in case Harris tailed me again. Luckily, it seemed he'd gone straight back to the House of Fire after searching the Spirit Agents' place, because I reached the castle without encountering anyone. I hardly believed he'd had the nerve to march into Miles's home, but a depressing number of guards who worked for the Houses were all too keen to use their authority to make trouble for people. Especially non-House mages.

I found the other Elemental Soldiers gathered in the break room. When I walked in, Cal, the Earth Element, gave me a dismissive look and returned to playing video games on the console hooked up to a flat-screen TV against the wall. Felicity, the Water Element, gave me a smile, but that was somewhat overshadowed, literally, by the lich lurking next to their group. It wasn't unusual to see liches everywhere in the castle, but the way that particular lich kept glaring at me was so personal that I wondered if I'd accidentally said something to offend them at some point.

"Is the Death King around?" I asked Ryan, the Air Element, trying to ignore their hostile companion.

"Not at the moment," they said. "Where have you been?"

"Talking to the House of Fire," I said. "I have an update I think he'll want to hear."

Ryan rose to their feet. "All right. If you're that certain you want to disturb him."

They accompanied me to the main hall. The Death King was nowhere to be seen, but Dex zoomed over to me when I entered.

"Hey, there," Dex said. "What's up?"

"Seen the Death King?"

"He's through there." He pointed to the door to the storeroom off the main hall, which I knew contained the Death King's personal cantrip collection. I wouldn't have thought he needed to use cantrips, considering his lich powers, but Ryan headed that way, pushing open the door.

Sure enough, the tall figure of the Death King stood within the room, for all the world like he'd been eavesdropping from the other side of the door.

"Bria," he said to me. "Have you come with an update from the House of Fire?"

As I told him about the day's events, he crossed the hall to the dais and took up his usual position, while Ryan retreated from the hall, leaving the two of us alone.

"So the House of Fire has lost their head jailor," said the Death King. "Unfortunate."

He sounded as indifferent as I did. I couldn't believe

I'd ever wondered if he'd secretly had an alliance with the Houses, because they seemed to be his lowest priority.

"The House of Fire's guards think Tay committed the murder," I added. "She was out of her cell at the time, and she won't say what she was doing."

"What do you think?" His tone was neutral, but he knew Tay and I had been friends. It was hard to keep anything from the King of the Dead.

"I don't think that's all there is to it," I told him. "For one thing, Adair is imprisoned in the same place as Tay is, and he has the ability to use mind control to influence people into doing his bidding. For another, if Tay actually committed the murder, she would have confessed by now. I don't know what she's doing by delaying. Unless Adair ordered her not to admit she did it, of course."

"I cannot comment on her innocence," he said, "but Adair doesn't seem to be in the securest place. The House of Fire's jail is primarily designed for mages, but not people like him. I understand that he already broke out of the Houses' securest facility, and they must know they're only delaying a repeat of the same scenario."

"It's your lucky day," I said. "The guards at the House of Fire said they were willing to consider negotiating an agreement if *you* take Adair off their hands and imprison him here in the Court of the Dead."

"Is that so?" he said. "What are his abilities, precisely?"

"He's half-elf and half-human," I said. "He can move faster than most humans, and he can influence anyone using mind control, but his power doesn't work on liches. That's why the House of Fire is confident that handing him over to you will solve the issue of his potential escape."

"Did they assume I would agree to their offer?" he queried.

"I'm not sure they cared either way," I admitted. "But the whole Family escaped from jail a month ago and they've only managed to recapture one of them. Not sure what your track record is, but it's gotta be better than that."

"Then I'll take him off their hands and ensure he is secured here in the Court of the Dead," he said. "Is there anything else you wanted to tell me?"

I reached into my pocket and pulled out the cantrip I'd taken from the House of Fire. "This was used to kill the jailor. It has the Family's signature on it, but I know for a fact that their old factories burned down five years ago."

"There's a strong possibility they may have rebuilt, isn't there?" he said. "I think we must assume they did."

"Yes, but this cantrip is new," I said. "They never used reusable cantrips before, and I don't know where this one came from. I don't know how it got into the jail, either."

"The reusable cantrips recently came into use in Arcadia before spreading through the Parallel," he said. "They're manufactured at the local warehouses. There have been a few incidents involving illegal cantrip trade in the city, as it happens, and I'm not convinced it has been stamped out."

"Oh?" I said, not sure what he was getting at. "I didn't think that was something that would interest you. Illegal cantrip trade, I mean."

"Anything that potentially threatens the safety of my Court is of interest to me," he responded. "I intended to send Ryan to ask a few questions at the warehouses, so I see no harm in you going with them. Do let them know, won't you?"

"Are you sure Ryan won't mind?" I asked.

"Ryan knows that it's best to have backup with them on dangerous missions," he said. "They'll understand."

Ryan was *not* thrilled at being asked to escort me to Arcadia. They didn't say a word to me on the walk out of the castle, and only laughed when Neddie the horse refused to let me mount him. In the end, I walked on foot to the outskirts of Arcadia while Ryan rode on horseback. By the time I reached the bare ground at the very edge of the swamp, I was in a bad mood, to say the least.

"Who's the cantrip manufacturer we're supposed to speak to?" I asked, kicking mud off my boots.

"You'll see." Ryan hopped off Neddie's back and gave the horse a stroke, letting him canter away back into the swamp. "Stay close behind me and don't wander off."

"Do you even know what your master asked me to speak to the manufacturers about?" I said.

"*Our* master told me to speak to the manufacturers myself," said Ryan. "If you get yourself into trouble, I'm not getting you out of it."

That's nice. "Noted."

The warehouses covered the edge of the city which bordered the swampland. The Houses of the Elements barely had a foothold here in Arcadia, thanks to the vampires being the ruling force. I only knew of one hangout for mages and it wasn't exactly reputable. I couldn't picture the Family walking through this maze of warehouses to the central one marked as the city's main market for all things magical. A steady flow of people walked in and out of the entryway: practitioners and mages, but also the occasional vampire, dressed in dark clothing and with their hoods pulled up to stave off the daylight.

Ryan and I joined the queue beside the doors, attracting a fair few stares thanks to our armoured clothing. The crush of people didn't help, and it came as a relief when we finally got inside the warehouse itself. The open space before us contained rows of tables selling everything from produce to everyday items imported from the other side of the nodes as well as cantrips and other magical devices. At the very back of the warehouse lay a long line of tables covered with dozens of golden cantrips engraved with runes. I hadn't seen such a big collection outside of the Death King's castle before.

"The Collective of Spells." I read the sign affixed to the back wall of the warehouse. "Is this the supplier we're looking for?"

"Hello?" said the girl behind the table, giving the Air Element a wary look. "Can I help you?"

"We're looking to speak to the manufacturer of the reusable cantrips being distributed throughout the Parallel," I said. "I take it that's you?"

The Collective of Spells. I'd never heard of them before, but I hadn't exactly been plugged into the legal business of acquiring cantrips. I'd mostly got them from Striker's network in Elysium before now.

The girl's gaze darted between us. While her wariness was understandable for anyone faced with two of the

Death King's Elemental Soldiers, did she know some of her cantrips might have been used to commit murder?

"Not just me," she said. "There are a lot of us. What is it you want to know?"

"Whereabouts are these cantrips manufactured?" I asked.

"Here in Arcadia," she said. "Why?"

"The Death King," said Ryan, "would like to know the names of the traders you work with, in Elysium in particular. You might have heard of the incident a couple of months ago where some of your cantrips were misplaced and used to create illegal spells, and we have reason to believe the same might be happening again."

Her face paled at the mention of the Death King. "All our sources are legitimate, but we can't control what people do with cantrips in their own homes. Despite that, we're closely monitoring all our contacts."

She might be telling the truth. Reusable cantrips might be used for any purpose and nobody would be able to trace them back to their source, but the cantrips on the table weren't marked with the Family's symbol. They wouldn't do something like that so openly, though, in case the vampires swooped in and shut the place down.

"Where can we get a list of the people you supply cantrips to?" I asked.

She chewed on her lower lip. "You'll have to ask the boss about that. He's at the warehouse next door."

"All right," I said. "Thanks."

As we turned to leave, a voice spoke from behind us. "Oh, hello, Ryan."

I turned to see an elf, startlingly attractive with a tanned face and pointed ears, walking through the crowd as though oblivious to the attention he was drawing from the other patrons. He stopped in front of Ryan, a smile on his face.

"Friend of yours?" I said to the Air Element.

"We both know Liv," Ryan replied.

Okay. Not an ally, then.

The elf turned to me with a curious stare. "Who are you?"

"Bria," I said. "I'm the Death King's new Fire Element."

"I'm Trix," he said. "Most humans can't pronounce my full name, so I go by Trix."

"Nice to meet you." He couldn't tell I was part elf—my cantrip hid my pointed ears—but it struck me that I didn't necessarily need to hide them anymore. I'd originally tried to make myself look less distinctive for the sake of maintaining anonymity, but as the Death King's Fire Element, I drew attention just by walking into a room anyway.

"We should go outside," said Ryan. "We're done in here."

The three of us wove through the crowd and out of the market into the open air, at which point the elf turned back to face us.

"What're you here for?" he asked.

"More trouble with illegal cantrips," Ryan said. "Allegedly, someone else is using reusable cantrips from the COS to create illegal spells on the side, though since it's Bria's claim, I can't verify its accuracy."

Hey! "I can show you the cantrip if you don't believe me, but flashing the Family's symbol in the market might get me arrested. Might have escaped your attention, but everyone in that warehouse was staring at us already."

"Illegal cantrips?" said the elf. "That sounds like Liv's area."

I groaned inwardly. Of course it did. Liv always seemed to show up where I least wanted or needed her.

"Not really," said Ryan. "It's more her friend Devon who deals with cantrips. She helped us track down the people responsible for creating illegal cantrips last time around."

"Who were they, exactly?" I asked. "Might it be the same people again?"

"We broke up all their safe houses," said Ryan, wearing a disgruntled expression. "The operation might've survived in some form, but I can't say how the cantrips ended up in Elysium."

"Did those cantrips…" I paused. "Did they have any kind of mark on them? Like a signature?"

"No," they said. "They were all reusable, though, which is a relatively new model created here in Arcadia itself."

Hmm. Maybe not the Family's doing, but they'd certainly stepped in pretty quickly. Cantrips which wiped themselves clean after use could be used to conceal all kinds of evidence.

"Who ran the operation?" I asked. "Last time, I mean? There's gotta be a figurehead."

"A vampire," said Ryan shortly. "None of the original perpetrators walks free, but those inferno cantrips didn't drop out of the sky."

"I know they didn't," I said. "The cantrip which killed the jailor in the House of Fire wasn't an inferno, though. I've never seen anything like it before."

"A cantrip killed someone at the House of Fire?" said Trix.

I hesitated for a moment, unsure whether I should be discussing it in front of him. While elves didn't tend to get involved with human politics, I didn't know the guy, even if Ryan trusted him. On the other hand, I'd already brought up the subject. "Yeah, but we don't know what the spell was. Or how it got there."

"Liv might know," said Trix.

"She has enough crap to deal with," Ryan said. "Last thing we need is to get her wrapped up in illegal cantrip business again. Right, I'll go and speak to the COS's people and get a list of who they sell their cantrips to outside of the city. It's this way."

While Ryan took the lead towards the warehouse on our right-hand side, Trix fell into step with me. "Are you an elf?"

I startled at the blatant question. "What? Why?"

"You move like one."

He was definitely sharper than he looked, that was for sure.

"Half elf," I said. "Half human. I never met my elf family."

"Shame," he said. "There aren't many of us left."

"No." I didn't know what he expected me to say, so I caught up with Ryan, who stood talking to a bulky security guard outside the warehouse doors.

"Are you with the COS?" Ryan asked.

"Who wants to know?" said the guard.

"The Death King," I said, figuring mentioning his name would speed the whole thing up. "He has concerns about your contacts in Elysium. Can you name them?"

"Ask my supervisor. He's in there." He jerked a thumb over his shoulder. "Don't touch anything."

Ignoring Ryan's look of annoyance, I entered the warehouse beside them, where we found ourselves in a small storeroom. Through a door on the left, I could see a larger room, full of people standing at long tables surrounded by heaps of carved cantrips. I found a man in a dirt-covered uniform with sideburns and a scarred face and waylaid him.

"Elysium?" He had to bellow to be heard over the noise of the warehouse. "Dawson's the only person we sell to there. Our main customer is the Order of the Elements. They buy in bulk and return them after use wherever possible. Rest of the Parallel hasn't caught on yet."

"The Order?" Damn. I'd thought they avoided dealing with Parallel-based businesses. Not that I knew very much about the Order except that they policed magic on the other side of the nodes and really hated spirit mages. Not to mention people like me.

"Is this Dawson the only person you deal with in Elysium?" Ryan asked. "Got an address?"

"Ask my assistant." He pointed to a young man standing nearby, who Ryan waylaid. I couldn't hear a word he said, so I made a mental note to ask Miles for the name of the Spirit Agents' supplier later. If there was only one major cantrip supplier in Elysium who bought supplies from Arcadia, I was pretty sure it must be the same one.

The question was, was said supplier involved in the illegal cantrip trade, or had the cantrip bearing the Family's mark come from somewhere else entirely?

I followed Ryan out of the warehouse, they promptly launched into a conversation with Trix which I couldn't follow.

"What in the world are you talking about?" I asked.

Ryan's jaw clenched. "Nothing."

"Dungeons & Dragons," Trix supplied. "We're designing Ryan's character's backstory."

"Okay…" I had only a rudimentary knowledge of popular hobbies on the other side of the nodes, but Ryan looked like they'd be more comfortable riding to war than sitting at a table partaking in fictional battles. "Dex plays, too, he told me."

"Want to join us?" Trix said.

"No," Ryan answered for me. "So there's one supplier in Elysium, who also sells cantrips to all the Houses. If *they're* the one illegally selling to the Family on the side, I hope you're ready to face a world of trouble, Bria."

Not really. Though it'd slipped my mind that this Dawson person must supply the Houses as well as the Spirit Agents. Either the Family was getting their cantrips from elsewhere… or they were closer to my allies than I'd thought.

5

Ryan flat-out refused to go to Elysium without reporting to their master first and proceeded to talk to Trix all the way back without saying a word to me. I felt distinctly like a third wheel as we walked back to the node at the edge of the Death King's territory, at which point Ryan called up a horse. Neddie, of course, growled at the sight of me and refused to let me mount him.

"I'd like to learn to ride one of those," Trix announced.

"I can teach you," said Ryan.

It'd have been nice if you'd offered the same to me. I bit back my protest and attempted to coax another horse over to me, to no avail. While the others rode ahead of me, I walked on foot, fuming, until I reached the castle.

"The Death King's in the hall," said Felicity, catching sight of us. "What's your friend doing here?"

"Visiting," said Ryan. "Trix, can you wait outside? I won't be long."

"What's the deal with him?" I followed them up the

steps to the castle. "I thought you didn't want anyone from outside to come in here."

"I'm careful not to let *untrustworthy* people in here," Ryan corrected.

"Ouch." I put a hand over my heart, eyeing the skull-covered pillars on either side of the doors. "Those things are creepy, you know. Has anyone ever tried improving them by sticking fake moustaches on them or something?"

Ryan didn't answer, pushing open the oak doors in front of us. We entered the hall and found the Death King standing on the dais at the back as though he hadn't moved since we'd left the castle.

"There's been a change of plans," said the Death King, before either of us could speak. "The House of Fire wants to hand over their prisoner now, and they've requested your help in restraining Adair while they complete the transfer."

"Me?" I halted in front of the dais. "Seriously?"

They couldn't possibly trust me to stop Adair from making a quick getaway, surely. Harris had all but accused me of working with him once already.

"I mentioned that you had a transporter spell," said the Death King.

Right, of course. "I do, but I'm not sure it would work on two people at once."

"Then use it to transport Adair through the node and into the castle grounds, and I'll have people waiting on the other side to restrain him," he said.

I could think of a dozen ways that might go wrong, but I had the sense that I might as well be talking to a brick wall. Besides, the hardest part would be getting

Adair onto the other side of the gates in front of the castle. Once he was there, the collective strength of the Death King's army ought to be able to subdue him and drag him into the jail, but that didn't mean Adair wouldn't try to initiate an escape attempt anyway.

Ryan cleared their throat. "We asked at the warehouse about the suppliers in Elysium, but it seems there's only one person in the city who buys cantrips from Arcadia's markets. I have the name and address."

"Deal with that later," the Death King said. "Bria, go back to Elysium as soon as possible and speak to the House of Fire about helping transfer their prisoner. Without taking any detours this time."

Had he known I'd gone to visit the Spirit Agents on my way back? "Can't I at least grab lunch before I leave? I've been on my feet all day."

The Death King's cold gaze turned on me, and I had the sudden mental image of him reaching out and ripping out Adair's soul. I couldn't deny that was an appealing thought. "You may stop at your quarters before you leave the castle."

From the looks of things, Ryan had zero intention of coming with me, and I was more than happy to leave the pair of them to hang out with Neddie the zombie horse instead.

I dropped by the break room to grab a snack bar for lunch and then left the castle, walking past the jail and the node which was designated for the Death King's private use. The node in question was impossible for anyone to use who wasn't a spirit mage—at least not without the aid of a transporter spell—but if I managed to shove Adair through the node without him making a quick getaway, he'd immediately find himself surrounded by liches as soon as he landed next to the jail.

As for me, travelling via transporter spell was not my favourite activity, so I walked out of the gates and towards the node on the other side of the fence, surrounded by swampland. From there, I transported myself to the centre of Elysium and retraced my steps to the House of Fire's headquarters.

Like before, Harris answered the door. "Back already?"

"Yeah, on the boss's orders," I said. "Which you probably know about."

"I expected you to give us a little time to get the prisoner ready," he said. "He's being uncooperative."

"It's his defining trait." I didn't want to deal with Adair's bullshit, but despite their arrogance, the guards weren't equipped to handle him in the slightest. "Most sedatives don't work on him for long. Tying him up is best, but don't use rope or anything he can break easily."

"Did I ask for your advice?" he said.

"Just trying to be helpful," I said, giving up on any attempts at civility. "At least you know I was telling the truth about being the Death King's Fire Element, right?"

He scowled. "It won't last. People like you always end up back in the same place."

"Doesn't look like you've moved very far to me," I commented. "Can I come in?"

"No." He planted himself in front of the door, arms folded, refusing to let me even get past the threshold. "I don't trust you, and if I had my way, you wouldn't be involved in this operation."

"Look, I'm not going to let the prisoner walk free," I said. "He tried to murder me the last time we set eyes on one another. Also, I'm the one who got him jailed. Twice, I might add."

"People like you have inconsistent loyalties," he said. "I hope the Death King knows that."

That stung. The Family might be known for cutting ties and switching alliances, but I'd always been loyal to those I cared about. It wasn't my fault people around me had an annoying tendency to turn out to be anything but loyal to *me*. Tay and Shawn were proof of that. I just hoped that Miles wouldn't end up the same way.

"Do all the Houses use the same cantrip supplier?" I asked him, deciding to change the subject before I ended up losing patience and socking him in the jaw. I already knew the answer, but he might inadvertently give me a clue which would help me figure out how that cantrip had got in here.

"What's it to you?" Harris said.

"A cantrip killed your jailor," I said. "And there's only one supplier here in Elysium. Haven't you looked into it?"

"The killer might have got the cantrip outside of the city," he said. "Your friend hasn't shared any more information with us."

That figures. What Tay was playing at, I have no idea. "Look, I'm trying to figure out where that cantrip came from. A cantrip bearing the mark of the Family shouldn't have ended up in the city to begin with."

There was no point in arguing with him at this stage, though. Since he'd stepped out of the door frame, I took the opportunity to slip underneath his arm and into the hallway, where I heard voices coming from downstairs.

"Hey!" he said. "Fine, you can come in, but don't touch anything."

Like he had anything worth stealing. I had no need for pickpocketing now I had a regular salary coming in, besides, so I sauntered past him and towards the stairs down to the lower level.

Harris tailed me. "I haven't given you permission to go down there."

"I thought it was implied." I descended the stairs, ignoring his grumbling behind me. If he didn't want me here, he shouldn't have accepted the King of the Dead's offer.

I reached the lower level, realising entirely too late that I'd have to walk past Tay's cell on the way to find my brother. I stepped out into the corridor to find her staring at me through the cage bars.

"What on earth are you doing?" she said.

"Moving our friend to a higher-security prison," I responded.

"You're getting him out of his cell?" Her face paled. "That's a ridiculous idea. He'll be waiting for exactly this."

"He's sedated," said Harris, from behind me. "And you will be, too, if you don't shut your trap."

"Tay," I said warningly as she began to speak. "Don't start anything right now. Unless you want to confirm that Adair had a role in the jailor's murder and save us the bother of interrogating him?"

She said nothing, so I walked the rest of the way down the corridor, following the murmur of voices. Harris and I halted behind a group of guards who'd gathered around a single cell with bars made of magic-proofed material.

Inside the cell was my brother, lying unconscious on the floor. Adair looked unnervingly like me for someone who wasn't a relation, tall and lean with his hair shaved to stubble where mine was long. His pointed ears were on full display and his face looked unexpectedly young in sleep, while the prison uniform contrasted the expensive clothes he'd worn the last time he'd seen him. I never did find out where he'd got them from. Probably from where the rest of the Family was hiding, wherever *that* was.

I pushed a slew of conflicting emotions aside, with difficulty. We might have grown up as siblings, but he had never treated me as anything other than a convenience. And he'd nearly killed me a week ago.

I cleared my throat. "Excuse me."

"What're you doing down here?" asked one of the guards, spotting me.

"She's here to help us move him," Harris growled. "Allegedly."

"I won't get under your feet," I said, "but if you run your plan past me, I can point out any issues. We don't want him walking free."

"We most certainly do not," said one of the guards. "He'll remain sedated while we transport him out to the nearest node. Then..."

"I have a transporter spell," I told them. "That will allow us to send him directly to the Death King's territory, where the liches can take him into the jail without any chance of him running free."

"Who made you the boss?" said Harris.

"One of you can operate the transporter spell, if you'd prefer," I said. "Or I can ask one of the other Elemental Soldiers to come here in my place if you really have that much of a problem with me."

"No," said Harris flatly. "We don't take orders from the Death King or his poor choices for soldiers."

Great. If Adair made a break for it, it'd be their fault, not mine. If I pushed them too far, though, they might take the transporter off my hands and lock *me* in the cell alongside Adair. I didn't know what they'd sedated him with, but I hadn't exaggerated when I'd said most magical substances were much less effective on him than they were on regular people. At most, we'd have half an hour before he woke and started taking his anger out on everyone within range.

Thankfully, the guards ignored Harris's complaints and hauled the unconscious Adair out of his cell. Without glancing in the direction of Tay's cage this time, I headed up the stairs, while two guards carried the unconscious form of Adair ahead of me. His hands were cuffed with the same magic-proofed stuff as the bars on his cage, but that didn't mean he wouldn't try to break out of them the instant he woke up.

We needed to get to the Death King's castle first.

Outside the House of Fire, we turned the corner and headed for the nearest node. I found myself regretting coming here alone. I wished I'd brought Harper at the very least. While I knew she didn't want to get close to anyone connected to the Family, being a lich meant she could pass through the node straight to the Death King's private node without the need for a transporter spell.

I reached into the pendant around my neck and removed the gleaming coin Shawn had given to me, but the guards continued to drag Adair towards the node without paying me any attention.

I cleared my throat. "I have the spell ready. Who wants to volunteer to send him through?"

To my horror, Adair's eyes snapped open, meeting

mine. He twisted out of the guards' grip almost at once, swinging his cuffed hands at them. The blow caught both guards at once, sending them flying into the air.

Shit. I knew this would happen.

I ran at him, transporter spell in hand, but he pivoted out of the way with a bellow of rage. I hadn't a hope of restraining him single-handedly, but the heavy chains on his wrists made it harder for him to keep his balance. Yet he was too damn fast, and too close to the node for me to risk a proper assault in case I ended up stranding us both in the middle of nowhere.

"Fuck off," he spat at me. "Let go of me and go away."

To my horror, I found my body automatically obeying his commands. His persuasive magic was still in full working order, and the lightness that seized my limbs urged me to run as far away as possible.

Instead, I shot a fireball at him. He dodged, tackling me around the middle and propelling both of us through the node. I fumbled for the transporter spell, too late, and it flew from my grip as we tumbled through emptiness and landed sprawling on hard ground.

I looked up, finding that we hadn't landed on the Death King's territory, but near the warehouses of Arcadia. Worse, I'd dropped the transporter spell somewhere on the other side.

Adair staggered upright, chains dangling from his wrists, and made another lunge for the node. I tackled him before he could reach it, using the momentum of our fall to pin his cuffed arms to the ground.

"Care to tell me where that cantrip of yours came from?" I said. "The one that was used to kill the jailor?"

Instead of answering, he twisted out from underneath

me, and I hit the ground on my knees, hard. He made a break for it, his feet skidding in the muddy ground and his cuffed hands swinging—and a skeletal horse walked into his path, headbutting him in the face. Adair flew back into the mud, swearing explosively.

"Thanks, Neddie," I said, genuinely grateful for the grumpy horse's sudden appearance. At least until he knocked me over, too, and I landed on my rear in the mud. "Ow."

"The horse is called Neddie?" Adair pushed to his feet, his nose bleeding.

I climbed upright and jabbed a finger at him. "He's the one who deserves a good thrashing." *Bloody zombie horse.*

"Get them!" a voice shouted from the direction of the node behind us, and several of the House of Fire's guards ran to surround the pair of us.

"Hey, I'm taking him to the Death King!" I said indignantly. "Or I would be, if this damned horse did anything I asked it to."

Neddie placidly stood at the side and chewed on some muddy grass while Adair turned on the guards. "Fight one another, not me."

The effect was instantaneous. Several fireballs flew among the guards, and alarm flickered through me. You'd think Adair's power would be somewhat dampened after his imprisonment, but every one of the guards had fallen under his spell—punching, throwing flames, and otherwise ignoring the pair of us.

I'd have to handle Adair myself. I ran towards him, careful not to make eye contact. "You shouldn't be able to do that."

A grin twisted his mouth. "These cuffs aren't made for the likes of us, Bria."

As I readied myself for a fight, a tremendous blast of wind struck both of us, knocking the guards' fireballs off course and causing Adair to overbalance again.

I never thought I'd be glad to see the Air Element, but Ryan looked at the uniformed guards with an expression of confusion on their face as they began hurling fireballs at one another again. "What's going on here?"

"I was bringing this guy to the Death King's jail," I told them. "He has mind-control powers. Don't look him in the eyes."

Ryan raised their hands and Adair's body flew into the air before he could rise to his feet. A second blast of air magic sent the House of Fire guards flying in all directions like bottles knocked over. "How long does it last?"

"Not much longer as long as he doesn't make eye contact with them again," I replied. "Let them fight it out. Serves them right for not trusting me to deal with this myself."

Adair kicked and yelled and shouted curses, but Ryan ignored him, levitating him all the way across the swamp without so much as breaking a sweat. When we finally reached the Court of the Dead, the liches at the gates parted to let us through, while their leader appeared at the top of the stone staircase and descended to meet us outside the castle.

Ryan faced the Death King. "What do you want me to do with him?"

"Take him to the jail," said the Death King. "His abilities don't work on liches, according to Bria."

"It's true," I added. "I'll open the doors."

I walked ahead to the blocky shape of the Death King's jail, opening the doors to let Ryan levitate Adair inside. "You know, this would have been much easier if you'd just done as you were told, Adair."

"This is a waste of time," said Adair. "This place won't last, any more than the House of Fire will."

"And just what is that supposed to mean?"

"Nothing," he said. "Yet."

"Quit talking." Ryan all but threw Adair into a cell, slamming the door on him.

With my brother safely behind bars, I left the jail before he attempted to work his magic on me. Yet his words crept into my thoughts despite my best efforts. The Family had never made an overt threat against the Death King, but they'd certainly been involved with the recent attacks on his territory. Might he be telling the truth? He'd have reason enough to lie purely for the purposes of screwing with me, but the fact remained that the rest of the Family was mysteriously absent.

Maybe biding their time… and preparing to strike at the heart of the new life I'd begun to build.

6

I didn't get the opportunity to update Miles on my close call with Adair until the following day. After receiving no instructions from the Death King other than leaving our new prisoner alone, I set out for Elysium the next morning. Miles seemed to be expecting me, because he answered the door in person this time.

"Shit, Bria," said Miles, when I'd explained the adventurous turn yesterday had taken. "I didn't know they'd make you move your brother to the Death King's territory so soon."

"I got the impression they didn't want me involved in their plan, but they needed my transporter spell," I said. "Which I lost somewhere in Elysium. Sorry."

"You mean this?" Miles reached into his pocket and held up the disc-shaped spell. "Wouldn't want that going missing."

"Oh." I took it from him with a rush of gratitude. "Thanks."

"Thank my brother," said Shelley, entering the room.

"Tate was watching for a distance. He saw the whole shit-show go down. I take it that dickhead of a brother of yours didn't escape?"

"He almost did, but the Air Element helped me restrain him," I said. "The House of Fire's guards were pretty much useless. They haven't come here again since the last time, have they?"

"No, but that doesn't mean I'm keen on the idea of them poking their noses into our business," said Shelley. "At least the Death King is a known entity."

The Death King wants an alliance with the Houses himself. But that would depend on the Houses' cooperation, and they seemed to have zero intention of listening to a word I said. While I'd be more than happy to leave them alone, they had Tay's freedom under their control, and maybe her life, too.

Even if she *had* killed the jailor, the odds were high that Adair had been the real culprit. Not that he'd made a confession, though the Death King hadn't sent anyone to talk to him yet. I suspected I was the only person Adair would speak to, regardless, but it would do no good whatsoever to go into the jail and risk him using his mind-control powers on me. Not without a plan, anyway.

"Yeah, he is," said Miles. "His jail is secure, for the record, so that guy won't walk free anytime soon. You know he offered to let us stay with him in the castle if we want, too?"

Shelley frowned. "I'm not leaving our base, not with the House of Fire sniffing around at every opportunity. Can't he help us with that? He's no friend of the Houses."

"He's not obviously opposed to them either," said Tate. "If he wants to make an alliance."

"It's the sensible thing to do," I said. "I'm not a fan of the Houses, but they're the ruling authority in the city. I'd rather they were on our side than against us, if there really is another war coming."

Shelley made a sceptical noise. "The last people who said there'd be a war are rotting in jail."

"Best to be prepared," said Miles. "I don't know about you, but if the Death King's taking it seriously, it means the crap will probably hit us first. Not that I'm keen to work with the Houses, mind. I thought that dude was going to walk off with our cantrip supply yesterday."

"Speaking of cantrips," I said, "you use the same supplier as the Houses, right?"

"We do," said Miles. "Why?"

"I spoke to the cantrip manufacturer in Arcadia and they said they only sell to one supplier in Elysium," I explained. "Which means either the cantrip someone used to kill the jailor came from there, or there's another illegal cantrip supplier somewhere in the city."

"Fair point," said Miles. "Want to talk to Dawson? Not like I've got much else going on."

Shelley cleared her throat. "Except for keeping the other Spirit Agents in line."

He shot her a grin. "It's a group responsibility. Anyway, it's worth checking out. We need to know if the Family has their claws in the local cantrip supplier."

"I bloody hope not," said Shelley. "Did the Death King tell you to speak to him, Bria?"

"He hasn't given me instructions," I said. "Other than not disturbing the prisoner, which I had zero intention of doing anyway. Admittedly, he didn't tell me to talk to the supplier..."

"He didn't tell you *not* to, did he?" said Miles.

"I like the way you think," I said. "No, he didn't, and since I'm already here, I might as well go check it out."

"Sure," he said. "Shelley, I'll be back in an hour."

"Don't get into trouble," she responded.

The pair of us left the Spirit Agents' house, walking along the path to the gate. A vampire chicken ambled past, its beak bloody. "Did it take a bite out of someone?"

"Nah, I think the kids have been feeding them dead rats."

"Lovely." They certainly seemed well-looked after, and I wondered if they had any intention of selling them after all. It might be useful to have an army of vampire chickens to attack intruders. "Any updates you don't mind sharing now they can't overhear us?"

"Hey, you can trust the others," he said. "You know that, right? They'll come around to trusting you eventually, too."

"Even after what happened with Shawn?" I said. "Do they really not believe there's going to be a war?"

His expression darkened. "They do. They just won't admit it. Shawn wasn't the only spirit mage traitor."

"No?" I turned to him. "Who else? Do I know them?"

"No." He drew in a breath. "Okay, the Death King doesn't want me to tell you this, so don't let it slip that you know, okay? But I know who the mastermind is."

I stopped in my tracks. "The Family? You've seen them?"

"No, but the person who organised the coup against the Death King is a lich named Hawker," he said. "Or should I say he *was* a lich. Before he came back to life."

My mouth fell open. "What? That's not possible."

"I didn't think it was possible either," he said, "but the Death King told me otherwise. Hawker used some kind of spell to turn himself from a lich into a living spirit mage again."

"The Family's cantrips." I dropped my voice. "You mean—there's a *cantrip* which brought him back?"

Of *course* the Family had been responsible. But did that mean they planned to use the same cantrips against the Death King? Was that what Adair had been taunting me about, when he'd implied the Court of the Dead was doomed?

"Looks that way," said Miles. "Spirit mages can't bring people back from the dead. Liches can turn human again after a short time if their death wasn't permanent, but that Hawker guy... he died years ago. Around the time of the war."

"I think I need to tell Harper," I said. "She isn't dealing well with being a lich. If there's a chance she might get to become human again, she'll want to know about it."

"Uh, not a good idea," he said. "There's usually a downside to powerful cantrips like those. There was one version a couple of months ago which brought liches back to life and then made them rot and fall to pieces."

"Nice." I pulled a face. "Okay, that's one hell of a downside. Still, if this Hawker person is alive when he used to be a lich, he must have made it work, right?"

"Liv is looking into it," said Miles. "That's what the Death King told me."

"Oh, he gave you an update and not me?"

"Don't get too excited," he said. "That's only one piece of bad news. The other is that the Order of the Elements is now assumed to be under Hawker's command."

Once again, I halted mid-step. "The Order was taken over by a rogue? Seriously?"

"Yep," he said. "They were infiltrated from the inside, as far as I can figure out. Personally, I think they were crooked anyway, with their policies against spirit mages, but the official line is that they're under new management."

"But… they're the Houses' liaison on Earth."

Whenever the Order found illegal mages they didn't want to deal with, they handed them straight to the Houses. Did the Houses know the Order was under the control of the enemy? Should I be the one to tell them?

"They know," Miles said. "The Houses, I mean. The Death King told them."

"He didn't tell me."

Maybe he didn't trust me at all. But Miles did, which was no small thing. Spirit mages like him and the Death King faced potential betrayal at every corner, and while it came as no particular surprise that the King of the Dead had kept information from me, Miles had elected to tell me despite the risk. I hadn't worked with another person since Tay's betrayal, and it'd taken me long enough to trust her with my life. Now, I didn't know if I'd be able to reach that level of trust with someone again, but Miles was a strong contender.

"The Houses haven't put out an official statement on the Order yet," he added. "I think they're keeping it quiet."

"Like the Family's escape," I said. "That's their policy: don't tell anyone anything and then deny all responsibility."

Miles resumed walking again. "Let's hope they haven't lost their cantrip suppliers to the enemy, too."

Dawson's place turned out to be located on a corner of a side street, not far from the Houses' headquarters. A red flag if I ever saw one, though maybe not, considering the middle of the city was also the centre for all things magical.

Miles led the way to the black-painted door and knocked, and a man with long grey hair answered.

"Hey, Dawson," said Miles. "I'm here from the Spirit Agents."

"Miles," he said, in an accent I couldn't place. "What's up? You want more cantrips?"

"Wouldn't mind a refresher," he said.

Dawson passed on the order to a broad-shouldered young man behind him, who moved to the shelves and started taking cantrips down and putting them into a cardboard bag.

"Who else do you sell to?" asked Miles.

"Who wants to know?" said the man. "The Houses of the Elements, plus a bunch of people like you. Practitioners, independent mages, whatever."

So they did sell to the House of Fire. Which... didn't tell me much. That cantrip which had killed the jailor might have been carved by anyone. I needed to narrow it down.

I pulled the cantrip in question from my pocket. "Can you identify this? It's a reusable cantrip, and I don't know which spell was used on it before it wiped itself clean."

"You'd need an expert to identify the previous spell used on it," he said. "I can do it myself, but it'll cost you."

"Nah, it's fine." If he identified the spell and it turned out to be illegal, it might come back to hit us instead of the person who'd actually carved it. Besides, identifying the spell wouldn't point to the person who'd actually created it. I flipped over the coin to show the mark instead. "What about this?"

"That?" He peered at the back of the cantrip. "That's a signature, isn't it? Some practitioners use them, but I reckon it's a waste of time."

His expression showed no recognition at the sight of the Family's mark. *Maybe he doesn't know.*

The assistant handed Miles the bag of cantrips. "Have a good day."

We couldn't have a snoop around inside the place without drawing too much attention, so we took the cantrips and left.

"Good call," Miles said to me. "Dawson isn't a bad sort, but I doubt your salary from the Death King so far will cover the cost of him identifying that spell."

"Figures," I said. "He didn't seem to recognise the mark, but I wonder if he was telling the truth. If we came back here later under an invisibility cantrip to have a poke around…"

"Bria, he's a cantrip supplier. Pretty sure someone's tried that one on him before at least once."

I shrugged. "Worth a shot."

"I'm not sure he knows the Family," said Miles. "He's a decent guy. Gives us a discount on all new cantrips."

"Is he the one who sold you the transporter spell?" I asked.

"No," he said. "Shawn *said* he got it from the market, but maybe the enemy gave it to him instead. Anyone's guess."

"His big mistake was handing it over to me," I said. "I'm not giving it up anytime soon."

"Wise decision there," he said.

"Yeah."

Never mind the transporter spell. If the Family had a hold over Elysium's cantrip supplier, they had links to every practitioner here in Elysium, as well as all four of the Houses of the Elements.

The Order has fallen to the enemy already. How long before the Houses followed the same path?

7

A week passed with no further instructions from the Death King about our new prisoner. My boss had reacted without any surprise when I'd told him we'd hit a dead end when searching for evidence of where the cantrip which had killed the jailor had come from, but I'd at least thought he might want me to talk to Adair. Whenever I went near the jail, it was to find glaring liches blocking my way, so I got on with the job and went to check up on the House of Fire in every spare moment I had.

I was more concerned with Tay than with my incarcerated brother, but by the fourth day, the House of Fire's guards had taken to slamming the door in my face whenever I tried to ask them for updates. I assumed she was still alive, but until Adair started talking, I'd have no evidence to draw on which might prove she wasn't responsible for Zade's death. By the seventh day, I'd put Adair to the back of my mind altogether, so it damn near made me jump out of my skin when I walked out of the castle that morning and heard Adair's loud shouts from the direction of the jail. The racket filled my ears as I crossed the grounds and addressed the liches guarding the Death King's prison. "Can't you shut him up?"

"No," said one of them. "We can tell him not to make a sound, but we can't enforce it. He can't use his persuasive magic on any of us, so all he can do is yell until he tires himself out. Sounds like he's found his voice again, anyway."

"Can I speak to him?" I said. "Maybe I can shut him up."

"Fine," said the lich, "but we'll be watching. No funny business."

"Hey, I work for the Death King, too." Even the *liches* didn't trust me? Maybe I didn't blame them, given how some of them had ended up being burned to a crisp during the trials, but it'd be nice to have a little cooperation against my delight of a brother.

I entered the jail and walked up to Adair's cell, covering my ears against his yelling.

"What is wrong with you?" I shouted over the noise, taking care not to make eye contact with him.

He stopped yelling. "Did they kill your friend yet?"

"Fuck you," I said. "You know you can't get out of here, don't you? You can yell all you like. Nobody's going to listen."

"I could make *you* let me out," he said.

"You could try." His ability didn't work if I didn't look him in the eyes. No matter what mind games he tried to play, he couldn't deny that simple fact. "Alternatively, you can shut the hell up and stop giving everyone a headache.

No amount of yelling will make the Death King acknowl-edge you."

"I don't give a crap about him."

Damn. Was it me whose attention he'd wanted to draw? At a guess… yes, he had, and I'd given him what he wanted. "If you wanted to speak to me, are you going to tell me how you got out of jail the first time?"

That was the question which had been preying on my mind for the longest. If he'd got out of jail by himself, that was one thing, but I still hadn't the faintest idea where the others were hiding.

"Your friend Tay made the mistake of coming to talk to me and now she regrets it," he said. "I wouldn't bother in future."

I knew it was him. "You made her kill the jailor?"

He laughed. "You think if I confess to murder it'll make them spare her life? They won't, Bria. They've already made up their minds."

Bile coated the back of my throat, and my hands itched to punch his lights out. "Look, if you know anything about the Family's location, then I'd appreciate it if you tell me before the Death King gets to you first. Even if you're all but immortal, I'm pretty sure you can still be turned into a lich."

"I can't," he said, in confident tones. "And I think I'll let you work their location out on your own. *Get out.*"

I averted my gaze, sharply, but his voice rose in volume until the words were unintelligible. He didn't need to use magic on me to make me want to run in the opposite direction, so I retreated from the jail, hands clamped over my ears again. Thank the Elements that only the liches were in charge of guarding the jail and not the Elemental Soldiers, because liches didn't have ears. Or heads.

I ran to the castle, up the steps and into the main hall, releasing a sigh of relief when the doors cut off the sound of his screaming. At first, I thought nobody was inside, and then I saw a fiery humanoid shape in front of the hall of souls.

"Bria," said Dex. "What're you running from?"

"I'm looking for the Death King," I said. "Where is he?"

"Is it about our new prisoner?"

"Please tell me you haven't been gossiping."

He gave me a mock hurt look. "I didn't even tell Liv."

"I should hope not," I said. "Given how she's incapable of leaving the hell alone."

Maybe I was being unfair on her, but she'd put a serious wrench in my plans to stop Shawn from breaking into the Death King's castle and I was pretty sure she still suspected me of conspiring against His Deathly Highness. I didn't need another enemy, so I'd prefer to keep my distance from her for the time being.

Before the fire sprite could reply, the Death King glided through a side door into the hall.

"Bria," he said. "What is it?"

"Death King," I said. "Adair just spoke to me—"

"I don't remember giving you permission to visit him."

"He was screaming the place down," I said. "Still is, in fact. He also heavily implied that he used his influencing power on Tay to make her kill the jailor at the House of Fire."

"Shouldn't you be telling them that, not me?"

"They're currently refusing to let me into the building or even acknowledge my existence," I said.

"Whatever happened to negotiating an agreement with them?"

"I hoped they'd be more accepting of you than they've been," he said.

You aren't the only one. I hadn't exactly expected to be welcomed with open arms, but their attitude was grating to say the least. If they were truly plotting to execute Tay no matter what, though, how could I possibly convince them to spare her?

"I guess not," I said. "I *was* their prisoner before, and I did tell you they didn't like me."

"Despite the fact that you turned your family in and ensured their imprisonment," he said. "The House didn't share the details of their location with you?"

"My brother is the one with the mind-control power, not me," I said. "I can't force the House of Fire to tell you how the Family escaped or where they're hiding. Nor can I convince Adair to tell me, though he implied he knows, too."

Even if they'd wanted to cover their own backs, you'd think the Houses would have at least tried to organise a search for the Family's hiding place. Or asked the Death King to help. I'd assumed he commanded respect even with them… unless they'd already chosen a side.

Before I could question my decision, I said, "You might have mentioned the Order of the Elements had fallen under the control of the enemy."

"Did Miles tell you that?"

"Of course," I said. "Why not mention it to me? You told the Houses, he said, but not me?"

"They refused to listen to my warnings," he said. "That was the reason for our disagreement."

Oh. "They didn't believe you?"

"They believe my source of information was misinformed," he said.

"You have someone spying on the Order?" I said. "Since when?"

"I did." There was an odd note in his tone which I couldn't place, but he didn't offer another word of explanation.

"Do you want me to go to the House of Fire, then?" I asked. "Maybe I can talk some sense into them and get them to believe the truth about the Order."

"Forget the Order," he said. "The Order's status only matters for the inhabitants of Earth, not the Parallel."

I wasn't so certain about that, but I hardly gave a shit about the Order myself, not with the Family at large, Adair being uncooperative and my former best friend potentially facing a death sentence. Yet I still found room to be irked at the Death King for hiring me as his Fire Element and still refusing to tell me pertinent information.

"Are you sure the same enemy hasn't taken over the Houses, too?" I said. "Why not send someone to check?"

"That," he said, "is supposed to be *your* job."

Oh. "I thought you wanted to join forces. Before the enemy gets there first. Isn't that the goal?"

"Something like that," he said.

"Then what am I supposed to do if it turns out they already made up their minds?"

"That's a decision you'll have to make on your own."

Annoyance flared inside me. As he turned away, I said, "Did you know the enemy has a way to bring the dead back to life using a cantrip?"

He rotated, his empty gaze piercing me. "Who told you that?"

I swear the entire hall got colder. "Miles did. He said… he said the enemy was a former lich who brought himself back to life and that he has a way of doing the same for the other liches, too. Have you told them?"

"They're well aware," he said. "However, we have yet to find out what the method is and if there are any potential downsides. In any case, it's of no concern of yours."

"My friend is a lich," I pointed out, but he was already drifting away across the hall. "What am I supposed to do now? Go back to the House of Fire and tell them they have one chance left to give you an answer?"

"If you believe that'll be productive, then by all means, try," he said. "Tell them my offer is still open."

That was a challenge if I ever heard one. "I will."

On the way out of the castle, I walked *through* a lich, which was about as fun as you might think. An ice-cold sensation slid through my body, and I yelped. "Ack."

"Ow," said Harper. "I can feel your fire, and liches are pretty damn flammable, you know. What did the Death King want with you?"

"He wants me to go back to the House of Fire," I said. "Or to be more accurate, he pretty much said it's impossible for me to get a straight answer out of them, so now I have an incentive to prove him wrong."

"Haven't you been going there every day this week?" Harper asked me.

"Only to make sure they haven't punished Tay," I said. "But given what I just heard from the Death King, they won't even tell *him* how the Family got out of prison."

"They won't tell the Death King?" she echoed. "Aren't they afraid of him?"

"You'd think," I said. "So I need to poke them a bit more. I know for a fact someone gave the killer that cantrip. It didn't get there by accident."

"Cantrip?"

"That's how the jailor died," I said. "Reusable cantrip, carved with a spell that killed him instantly. Even if the killer came from inside the House of Fire, they got the cantrip from outside. Someone gave it to them."

"I'm hearing weird shit about cantrips lately," she said. "Like those infernos."

"Yeah, and the cantrips the enemy is allegedly making to bring people back to life," I added. "Did you—"

"There's a way to come back to life?" Her tone sounded shocked. "What? You're joking."

"Sorry, I thought you knew." Now I wished I hadn't mentioned it, so I didn't get her hopes up if there turned out to be a massive downside like Miles had implied.

"I didn't." Hurt underlaid her tone. "Where do they come from, then?"

"I don't know," I said. "Miles said the enemy used one to turn himself from a lich into a human again, but he won't tell anyone how he did it. Usually there's a massive downside to that kind of magic."

"That figures," she said. "I'll see you later."

As she left, I made for the node, regretting bringing up the subject. I hadn't wanted to give her false hope, not after she'd lost so much already. Her brother had died, while her own life had been put on hold, and I didn't blame her for looking for a way out.

I returned to the House of Fire to find Harris on duty,

as usual. This time, I wedged my foot in the door to stop him from shutting me out.

"Another guard died outside the House," he said. "Murdered using the same method which killed Zade."

"Shit." Adair was now in the Death King's hands. He couldn't have done it. And from the smirk on Harris's face, he knew it, too. "Was Tay out of her cell again?"

"No."

Huh. "Then she can't be a suspect."

"That's for us to decide, not you," he said. "Go away."

"The Death King sent me to discuss Adair." I had the suspicion they'd respond more readily to that than to another request for them to spare Tay's life.

"What about him?" He stepped back from the door, allowing me to enter. It seemed bringing up my brother was the key to getting them to let me in.

"When did the murder happen?" I asked.

"Last night," he replied. "I came down to relieve him of guard duty and tripped over the body outside."

So he died outside. If he'd been killed by the same kind of cantrip as the one which had killed Zade, it hadn't necessarily come from inside the building itself. Anyone might've been the culprit.

"What did you want to say about that brother of yours, then?" Harris glanced over his shoulder, an air of uneasiness about him. If I wanted to probe him for information, I couldn't have picked a better time to take advantage of his distraction.

"He likes screaming and rattling the cage bars, doesn't he?" I said. "He also strongly hinted that he hypnotised Tay before the jailor's death."

"If you're looking for me to take pity on your little

friend, you're out of luck," he said. "All evidence says she's the killer."

"Then tell me how Adair got out the first time," I said pointedly. "You have nothing to gain from keeping that information from me. He's still in jail, but I want to make sure he stays there. Preferably for the duration."

"Then I'd suggest you discuss your security measures with the Death King."

"You don't trust the Death King either, do you?" I said. "What's your problem with him?"

If the Death King headed the original House of Spirit, he'd once been on an equal footing with them. While being a lich meant being cursed to spend an eternity as a zombie, there was no denying that his magical prowess far outmatched the other Houses. Perhaps Harris felt threatened by him. It was as good a guess as any.

"He has no right to send you here to tell us how to take care of our prisoners," said Harris.

Maybe he does, given your track record. "Was the guard who died killed by a cantrip?"

"So it appears," he said. "I seem to remember *you* took the other one."

I threw my hands up. "Just consider for a moment that I might be trying to help find who's killing your people. Also, you might want to listen to the Death King's warnings. I know for a fact that he told you the Order of the Elements is under the control of the enemy—"

"Get out," he said. "I've heard enough from you. Tell the Death King that there will be no alliance between our House and his as long as he keeps information on the nature of the enemy from us."

Okay, that made no sense whatsoever. "He's not keeping anything from you."

He looked down at me. "Then he doesn't trust you so much after all."

Anger scorched my cheeks with heat, but I managed to refrain from tossing a fireball at him. If I lost my temper, I'd end up in a cell myself, so I turned heel and left, retracing my steps to the node.

After I landed in the swampland, I walked back towards the gates, fighting the urge to go and pick a fight with Adair. It wouldn't do any good to start anything with him while I was already hopping mad.

Ryan accosted me on the other side of the gates. "Where've you been?"

"The House of Fire," I said. "Another guard died the same way as the head jailor did."

"With a cantrip?" they asked.

"Apparently," I said. "Also, the guard at the House of Fire told me that he won't cooperate with the Death King as long as he supposedly keeps secrets on the nature of the enemy from everyone else. Including us."

Ryan's eyes narrowed. "He *what?*"

"I'm not sure if he was telling the truth," I said hastily, "but I think it's safe to say the Houses have cut us loose."

"They can't have," said Ryan. "We took their prisoner off their hands, and they need to keep up their end of the bargain if they want the Death King to stay on their good side."

"I'm not sure they care either way," I said. "Harris pretty much shoved me out the door. Wouldn't give me the cantrip to look at either, so I can only assume it's the same as the last one."

"What about that supplier?" they said. "Did you speak to them?"

"We did," I said. "The Spirit Agents don't think Dawson is guilty of making the cantrip himself, but I didn't want to pay him to identify the spell for me. Also, I'd rather not put a target on my back by asking an expert."

"I bet Liv's friend Devon can figure out what it is," said Ryan. "She won't tell tales, either."

Liv. Again. "Can she identify the person who carved it?"

"No," they said. "But she can take a reusable cantrip and identify the previous spell used on it. I've seen her do it."

"I guess it can't hurt." I was all out of ideas, and besides, it wasn't like I had anything to lose by asking. "All right."

I'd expected the Air Element to ask the Death King's permission, but instead of going to him, they went to one of the rooms near the Elemental Soldiers' quarters which had once been used as a dormitory for the contenders during the Fire Element contest. On a bed inside the room sat a woman of around Liv's age, with heavily bandaged hands. Her short brown hair stuck up in all directions as she looked up from the book she was reading. "You're the new Fire Element, right?"

"That's me," I said. "I'm told you're an expert on cantrips. Can you look at this one for me?"

She dropped the book onto the bed. "Sure. Not much else I can do until my hands heal up."

"What happened?" I asked.

"Got on the wrong side of one of those inferno spells."

I winced. "Sorry."

She took the cantrip from me in her bandaged hands. "What're you looking for? It's blank."

"I hoped you could uncover which spell was used on it before it wiped itself clean," I said. "It was used to kill a guard in the House of Fire."

She laid it down on the bed. "You might've led with that part before dumping this on me. Liv does this kind of thing all the time."

I'd rather she stayed out of this one. "Doesn't she work for the Order?"

Did *she* know they were under the control of the enemy?

"Not exactly." Devon turned the cantrip over in her hands. "I'll have a look at this and get back to you later."

She wanted to keep her friend's secrets, then. Understandable. If the Death King knew of the Order's corruption, it was a safe bet he'd told Liv, too, but what if the enemy's influence on the Order was creeping into the Parallel, too? That might account for the Houses' sudden reticence to consider a deal with the Death King, even after we'd kept up our end of the bargain. The Family's signature on the back of the blank cantrip was a screaming reminder that they were never as far away as they seemed.

I halted in the doorway. "That signature on the back of the cantrip... have you seen it before?"

"This?" She peered at it. "Nope. I can't identify a signature unless I've already encountered the practitioner who carved it. I don't know this one."

"No worries," I said. "Thanks for the help."

I walked out of the dorm, my head spinning. I hadn't

thought Devon might be linked to the Family, so at least there was little chance of word making it back to them. Yet I had the sinking feeling they'd left their signature on the cantrip partly as a message to me. Adair had already goaded me about the Family hiding in plain sight, and while I hadn't had cause to pay any attention to the Order of the Elements before now, I had yet another reason to have a bad feeling about the situation in the Houses.

What if the worst had happened, and the Houses already did the Family's bidding?

8

———

After leaving Devon in the dorm, I walked with Ryan back to the main hall.

"So you're going to wait for her to figure out what kind of spell was on the cantrip?" they said.

"Not much choice," I said. "I mean, we can go back to the supplier in Elysium again, but I doubt anyone would tell us directly if they're working with the Family. So I thought Miles and I could grab some invisibility cantrips and take matters into our own hands instead."

"That sounds more like bending the rules than I'd like," said Ryan.

"Two people have died," I told them. "I don't know about you, but the idea of a cantrip which can kill people with hardly a trace is pretty unnerving, and I don't see any harm in snooping around the supplier's house. You don't have to come."

"Did you say snoop around?" said Dex, flying over my shoulder. "I'm in."

"You weren't invited," said the Air Element.

"That's not very nice," he said. "I won't tell Liv, honest. I want to come."

"You don't even know where we're going," I said.

"To spy on someone?"

"No, to sneak around the cantrip supplier in Elysium and see if we can find evidence linking them to whoever used two unknown cantrips to commit murder at the House of Fire," I told the sprite. "You can come along if you don't draw attention."

"I would never," he said solemnly. "I'll not make a peep."

"Uh-huh," I said. "I think we should go after they close up for the night. Ryan, are you in?"

"I have plans tonight," they said. "Surely your friend Miles can help you instead."

"I haven't asked him, but I'm sure he will," I said. "If it turns out the suppliers *are* involved in creating these illegal cantrips for the Family, though, we need all the backup we can get. What plans do you have?"

"None of your business."

I frowned. "No need to be rude. It's not like the Death King has given us any specific instructions. He didn't say we couldn't leave the castle."

"He also didn't give you permission to start a feud with Elysium's only cantrip supplier."

"I won't get caught." When they rolled their eyes, I added, "Trust me, I'm good at stealth."

"No doubt, given how you cheated your way into the Fire Element contest."

Okay, that was unfair. "The Death King gave me the

job because he wanted me to negotiate with the Houses of the Elements. The House of Fire won't speak to him because they're too preoccupied with the fact that two of their people dropped dead in the last week. If I can find out who did it, technically I *am* doing my job."

"If you say so," they said. "Then go, but for all our sakes, please don't get caught."

When I left the castle later that evening, I found the dark shadowy form of a lich waiting for me outside.

"Where are you going?" asked Harper. "The House of Fire again?"

"Nah, the cantrip supplier in Elysium," I said. "Might end up in the House again if the clues lead that way, though. What're you up to?"

"Well…" she began. "I'm kind of running an important mission for the Death King, too."

"Really?" I said. "He never mentioned it."

"It's because his enemies are specifically recruiting liches," she said. "They want the Death King's forces on their own team. So I'm taking advantage of that."

"Huh," I said. "I didn't know."

Still, at least she had something to do with her time. I'd felt bad for leaving her out of my plans, but I knew how much she hated the Houses, and I didn't want to freak her out by insinuating that the Family were back to their old tricks, either.

Nobody else was outside except for Neddie the horse, so I walked over to him while I waited for Dex to join me.

The horse whinnied when he saw me and tried to bite my fingers.

"I think you're going to have to give up on your ambitions to ride a zombie steed, Bria," said Harper. "They really don't seem to like you. If you ask me, they have a thing against fire mages."

"Guess I don't blame them for that." I spotted Dex approaching from the castle. "See you in a bit, Harper."

Dex and I left the castle via the gates and passed through the node, heading to the city of Elysium. We emerged down the road from the Spirit Agents' house, where Miles waited for me outside, as we'd arranged, wearing a dark coat with the collar turned up against the cold evening air. "Hey, Bria."

"Hey." I glanced down at the sight of movement at my feet, but it was only a curious vampire chicken. "I thought someone was supposed to be picking those things up."

"They were," Miles said. "Haven't heard a word. I reckon they got distracted by all the crap happening in the Houses."

"What are you two doing?" Shelley said from behind him.

"We're going to pay another visit to Dawson's place," I said. "To have a poke around and see if there's anything he's not telling us about who he sells to."

"Really, Miles?" said Shelley. "Did you really want to alienate one of our few allies?"

"We won't alienate anyone if we don't get caught," he replied. "Which we won't."

"We could use some backup," I added, as Dex flew overhead and hovered above my shoulder.

"Is that a fire sprite?" said Shelley.

"That's Dex," I said. "He'll be helping us out. He can get in and out of places with being seen… provided he doesn't set them on fire, that is."

"I won't start a single fire unless you ask me to," he said.

"Let's hope I don't need to," I responded. "Anyone want to back us up? We're not going to start any fights if we can help it. I just want to know if the suppliers are selling cantrips to anyone who might be linked to the Family. We need to know if they're knowingly involved or if the people who murdered the guards at the House of Fire got the cantrips from elsewhere."

"All right, I'll come," said Shelley. "Only to stop Miles from getting into trouble."

Miles grinned. "I'll be on my best behaviour."

We made our way down the darkened street. I didn't have much reason to fear what lurked in the eerie silence —not when I'd spent the last few weeks hanging out with liches and zombie horses—but I still tensed at every small noise. Then a familiar squawk from behind us made me spin around. Sure enough, something small and feathered lurked behind us.

"Er, Miles, one of the chickens followed us."

"Ah, hell." He stepped in and picked up the chicken around the middle, and when it let out an indignant sound, he covered its beak with his hand.

I stifled a laugh. "Nothing ever goes without a hitch, does it?"

"I'll hold the chicken," said Shelley. "Since we're not starting any fights, *are* we, Miles?"

Bloody hope not. After Miles passed her the chicken, we

walked on until we reached the supplier's house, at which point I used a cantrip to turn invisible.

"Dex, we're going in," I whispered to the fire sprite. "If anyone shows up, can you distract them?"

"On it," he whispered back.

"I'll be right behind you," added Miles.

An unlocking cantrip took care of the door, and I slipped into the darkened room. Boxes of cantrips filled the space, all marked with labels indicating who they were meant for. And all of them held the COS's logo, too. That meant they were reusable cantrips from Arcadia, but that didn't mean they hadn't made another stop en route.

I peered into a couple of the boxes. It was too dark to see if the Family's logo was on any of the cantrips, but I assumed they wouldn't be that blatant. If there were clues in here, they'd be hidden away.

Dex landed on my shoulder, making me jump. "There's two shifty-looking guys outside. I think they're on their way here."

"Shit." I ducked around the boxes and crossed the room to the door, darting outside into the night. Miles and Shelley must have hidden themselves nearby under the guise of invisibility cantrips, because nobody was within view. The murmur of voices sounded from the adjacent street. I walked on silent feet, holding my breath, and ducked within an alley as two men dressed in dark clothing approached the shop and eyed the closed door.

"He's late," one of them said.

"Probably checking for spies," his friend replied. "You know how hard it is now they're watching the COS so closely. They're scared they'll come here next."

"They can't watch everyone," his friend responded.

"That's the beauty of reusable cantrips. The evidence is wiped clean."

"Not to experts," said the first guy. "Luckily, that's not most people."

"Yeah, and soon enough it won't matter," said his friend. "The COS was always a front and even with the guy who started the operation rotting in the ground, someone will get a foothold in soon enough."

"We have to do this by the book until then," said the first guy. "Man, I can't wait until the Houses come out on the right side."

What is that supposed to mean? These guys were definitely up to something shady, but I couldn't see anyone from the supplier nearby. At least until a broad-shouldered figure walked into the alley beside the shop, carrying a box. There must be another entrance around the back, and I thanked my invisibility cantrip for keeping me hidden from sight. Regardless, I pressed myself against the wall as he walked past, recognising him as the assistant who worked at Dawson's place. *Does his boss know he's hanging out here at night?*

"There he is," said one of the men. "About time."

The assistant approached them, and they conversed in low voices over the box. Did Dawson know his assistant was selling cantrips to dodgy-looking strangers? Whether he did or not, I didn't need to be able to see their faces to know the two men for mages. *They're from one of the Houses.* Not the House of Fire, I didn't think, but in order to find out which House they belonged to, I'd have to follow them.

One of the two men took the box in his hands, and the pair of them walked back down the alley. I waited for

Dawson's assistant to return to the shop before following them silently. I didn't see Miles or Shelley, but I wasn't about to let the pair of them out of my sight until they reached their destination.

The two mages kept walking, speaking in low voices. I sensed Dex's warm presence nearby and spotted the flicker of the fire sprite's light, but I didn't dare speak to him in case I alerted their attention.

"This stealth shit is getting old," said the first guy, who carried the box. "Wish the other Houses would hurry up and capitulate."

The two mages rounded a corner and came to the central headquarters of the House of Earth. The building resembled the House of Fire from the outside, except with a brown door and fittings instead of red. I'd never met the person in charge of the House of Earth, but did they know these two men were breaking the law? Nobody bought cantrips in the dead of night unless they had something to hide—from the other Houses as well as from their own. I glanced across the street to where the House of Fire stood at the far corner, but I saw no signs of movement outside.

If the House of Earth had already been infiltrated, who would be next? Was that what the cantrips were truly intended for? If they were designed to silently kill, like the ones which had taken out the jailor and guard at the House of Fire, then snagging those cantrips would solve the murders *and* remove the heat from Tay in one fell swoop.

My gaze picked out the outline of the fire sprite nearby, hovering above my head.

"Dex," I whispered. "Do something to distract them."

"What kind of diversion?" he muttered back. "Loud enough to alert the other Houses?"

"Not sure they're paying attention," I whispered. "Go on, throw a couple of fireballs behind their heads so the mages think it's the House of Fire."

Chance would be a fine thing, but if I couldn't stop all the traitors in the House of Earth at once, I could at least make their life difficult by taking their illegal cantrips off their hands.

At a snap of Dex's fingers, sparks flew out and coalesced into a flame which shot over the mages' heads.

The two mages exclaimed in surprise, and the box of cantrips fell to the ground. Another fireball shot from Dex's hands, causing the mages to dive to either side to avoid being hit. I darted forwards and grabbed the box in my hands, dragging it into the shadow of a nearby alleyway.

"Hey!" one of the men shouted. "Who's out there?"

"Quiet," hissed his friend. "We can't have the other Houses hearing. Go on, you get the box back."

I lifted the box's flap, and a single glance inside confirmed my worst guesses. The cantrips within all bore the mark of the Family.

Another fireball soared overhead, and one of the men flung himself around the corner, cursing. The second guy, however, took a step back and disappeared below the earth. An instant later, he surfaced directly in front of me, hands grabbing the box and drawing both of us downwards into the ground. *Shit, I forgot earth magic could do that.*

I clung to the box, suddenly submerged to my waist in

the earth. He might not be able to see me, but I was stuck, unable to stop him from wrestling the box out of my grip.

"Who are you?" hissed the mage. "Show your face."

I lunged forwards and tugged at the box, but he held on fast. The sound of pounding footsteps reached my ears. More mages had come out of the House of Earth, hearing the ruckus.

Abandon ship!

I let the box go and scrabbled to get back to the surface before I ended up being dragged even deeper underground. Seven, eight mages ran out of the building. Too many to take on alone, not when I couldn't see Miles or Shelley anywhere.

"Where's that fire mage?" one of them shouted. "Hey!"

Sparks flew, and the smell of flames singed my ears. Silently thanking Dex for keeping them occupied, I got my feet back on solid ground and sprinted down the street, heading for the House of Fire. I didn't believe they'd help me out even in a dire situation like this, but if I got their attention before the earth mages got that box of theirs out of sight, they wouldn't be able to deny they were carrying illegal cantrips.

The door to the House of Fire was locked, but I hammered on it with my fist, turning off the invisibility cantrip as Harris's irate face appeared in the gap between door and wall. "You again?"

"There's mages breaking the law back here." I jabbed a finger wildly over my shoulder. "Members of the House of Earth are carrying illegal cantrips marked with the Family's signature."

"What are you doing here?" he said. "No bullshit."

"I told you," I said, "the House of Earth's mages are

buying up illegal cantrips, but when I tried to get the box off them, they brought out half the House's security. I think the whole House is in on it."

"Fuck off," he said. "You think I'll believe a word you say?"

"It's true," I said, irked. "Look, they're right over there."

He looked where I pointed, but of course, it was too dark to see anyone. As I attempted to wedge my foot in the door, he gave me a shove off the doorstep. "Go away."

Seriously? I backed away from the House of Fire and fumbled for my cantrip to turn invisible again, determined to physically drag one of the earth mages here if that's what it took.

Then I heard a familiar squawking noise in the shadows. Oh, hell.

"Miles?" I hissed. "Please tell me you didn't leave that chicken unattended."

"Bria?" said Miles's voice. "Damn. Thought you were fighting those earth mages."

"They brought out their House's security," I said. "The House of Fire didn't believe me, but if they end up getting taken over from the inside, they can't say I didn't try to warn them."

"Want me to release the chicken on them?" said Miles.

"Tempting." I tensed as the ground trembled underfoot. "Shit. I think some of those mages are still underground."

Were they coming after the House of Fire? If so... we were standing right here.

"Miles," hissed Shelley. "Get over here. Both of you."

The ground exploded as two mages surfaced at once,

narrowly missing both of us. Glowing cantrips flared in their hands. *Infernos.*

"Run!" I shouted over my shoulder. We pelted down the road, and Dex zipped overhead, his own fire a warning signal before the inferno rippled through the air. The entire area in front of the House of Fire went up in flames, heat searing my back and feet. I kept running, not daring to look over my shoulder.

Holy shit. They'd been aiming right for the House of Fire, and even fire mages couldn't stand up to those flames.

"This way!" Miles's voice sounded. I sprinted onward, my hands flickering in and out of sight. Great. As if our situation wasn't dire enough, it looked like my invisibility cantrip was on the brink of burning out. Which meant—

In a blink, all three of us appeared before we reached the next corner, vampire chicken and all. Beneath our feet, the ground trembled again. The earth mages were *still* tailing us. Could we even outrun them on foot? If we returned to the Spirit Agents' base, we might well be dooming everyone inside the house.

"There's no way the other Houses didn't see that," Miles breathed.

"They'll think a fire mage set off that cantrip," Shelley pointed out. "If Bria stays here, she's the perfect scapegoat, especially as she knocked on the House of Fire's door not a minute before the blast went off."

"Dammit," I said. "They did that on purpose."

Dex cleared his throat. "You might want to run."

The ground gave another heave, prompting us to break into a sprint again.

"At this rate we'll lead them right back to our base," Shelley gasped out.

"We can't run in circles all night either," Miles responded. "Dex, can't you do something?"

"I can't deflect fire, can I?" he said. "Escape through a node."

"Where?" I spotted the gleam of a node ahead of us. "To the swamp? That could work."

"I've a better idea," Dex said. "Come on. I'll take us to a safe house."

We picked up speed, hurrying down the street and trying to ignore the ongoing tremors beneath our feet. Dex reached the node first, and when we caught up with him, light enfolded around us.

"This better work!" I grabbed Miles's arm for balance, and we vanished into the node's light.

A second later, I slammed down onto a wooden surface, landing in a crouch. I raised my head, looking up at several bewildered faces.

Uh-oh. We weren't in the Parallel, but in a room containing a long table covered in what looked like a giant cardboard castle and a number of handmade figurines. Devon and Liv sat at the table, along with Trix the elf, who looked as baffled as the rest of them. And Ryan, who glared daggers at me. That answered the question as to what Ryan's plans for the night were, then.

"What the hell are you doing?" Liv demanded.

I straightened upright. "Long story."

Miles and Shelley picked themselves off the floor, while Dex flew over to the table to address Liv. "We were being chased. Had to make a quick getaway."

"Into my house?" said Devon. "Dex, that is *not* cool."

I shot the sprite a glare. "Dex, you never said the node landed in her house!"

Before she could reply, a loud squawk sounded as the vampire chicken landed on the table in the ruins of the model castle.

"Are we fighting a vampire chicken now?" Trix said uncertainly.

"I'll get rid of the chicken," Ryan said, reaching to pick up the vampire chicken. Its teeth sank into the Air Element's hand, and I stifled a laugh despite the seriousness of the situation.

Liv glared at the fire sprite. "Please don't tell me whoever was chasing you followed you into the house."

"No, I think we're good." He cleared his throat. "So… want to do battle with a vampire chicken now?"

"I think we should go," said one of the other players.

"No!" Devon marched over to our bedraggled group. "Get out of my house. And I swear if whatever's chasing you lands up in here, I'll shut you in a cantrip delivery box and send you to the Order."

The Order? I left the room, along with Miles and Shelley. Miles started laughing when we reached the door.

"Damn, Dex," he said. "We just landed on Liv's shit list. Again."

"Why do they live on top of a node?" I said.

"A lot of practitioners do," said Shelley. "It's the best way for them to access magic outside of the Parallel."

I'd assumed Devon was staying in the castle. It was also safe to assume she wasn't working on any cantrips at the moment either, given the state of her hands.

"Did she say she'd send us to the Order?" I said. "I thought Devon was safe."

"She used to work for the Order," said Dex. "What? Why are you looking at me like that?"

"If the Order arrests us for using a node illegally, we'll know who to blame."

On the plus side, we'd escaped death by inferno cantrip. On the minus side, we'd just pissed off the castle's resident cantrip expert, Liv *and* Ryan all at once.

More to the point… the Order was under the control of the enemy. And now we had definitive proof that at least one of the Houses was, too.

9

"That could have gone better," Miles said. "At least we managed to shake off those earth mages. We'll head back to base and make sure the others know there are rogues from the House of Earth roaming the city."

"We'd better hope they don't remember our faces," Shelley added. "Also, I think we just lost our suppliers, too."

"It might've just been the assistant who was dealing with those guys," said Miles. "I didn't see Dawson himself there, did you?"

"No, but it's safe to say they're not on the straight and narrow," I said. "Those cantrips they were trading all had the Family's mark on them. It didn't get there by accident."

"Why would the Family put their signature on a cantrip?" said Shelley. "Seems a dead giveaway for someone who wants to lie low."

"Nah, they're suckers for attention," I said. "They like

thinking of themselves as notorious. They'll have someone carving their mark onto cantrips, so everyone knows who they're dealing with."

"They also started a fire back there," said Miles. "That inferno didn't hit anyone in the House of Fire, did it?"

"If Harris didn't open the door when he heard the noise, he might've been lucky enough to escape," I said, with a grimace. "Problem is, he wouldn't listen to me when I said the House of Earth had been compromised, but I bet he'll be all too eager to pin the blame on me for the attack. Better hope he didn't see you two as well."

"Yeah." Miles's expression was unusually grim. "Question is, whereabouts are the Family manufacturing those cantrips?"

"Haven't a clue," I said. "I eavesdropped on those mages, but they didn't give it away. They did say it *wasn't* the COS who're carving them because they're being watched closely, so it might not be taking place in Arcadia. Hell, the operation might well be in Elysium for all we know. Somewhere underground." Literally, considering the earth mages' penchant for moving around under the city.

I heard shouting from the direction of Liv's house and tensed, then relaxed as then Dex flew past us. "There's a node this way. Come on. I don't think Devon is going to let you back in her house."

"Figures," I said. "What're they shouting at?"

"Dice."

"Right," I said, as if that made any sense to me whatsoever.

"What about us?" said Shelley. "I know the earth mages

didn't recognise us, but our base is way too close to the Houses for my liking."

"The Houses already know where we live," Miles reminded her. "We'll be okay. We can use the node from the Death King's territory to hop back to Elysium. That way we won't have to spend too long outside of our base."

Unless the earth mages decide to tunnel up through the floor. I didn't think they *had* seen Miles or Shelley, so they shouldn't target the Spirit Agents, but the Family was up to its old tricks, all right. That they were recruiting mages from within the Houses didn't come as a big surprise, but the fact that the House of Fire still refused to believe a word I said annoyed the shit out of me. I hoped the blast might have shocked some sense into them, but there was a depressingly high chance of the blame landing on yours truly. Again.

———

The Death King, to my consternation, remained absent all weekend. Whatever he did with his free time was beyond me, but I had no opportunity to give him the unwelcome update on my failed attempt to expose the traitors within the House of Earth. At least Miles and Shelley had made it back to their base in one piece and told me later on that the House of Fire had escaped the inferno cantrip by mere inches, only losing their door to the blast.

But the fact remained that the House of Earth were now holding an entire box of illegal cantrips marked with the Family's signature, some of which might well have been able to inflict a silent death on anyone who threatened to expose their secret. To top it all off, Devon still hadn't brought me an update on the cantrip I'd given her to identify, most likely due to her annoyance at me for crashing her game night, so I had yet to figure out what kind of spell had caused the deaths of Zade and the second victim.

With nothing better to do, I found a bag of costume props in the break room which presumably belonged to Devon or Liv, and spent a productive hour sticking googly eyes and moustaches onto the skulls in the pillars on either side of the entrance hall.

"Perfect." Dex snickered. "Much better."

"I agree." I tweaked the eyes in the sockets of a lopsided skull. "Has Devon forgiven me yet?"

"Ask her yourself."

"Wait, she's here?" I stepped back from the pillar. "Oops. I think I may have swiped her costume supplies."

While part of me expected her to start lobbing dice at me if I disturbed her, I wanted to find out what kind of cantrip had killed the jailor, even if the House of Fire was about as likely to ask for my help as the Death King was likely to be amused by my new decorations.

I walked down the corridor and found Devon in the dormitory, sitting on the bed. Her hands were no longer bandaged, her face screwed up in concentration as she used a delicate tool to carve runes into a cantrip.

"Bria." She put down the cantrip. "Come to apologise for crashing our game?"

"Uh," I said. "Yeah. I really didn't know the node led into your house. Dex didn't say."

"I'm inclined to believe it was his fault, to be honest," she said. "What was chasing you?"

"Turns out the Houses have a few traitors within their

ranks," I said to her. "The House of Earth does, anyway. We were trying to get some illegal cantrips off their hands, but they outnumbered us. If we hadn't gone through the node, their inferno cantrips would've burned us to cinders. We barely made it out. Sorry I wrecked your game."

"Apology accepted," said Devon, reaching behind her and retrieving another cantrip, this one blank and gleaming with the Family's symbol. "This cantrip, though, it's a nasty piece of work."

My heart skipped. "You figured out what it is?"

"Eventually," she said. "The last spell used on it was like a mechanised magical virus which breaks down the body from the inside."

"That's how Zade died?" Damn. "Guess it's less flashy than an inferno cantrip."

"Just as lethal, though," she said. "If the killer wanted to hide how they did it, they shouldn't have used a reusable cantrip."

"Maybe it's all they had on them," I said. "The cantrips the House of Earth was smuggling in were the same sort, I think. But I don't think they were carved in Arcadia."

Curiosity flickered in her eyes. "Then where?"

"I have no idea," I admitted, "but this isn't a spell you'd find on the market. And that mark on the back... it belongs to the Family. It's their signature."

She lowered the cantrip in her hand. "Gonna tell me who the Family is?"

"Only if you promise not to say a word to the Order," I said. "I heard you work for them."

"I did," she said. "I mean, technically I still do. They thought I was dead for a while... it's complicated, but they're one of the few organisations who buy cantrips on Earth. I don't like them, but I need to pay my bills. If they knew I was here in the castle, though, they'd slap me with a black mark for all the times I've used the nodes without their permission. I'm not on their side, and I'm sure as hell not reporting to them."

"Does Liv know?" I asked.

"She knows," she said. "She isn't happy about me risking my neck by staying in their employment, but I figured we could use an inside source on the Order. If you haven't heard, a group of renegade spirit mages took over the upper management from within, and most of the other Order members don't have a clue."

"How'd you find out, then?" I said.

"Because the people who nearly killed me with that inferno cantrip were working with someone inside the Order," she said. "They caused a diversion and then staged a coup."

"Damn." The Order was known for punishing mages harshly, but that didn't mean I could ever have pictured them being taken over by spirit mages from the inside. "Are they still working with the Houses of the Elements, even now?"

"The Order is no longer handing prisoners over to the Houses," she said. "Obvious reasons. I don't know if their ambassadors have met in person since the incident, but if it's true what you say and at least one of the Houses is working with the enemy as well, I can imagine they're more closely involved."

"Great," I said. "Problem is, the House of Fire won't listen to a word I say whenever I try to warn them.

What're the odds that they've already been taken over as well?"

Was *that* why they hadn't executed Tay yet? For all I knew, they'd been the ones to set the Family free in the first place. On the other hand, that inferno cantrip the House of Earth had thrown at me had damn near struck the House of Fire's base as well. Not exactly what I'd expect from their ally.

"No idea, but I'm done with this cantrip," said Devon. "Let me know if you need me to look at anything else."

"I don't yet," I said, "but... how tricky is that virus cantrip to make?"

"Very," she said. "It's also highly illegal on both sides of the nodes because it's so damn contagious. If this cantrip was active in any way, I'd have dropped dead the instant I touched it."

"Damn." I looked at the deceptively innocuous golden coin. "Lucky it was inactive when I picked it up, then."

"I can think of a dozen possible uses for a spell of that nature, none of them pleasant," she said.

Yeah. "They wouldn't be much use against the Death King."

Then again, according to Miles, the enemy already had a potential way of killing a lich... or rather, bringing them back to life.

"Don't speak too soon," said Devon. "You want this back?"

"Nah, keep it," I said. "I'm no practitioner. Thanks for the help."

After walking out of the dorm, I left the castle via the back door. I hadn't visited my brother since his temper tantrum the other day, and while he was a manipulative bastard, his power was limited while he was in jail. Since the Death King seemed to have no intention of interrogating him and he'd given me enough clues to guess that he'd manipulated Tay into killing the jailor, maybe I could coax some more information out of him on how much he knew about the virus-laced cantrips—and where they were being manufactured.

I approached the two liches guarding the jail. "May I see Adair?"

"No," responded the lich on the left-hand side, in the same cold echoing voice all the liches possessed.

Worth a try.

"I think I'm the only person he'll speak to," I went on. "He definitely has information the Death King will want to know, but he's too stubborn to talk to anyone else. I won't look him in the eyes or give him the chance to use his powers on me."

"If you insist on going inside," said the lich on the right, "we'll be watching you."

"Fine, but that might cause him to clam up." I'd lose nothing for trying, though, so I entered the prison via the door and let the two liches trail in behind me.

"You again," Adair said. "I knew you'd come crawling back."

"Who let you out of your cell?" I said. "The first time around?"

He laughed. "The Death King."

"That's not funny."

"I thought it was pretty fucking funny." He sat back on the bench inside his cell. "Lighten up, sister."

"Not your sister." By designating us as siblings, our guardians had hoped we'd mirror each other's behaviour, but he'd always been crueller, sharper than I was, and had stamped out what little conscience he'd possessed when we were kids in an effort to emulate Lex and Roth.

"You are," he said. "You're just like me, deep down. You locked me up here because you couldn't face the truth."

I shook my head at him. "How many people in the House of Fire are allied with the lich named Hawker and the spirit mages who took over the Order of the Elements?"

He was silent for an instant. "Huh?"

I risked a glance at him and saw puzzlement on his face. I'd wanted to catch him off guard, and it'd worked. Unfortunately, I hadn't exactly planned where to go from there.

"You heard me," I said. "How many members of the House of Fire have joined his side? Is it an open secret like in the House of Earth?"

"Makes no difference whether you know or not," he said. "It's already too late."

His words wormed beneath my skin. *So the enemy is already there.* "I beg to differ. I'm assuming not everyone in the Houses is working for the enemy, or else they wouldn't have seen to it that you stayed behind bars."

His face flushed. "Watch it."

"It's true, isn't it?" I said. "Even our guardians just left you locked up in there. Anyone would think they didn't care."

I averted my gaze, but I felt his sharp eyes on me all the same. "You need to watch your mouth."

"Tough talk from a guy behind bars," I said. "Why'd you kill the jailor using a cantrip laced with a virus, anyway? Fancied a change, or didn't you feel like being as violent as usual?"

"You don't have a clue what's coming, do you," he said. "It'll make those inferno cantrips look like a blessing."

Too late, I recalled Devon's words about those cantrips being deadly to anyone who laid their hands on them. Less violent than Adair's usual methods, yes, but if the box of cantrips those mages had been carrying had contained countless copies of the same cantrip, they might be lethal to large numbers of people. Yet all my warnings to the House of Fire had fallen on deaf ears. This one would be no exception.

I did my best to keep my face blank as I addressed the cage bars. "I know what's *not* coming. Lex and Roth. They don't give a crap about you."

At the sound of the names of our guardians, he roared in anger and rose to his face, and I turned away to avoid making accidental eye contact with him.

"Hawker will be here soon enough," Adair called after me as I left the jail. "He'll be the one who takes power from the Death King. Mark my words."

A likely story. It was past time I found the Death King, wherever he was. He definitely wasn't playing video games with the Elemental Soldiers, but his own quarters were the only part of the castle which were out of bounds to the rest of us. Regardless, Adair's warning had awakened a sense of urgency I couldn't shake. I entered the castle via the front doors and made my way to the far corridor, where a wooden door led to the private staircase belonging to the King of the Dead.

Before I could knock on the door, the Death King floated through the wooden surface. I stumbled back, damn near tripping over my feet. His cold stare sent a wave of chills down to my bones, and I swore the very fire inside me extinguished itself.

"Ack!" My voice sounded entirely too squeaky for my liking.

The Death King studied me. "If you've come to redecorate my quarters as well as the entrance hall, then I'd advise you to banish the notion."

Oh shit. He'd noticed the improvement I'd made to the skulls in the pillars. "I thought you were out of the castle."

Why had I thought redecorating his creepy pillars was a good idea again? I'd ticked off Striker to no end when I'd worked for him, but this was the first time I'd had a boss who could genuinely rip out my soul if he felt like it. For all I knew, that would be a permanent end even for the likes of me.

"You have an update for me, don't you?" He drifted past me into the entrance hall, and I followed, relief sweeping through me at the notion that he wasn't going to kill me after all.

I gave him a quick rundown of the events of last Friday evening, including my recent discovery about the House of Earth's loyalties. He didn't react with any surprise whatsoever to my pronouncement that several of their number seemed to be obtaining illegal cantrips from the enemy.

"So you knew," I said. "You knew the Houses were being taken over from within."

"I suspected there was a strong possibility."

My hands clenched. "Then what am I supposed to do? I take it you want me to stop trying to pursue an alliance with them?"

"I didn't have the impression you were having much luck in that regard anyway," he said.

"Then why bother taking the House of Fire's prisoner?" I said. "Why'd they let you bring Adair here if they didn't want any kind of alliance with you?"

"Presumably, they wanted him off their hands," he said. "I imagine it was a relief to be rid of him, one way or another."

"You're telling me," I said. "For the record, I also figured out the jailor at the House of Fire was killed by a cantrip containing a magical virus. Devon worked it out."

"Good for her," he said. "I'm glad you found a way to entertain yourself which didn't involve breaking the law or redecorating my property."

Unbelievable. "Don't blame me when the Family shows up on the doorstep to retrieve their missing member. Aren't you the least bit concerned about the Houses?"

"Yes," he said. "I am. That said, I suspected they'd be reticent to join forces with me. We don't have a pleasant history with one another."

"I'm not their biggest fan either, but the idea of someone like my brother, the Family, having access to their resources…" I broke off. "Cantrips that can kill at a touch and Elysium's only supplier being on the enemy's side ought to warrant a little more attention, surely. I can't even convince the House of Fire's guards there's a problem."

"Then they'll have to learn the hard way," he said. "Like the House of Earth did, I imagine."

"You used to belong to the House of Spirit," I said. "The Court of the Dead is all that's left of the fifth House. Miles told me."

"Your point?"

I threw up my hands. "I know you don't like the other Houses, but can't you… I don't know, send someone else to give them a warning? I'm not the person to do it. We have too unpleasant a history."

"As a matter of fact, I always thought you were uniquely suited to the job for a reason." He studied me. "Maybe you just aren't asking the right questions."

What was that supposed to mean? He was being spectacularly unhelpful, considering he must know perfectly well there was a strong chance the Houses had already fallen under the control of the Family.

Unless… wait a moment.

My mouth parted. "You mean you want me to pretend I'm working with this… Hawker person myself, right? Or with whoever's calling the shots? You don't think that wouldn't end badly for me?"

"That's your risk to take," he said. "If you ask the right questions, then you'll be able to narrow down the list of traitors pretty easily."

"Assuming they don't just lock me up." Which was a strong possibility, given that I didn't know for sure how many of the House of Fire's members were working with the enemy.

"I'm sure you can find a way to avoid it. You walked out of there at least once before."

Yes, I did. Three times, in fact. This, though, was different. Higher stakes. Potentially deadly.

Not that I was one to back down from a challenge.

ex waited for me at the other end of the hall when I left the Death King, hovering beside one of the newly decorated pillars.

"Off on another mission?" he said.

"You might say that," I said. "I'm going back to the House of Fire. Want to come?"

"Wouldn't miss it," he responded. "Those earth mages won't still be looking for trouble, will they?"

"They ought to have given up by now." I was more concerned with the House of Fire, and the impossibility of weeding out the traitors without getting locked up myself. Especially if Harris turned out to be one of them.

Once again, the pair of us travelled through the node to Elysium. The citadel towered over the rooftops, the sky was overcast, and the street was mercifully earth mage-free. The House of Fire's door had presumably been replaced after the inferno cantrip had blasted the old one to pieces, but the only change to its design was that a heavy lock now bolted it shut from the outside. That did not look welcoming in the slightest, but I rapped on the wooden surface with my knuckles anyway. Nobody answered.

"What's going on in there?" I tried peering into the building, but the windows were tinted so it was impossible for me to see if anyone was inside. "Dex, can you see anyone in there?"

"Two guards are downstairs. Want me to flush them out?"

"No," I said. "Hang on."

I walked around the side of the building to the back door and peered through the small pane of glass at the top. If I broke in, I could say goodbye to gaining the House's cooperation. On the other hand, nothing said 'go away' like a massive lock on the door. Who was I kidding? The earth mages had blown up their door with an inferno cantrip, and there was absolutely no way in hell Harris would believe I hadn't been involved. Even if by some miracle I made my way past him, I didn't have the patience to talk to every member of the House until I found whoever had joined up with the Family, not when most of them were plainly not in the know and were more likely to think *I* was the one trying to recruit them. I might as well have put myself in a cell already and saved them the bother.

Screw that. Instead, I reached in my pocket for an unlocking spell and an invisibility cantrip. "Forget the espionage shit. They clearly aren't open for business, so I'll go in the back way."

Dex hovered above the door, excitement fizzling around him in the form of fiery sparks. "Want me to slip inside and make sure nobody's watching?"

"Please." I used the unlocking spell and pushed the door open a fraction, and he darted ahead of me. Turning on the invisibility cantrip, I followed him.

Unnatural silence filled the space within. While the stairs leading down to the cells lay at the opposite end of the corridor, past the guards near the front door, I found myself wondering why it was so damn quiet in here. Had the House decided to close up entirely? Where in hell was everyone?

I debated looking for the cantrip that'd killed the guard, but I'd bet it was long gone by now. I climbed the stairs leading to the upper corridor and halted beside the closed door to the jailor's office. Zade might be dead, but I doubted anyone had cleaned out the place afterwards. Which meant there might well be evidence sitting in there pointing to the culprit. Even if not, the files on every prisoner, past and present, were inside that office. Including me... and including the Family.

If Harris wouldn't tell me how they'd escaped, then I'd find out for myself.

One unlocking spell later and I entered the former jailor's office, closing the door behind me. The neat, sparsely decorated room brought a shudder of revulsion as I recalled being hauled in there for my first interrogation. Zade's sneering face flickered in my mind's eye, his taunts echoing in my mind. I felt no sadness at his death. Rather, relief... and suspicion. The office was a little *too* pristine, as though someone had gone through and cleaned it up after his death after all. *Damn. Should have known it wouldn't be that easily.*

I walked over to the cabinets at the back, which contained records of all the prisoners here in the House of Fire. For a moment, my hand hovered on the case file of my own name before I forced my gaze away. That wouldn't do anything but bring up bad memories. I moved on to the next row, finding Adair's file next to a joint folder belonging to Lex and Roth, our guardians.

I pulled out the folder and skimmed to the final page, which ended on the words, *moved to another facility.*

I stared at the words for a moment. Moved to another facility? The House hadn't actually acknowledged that the Family had escaped? Weird... or not, considering their reluctance to let the word get out of their escape. I flicked through the file for more details, then did the same with Adair's, but nothing leapt out at me that I didn't already know. They hadn't noted down Adair's relocation to the Death King's jail, either, but of course that'd taken place after Zade's death.

Still...

I slid the folder back into place, heading for the jailor's desk. I knew where he'd kept the keys to the cells, and for a moment, temptation seized me. If they were going to be cavalier with their security, it'd serve them right if I went down to Tay's cell and liberated her before anyone realised I was here.

I unlocked the drawer and found it empty. Ah, shit. *Should have known it wouldn't be that simple.* No keys, and nothing else either. The other drawers were empty, too. Someone had cleaned out the place, all right. So the new head jailor could move in... or because they'd wanted to hide something.

My suspicion rising with each passing second, I searched every inch of the office, even under the carpets. Finally, I found a slip of paper half-hidden underneath a cabinet and pulled it out. It appeared to be a letter, scrawled in Zade's messy handwriting, which had been written before his death.

Yes, we got the cantrips. Are you sure about using the WO as a trading spot, considering their location?

Cantrips? My heart missed a beat, and I reread the note, unable to deny the implication. The House of Fire *hadn't* been compromised... at least, not in the way I'd thought. The *jailor* was the one who'd worked with the enemy.

And it seemed someone had killed him for it.

Given the letter's location, it had never reached its recipient, whoever *that* was. Did that mean he'd been murdered by someone trying to protect the rest of the House? It still didn't explain how the cantrip had got all the way downstairs, but perhaps Tay had taken it off the jailor and used it against him herself. Maybe it didn't matter, but if Zade himself had turned on his fellow members of the House of Fire, they couldn't sentence Tay to death for murder even if he'd died at her hand.

First, though, I needed to get her to confirm what I suspected.

I left the office and went back downstairs, heading for the staircase leading to the lower floor. I passed Dex on the way, and at a whispered instruction from me, he flew ahead of me to distract the guards by throwing sparks around the opposite end of the corridor. The guards headed that way, snapping at the prisoners to quit fooling around, while I silently approached Tay's cell. She sat on the floor, her gaze fixed at some point in the distance.

I didn't quite dare take off the invisibility cantrip, but I moved right up to the bars and whispered, "Tay."

She glanced up at the spot where I stood. "Bria? What are you doing down here?"

"I think I know why the jailor was murdered," I told her in an undertone. "Zade was working with the Family."

Her breath caught. "You shouldn't be in here."

"Tay, do the rest of the House know?"

She didn't answer.

"Tay, everyone else in here is vulnerable if you don't tell them," I whispered. "You have nothing to lose. If anything, they'll thank you for it. They'd want you to warn them the Family is recruiting allies from within their own ranks."

"When did I ever say I cared about the House?" she muttered. "They can all rot for all I care."

Oh, damn. So that was the problem. She was more than happy to watch the Houses crumble, and at one time, I might have agreed with her. On the other hand, I'd rather tear off my own arm than let the Family gain power over the ruling force in Elysium.

"The Family already took over the House of Earth," I said in a low voice. "Maybe the others, too. Look, I don't much care about the Houses, either, but I care about you. If you're in here when it all blows up, the backlash will catch you, too."

She sighed. "The House doesn't care about me any more than I care for them. Besides, they deserve what they get."

"You don't think they'll leave a power vacuum if they all drop dead at once?" I said to her. "Besides, those cantrips are lethal. I've seen them. The House of Earth's mages are buying them up in bulk, and when I tried to confront them over it, they threw an inferno cantrip at me and nearly took off the doors to this place."

Tay hissed out a breath. "I wish you didn't insist on putting yourself in harm's way, Bria. There's no need for you to be involved in this."

"Tay, it's my job to get involved," I said. "Also, Adair is still taunting me about the rogue spirit mages coming to take over the Court of the Dead. Was it really him who told you to kill Zade, or did you decide to take the decision into your own hands?"

"Does it matter?"

"Yes," I said, "because I'd like to know if you're still working with the Family or not. I want to know if I can trust you." As far as it was possible to trust someone who'd betrayed me once already, at any rate.

"I'm not working with anyone," she said.

"Were there any others?" I pressed. "Aside from Zade? Was the second guard who died a traitor, too?"

She didn't reply. Then I heard footsteps from the direction of the stairs. Cursing inwardly, I backed away from her cell, trusting the invisibility cantrip to keep me hidden from the guards. Two of them walked past, and I waited for them to disappear around a corner before making my way back upstairs. I glimpsed Dex hovering beside the back door as I approached and walked outside into the street.

"Dex," I whispered. "Hey—Dex. Over here."

"There you are," he said. "This is worse than talking to a lich."

"We aren't all eight inches tall with the ability to fly through walls," I pointed out.

"Most walls," he said. "Not in that place. I tried."

The House of Fire must be shielded against sprites, and presumably spirit mages as well. Despite the odds being against me, though, I'd managed to get my hands on some genuine proof of Zade's treachery, but I knew better than to take said evidence to a certain guard. Especially if *he* turned out to be one of the Family's insiders.

"What were you even doing in there?" Dex wanted to know.

"I got some evidence from the jailor's office pointing to his involvement with the Family," I murmured. "Not sure the House will believe me, though. I'm going to talk to the Spirit Agents."

"I'll keep an eye out for rogue earth mages, then," he said.

Thankfully, nobody ambushed me on the way to the Spirit Agents' base, earth mage or otherwise. After turning off the invisibility cantrip, I knocked on the door, and Miles answered a minute later.

"Hey," I said to Miles. "I just dropped by the House of Fire."

"And you didn't invite me?" He sounded insulted.

"The Death King sent me to ask them some questions to find out whether or not they're compromised, but they locked the place up," I explained. "So I did some snooping instead."

"And?" he said. "Are they compromised?"

"Not all of them," I said. "But the jailor was. *He* was the one in contact with the enemy, and I think that's why he was killed."

"Tay was trying to stop him?" he said, drawing the same conclusion I had. "That's why she wouldn't admit to committing murder?"

"I don't know, but it fits," I said. "Problem is, she doesn't care about the House itself. I can't really blame her for that, really, but as long as she refuses to admit the truth…"

"Do you think the rest of the House will believe her?"

"No." And therein lay the problem. "The records in the jailor's office also said the Family was moved to another facility, not that they escaped. Which might well be bullshit."

"Yeah, that sounds dodgy to me," he said. "Find any cantrips?"

"No, but someone cleaned up the jailor's office after his death." I pulled out the letter. "This is all I found, which is proof Zade was in on the illegal cantrip business. Is it too much to hope that the rest of the Family *is* in another facility, like Adair?"

"Probably." Miles took the letter from me and read it. "Yeah… it definitely sounds like he was involved with those cantrips. What's the WO?"

"Haven't a clue." I took the letter back from him and slipped it into my pocket. "Not the Withered Oak, surely?"

"It's the only mage hideout I know with those initials," said Miles. "Not exactly a reputable place, either."

"And it's in Arcadia," I added. "Same place as those reusable cantrips…"

"Exactly," said Miles. "Might be worth checking out. If I were trading illegal cantrips, I'd pick a place like that where nobody asks questions."

"The Family was never based in Arcadia, though." The question of their true location rose to the forefront of my thoughts, as much a mystery as ever. Adair hadn't given anything away, and even the files had been filled with lies. "They've always been near Elysium."

"I never even heard of the Family before now," he commented. "Not when they last walked free, anyway."

"They're secretive," I said. "It was mostly the Houses they were a threat to, and the Houses don't like letting everyone know their weaknesses. Anyway, until they recruited Shawn and his friends, they never showed an interest in spirit mages."

"Lucky us," he said dryly. "Also, nobody has mentioned the Family at their meetings in the citadel."

"Whose meetings?" I frowned. "You don't mean Shawn?"

"Hawker's," said Miles. "I've been snooping around spying on the liches, like I told you. Hawker's trying to recruit my people again, like he did with Shawn."

"Shit, Miles. You never said."

"It's not a big deal," he said. "I already had a pretty good idea who might be the next to defect, so I've taken precautions."

"But—that means some of the other Spirit Agents are working against you right now." I glanced up at the ceiling, wary that someone might be listening in.

"Relax, nobody in this house is working against us," he said. "We also worked out a scheme to give the wrong information to the enemy so they can't keep track of our plans."

"That'd be hard if the Houses start nosing around here again."

And to think I'd been more worried that the Houses would arrest Miles and his friends for hiding the Family in their house. This was far worse.

"We'll burn that bridge when we come to it."

"Hey, I'm the fire mage here," I said, earning a grin. "Unless I can somehow get my brother to talk, I can't make any definite assumptions about where the Family is hiding and how many cantrips they have floating around with their signature on them. All I know is that the House's official stance on the Family is that they're in another facility. They won't openly admit to their escape."

Which was nothing new, really, but it put a wrench in my plans to convince them of the danger within their own ranks. Let alone convince them to help the Death King.

"It doesn't sound like Adair has any intention of being cooperative."

"Nah, I'm the nicer of the pair of us," I said. "I hope I am, anyway. Granted, I've met vampire chickens with more charm than he has."

"You aren't wrong." He gave me a dimpled smile which made my heart forget how to behave normally. I sternly told it to calm down. I knew better than to get distracted. He might be charming—and keener on spending time with me than any of the other Spirit Agents were—but that didn't mean now was the time to develop an inconvenient crush.

After all, we had bigger problems. If the Houses were in denial about the true nature of what lay on the horizon, it was only a matter of time before what was left of their authority came crashing down around them.

———

The next couple of days passed without any new instructions from the Death King, nor any opportunity for me to update him on my failed espionage mission. The House of Fire's headquarters remained locked and quiet, leaving me at a loose end, and the only noteworthy improvement was that Ryan had finally stopped giving me the cold shoulder. I suspected the Death King had spoken to them, or Dex. Either way, I had an official invitation to play video games with the Elemental Soldiers. Neddie the zombie horse still didn't like me, but you couldn't have it all.

I left of the castle on Thursday morning and walked straight through a lich. The shock of cold drew a yelp from me. "Ow. Damn, Harper."

"Sorry," she mumbled, sounding more human than lich.

I rubbed my arms, where goosebumps had sprung up. "Harper, are you okay?"

"No," she said. "I was spying on Hawker's allies when two of them recognised me. They must have seen me back when I was working for... for Shawn and those rogues from the House of Fire."

My heart gave a sickening swoop. "What? Where are they now?"

"They're dead, don't worry," she added. "Liv killed them before they tailed us back here, but it freaked me out. I thought everyone who knew my brother and me was dead or in jail."

So Liv was spying on Hawker, too. Interesting. "Glad you got out of there without being caught."

"No more espionage for me," she said. "Never again."

"Did you learn anything useful?" I asked.

"Only that Hawker is working on seducing all the Death King's liches onto his side," she said. "Nothing new there, really. What about you? Learned anything from the House of Fire?"

"You might say that." I drew in a breath. "Turns out there's a strong possibility the jailor was the one who betrayed them."

"Is that why he was killed?" said Harper.

"Possibly," I said. "No idea if he was the only rogue or if there's a whole bunch of them, but they locked the place up after the rogues from the House of Earth tried to blow the doors off. They also have no information on where the Family might be hiding. Did you hear anything when you spied on Hawker?"

"No," she murmured. "I never saw the Family in person, even when I first got recruited by those rogues. Except..."

"Except for Adair." I glanced in the direction of the jail and spotted Miles hovering nearby, having presumably astral projected in from the Spirit Agents' base. When he saw me, he gave me a wave. "Miles might have an update for me. He's been spying on Hawker, too."

"I know," said Harper. "I'm surprised he hasn't been caught yet."

"Better hope it stays that way." I approached the spot where Miles floated above the ground. "What's the occasion?"

"I came to update the Death King," he said. "On our findings from Hawker's meetings. Nothing too exciting."

"Harper told me two people recognised her at the meeting," I said. "She said Liv killed them."

"I miss all the fun, apparently," he said. "What's going on with you?"

"Nothing whatsoever," I said. "The Death King hasn't asked *me* for an update. I think he likes you more than he likes me."

"Nah, he's just got enemies in a thousand places."

"Speak for yourself." I gave an eye-roll. "Have you been near the House of Fire in the last couple of days?"

"Not exactly," he said, "but I may have dropped by the Withered Oak earlier."

"Oh?" I raised a brow. "Did you see any illegal cantrips being passed around?"

"Not openly," he said. "I tried asking a few questions, but I hit a dead end. They're still not fans of spirit mages over there."

"That place has always seemed dodgy to me." They had zero restrictions on who could stay there, only that they had to be mages. And it was the only place in Arcadia with known links to the Houses. "Want to go back there and try again?"

"Exactly my thinking," he said. "I *did* find out they're expecting a group of new arrivals in town today, which might be a sign they're stepping up their game. If we get there first, we might be able to intercept them."

I doubted it'd be that simple, but part of me was crying out to *do* something before the enemy struck us first. We stood directly in the path of a storm, and it was only a matter of time before it broke.

11

I already wore my armoured clothing, but I grabbed a sword from the weapons room before leaving the castle with Miles, figuring that now was the time to put my newfound authority to good use. Not that the Death King had actually given permission for me to go to the Withered Oak. In fact, I still had yet to tell him that my plans to spy on the House of Fire had gone up in smoke, or that the jailor had been the traitor all along, but it was his own fault for leaving me to my own devices.

Miles, meanwhile, astral projected back to the Spirit Agents' hideout to get a couple of his friends to come and back us up, before meeting me at the node near the Death King's castle.

"I'd offer to let you ride a zombie horse to storm the place," I said to Miles, "but Neddie almost bit my finger off yesterday."

"Neddie?" he said. "Who names a zombie horse *Neddie?*"

"I never thought to ask," I responded. "All right, let's do this."

We crossed via the node into the centre of Arcadia. As Miles had promised, two spirit mages waited on the other side, joining us as we walked down the winding street towards the Withered Oak. The mages' hangout was an unassuming building whose brick walls bore faint scorch marks which suggested at least one fire mage had got into a fight outside at some point or other. I squinted through the dusty window, figuring I'd rather identify any potential threats before barging in.

"See anyone you recognise in there?" Miles said.

My gaze snagged on three mages standing near the window, including a stocky guy with a shaved head, idly playing with a flame he'd conjured in his hand. *Bark.*

"That guy was in the Death King's contest," I muttered to Miles. "Thought he was dead, but I guess not."

"Want to lure him out?" he said.

"Nah, if he has the nerve to hang around in here, he clearly has no idea we're coming," I said. "I reckon we can back him into a corner."

"If you say so," he said. "All right. You guys wait outside."

While the other spirit mages stood back out of range, the pair of us entered the pub. The grey-haired owner of the Withered Oak stood behind the bar, while his assistant was serving drinks to a couple of shifters. The muscular black man spotted us and moved over to exchange words with his boss. *Uh-oh.*

I took the lead and approached the fire mages near the window. "Hey, there."

Bark reacted as though he'd expected me to attack. He

swung around, fist in the air—which I dodged. Instead, Miles's punch knocked him flat on his back, and the other two mages leapt to their feet with exclamations of fury.

"You again?" growled the Withered Oak's owner, crossing the room at speed. "What trouble are you causing this time?"

"This man," said Miles, indicating the fallen mage, "was a contender for the Death King's new Fire Element before he got kicked out of the contest for conspiring against the Court of the Dead. Trust me, you don't want him in here."

"I don't want you in here either," said the grey-haired man. "You and your friends are always hanging around breaking shit."

"Hey, I haven't been here in weeks," Miles said. "Have you seen a spirit mage recently, then?"

"That's confidential, that is."

Everyone was staring at us. Okay, there were only about ten people in the room, but maybe drawing attention hadn't been the smartest idea. *Did the ex-Spirit Agents who betrayed Miles come here? They had some nerve showing their faces in public, but then again, the enemy already had one of the Houses dancing to their tune. Made sense that their allies would have started getting bolder. Especially if the dude who owned this place gave shelter to known criminals.*

Bark dragged himself upright and glowered at Miles. "I'm not breaking the law."

"Uh-huh," I said. "We'll just forget how you used an illegal cantrip to cheat in the Death King's trials and were then caught in the act. Still keeping up old habits?"

Two of the other patrons rose to their feet and made for the door. The three fire mages, meanwhile, approached me, and I smelled the smoke before they conjured flames into their hands.

"Stop that!" yelped the bartender. "We barely cleaned up the last fire."

"You ought to invest in a fireproof bar," I told him. "Really sorry about this."

I ducked under Bark's arm and kicked him in the back of the kneecap, causing him to face-plant, before flinging a paralysing cantrip at the other two fire mages. They froze midmotion, flames dying to a flicker in their hands.

Miles, meanwhile, ran at the two men who'd made a hasty retreat, and a cantrip flashed in his hand, causing both of them to collapse into a heap on the spot.

Miles grabbed one of the men's hands and retrieved a gleaming coin. "Inferno cantrip. This could easily have killed everyone in the building."

"Fuck." The bartender paled. "You lot—don't move."

I looked around the bar at the remaining patrons. "Anyone else want to make any confessions?"

Nobody said anything. Bark groaned at my feet, while the other two mages unfroze only for the black man from behind the bar to use air magic to levitate their flailing bodies into the air. I flung another paralysing cantrip at them to make it easier for him to move the intruders out into the corridor, then employed a similar cantrip on Bark before he launched into another attack.

"Good job we showed up when we did," I murmured to Miles.

"I hate to break this to you, Bria, but I reckon we're the reason they brought out that inferno," he whispered back. "They figured we know what their game is."

I grimaced. "What're the odds of there being more

illegal cantrips hidden in their rooms?"

"Good point." Miles addressed the owner. "Where were they staying?"

"This dude was in the first room on the right." He indicated Bark's limp form.

"You might want to vet your guests in future." With Miles behind me, I hurried upstairs and ran up to the room on the right.

To no surprise, I found the door locked, and not with an actual lock either. From the electric charge in the air, he'd sealed the door using magic. I reached into the pendant at my neck for an unlocking charm, hearing some odd scuffling noises from inside the room.

The door sprang open as I activated the spell, revealing a large hole in the floor—newly created, judging by the splintered mess of floorboards at my feet. A box of gleaming cantrips lay at the far edge. I trod carefully around the hole and reached for the box, only for a pair of dirt-stained hands to snatch it away from me. "What the—?"

A wild-haired mage stuck his head out of the hole. "Who are you?"

I blinked down at him. "I'm the Death King's Fire Element. I take it you're one of the dickheads who's using this place as a base to trade illegal cantrips?"

He gave a high-pitched laugh. "We're trading a lot more than that, sweetheart. Be seeing you."

I lunged for the box, but he vanished through the hole in the floor. The whole building gave an alarming shudder as the earth mage tunnelled his way down, and I caught my balance before I tumbled headfirst into the hole. Unlike an earth mage, I didn't have the inbuilt ability to navigate underground tunnels without suffocating to death.

I ran out of the room and found Miles looking up at me from the hallway. "What's going on?"

"There was an earth mage in there. He took his box of contraband underground." I took the stairs two at a time and caught him up by the door. "I'd follow, but I don't trust this place not to collapse on my head. Pretty sure the moron took out the foundations."

"Then we need to evacuate." Not that there were many patrons left. The bartender's assistant ushered the rest of them out of the door, while we ran outside to find two of the fire-wielding mages attempting to make a quick getaway. Miles's spirit mage friends barred their path, adding to the general confusion, but I was more concerned with the rumbling sound below our feet.

"Dammit, I need an earth mage to track him." I didn't know any, except… wait. "I'll go back to the castle and get backup. See if I can convince the Earth Element to help."

"Good, because we're outnumbered." Miles ducked as a fireball shot overhead. The mages had brought backup of their own, it seemed. If all else failed, surely the Death King had a good reason to pay attention this time. "I'm gonna run to the vampires' council house and see if any of them will lend a hand with these mages."

"Be careful." I left Miles and the others and used the node to travel back to the swamp. Near the gates, Ryan stood in conversation with Trix and one of the Death King's liches.

"Problems?" Ryan said.

"You might say that," I said. "Someone attacked the Withered Oak. I'm going to find the Death King."

"The Death King isn't in," Ryan called after me, but I was already breaking into a sprint through the gates. From there, I ran up to the castle doors and inside the main hall, skidding to a halt on the polished floor.

"Death King!" I shouted.

No response. *Dammit.* Ryan was telling the truth. I ran down the main corridor and to the break room, and Felicity and Cal both jumped to their feet when I dashed in.

"Bria," said Felicity. "What's going on?"

"Trouble," I said. "Some of the surviving fire mages who infiltrated the trials were using the Withered Oak to trade illegal cantrips, and an earth mage took their stash underground. I need an earth mage's help to track them."

Cal scowled. "Really?"

"Yes." I braced my hands on my knees, breathless. "I'm going back no matter what, but if one of you could tell the Death King what's going on, it'd be appreciated."

"I can stay here and wait for him to come back," offered Felicity. "Go on, Cal. It's not like she's got anything to gain from lying to you."

Cal gave me a sideways look. "If you're trying to trick me, I'll bury you alive."

On that promising note, the Earth Element and I left the castle and headed for the gates. Ryan and Trix had both disappeared, along with the lich they'd been talking to. I hoped they were on their way to the Withered Oak, because we needed all the allies we could get.

Cal and I reached the node without speaking a word to one another. He acted more of an ice mage than an earth mage most of the time, but as far as I knew, the guy wasn't friendly to anyone, so I didn't take it personally.

By the time we got to the Withered Oak again, the place was ablaze, and the smell of burning drifted outwards, along with creaking noises which suggested the entire building was on the verge of collapse. I halted at a safe distance from it and addressed the Earth Element. "Can you track an earth mage from here?"

He crouched and pressed his palm to the ground. "Not when the building's shaking like that. I'd need to go somewhere more stable."

"The tunnels?" I suggested. "There's got to be an entrance somewhere nearby. Those tunnels run all over the city."

I looked around and spotted Miles duelling one of the escaped mages. He dodged a fireball and slammed his palm into the mage's chest, striking him with spirit energy that sent him crashing into the wall. The mage slid to a halt in the doorway of the Withered Oak, and I caught up to Miles. "Backup's here."

"Hey, there," said Miles. "Who's that guy?"

"The Death King's Earth Element," I said. "We need to get to the tunnels to track that earth mage."

A hollow *boom* rang out. An instant later, a conflagration rose to consume the remains of the Withered Oak from the inside. *Shit. Hope nobody was left inside there.*

"That," I said, "looked like an inferno cantrip. We'd better move."

We backed further down the street, where Miles pointed out a hidden stairway leading deep into the earth. "Doesn't seem a good time to go underground."

"Nobody asked you." Cal descended the stairs without looking back, disappearing into the tunnel.

"Touchy, isn't he?" Miles said in an undertone.

"That's his natural state, from what I've seen," I muttered back. "C'mon. Let's hope his tracking skills are up to scratch."

We climbed down the narrow staircase into one of Arcadia's many underground tunnels. Cal stood in front of one of the earthen walls, his hands pressed to the solid surface.

"How close do the mages need to be before you can track them?" I asked.

"Close, but if I can find them, then they can find me, too," he answered.

Ah. "Can you sense anyone now?"

Cal removed his hands from the wall. "Yes."

"Where?" I asked.

"Right about... there." He pointed at our feet. *Oh, no.*

An earth mage exploded out of the ground, covering all of us in dirt. Cal collided with him in a literally earth-shaking thud which made me concerned that the tunnel itself would collapse on all our heads. As the mage flung Cal aside, Miles blasted him in the face with spirit magic. The mage hit the wall, which swallowed him up. *Uh... that's new.*

An instant later, he burst out of the wall again. I spun around and flung a paralysing cantrip into his face, while Cal grabbed his shoulders and dragged him into view. I could see something glinting at the back of the tunnel he'd made.

"I think that's our cantrips," I said. "I'll get them."

As I dove into the tunnel's opening, the mage unfroze and grabbed my ankle. Cal punched him, causing him to let go, but another alarming tremor shook the ground.

Another earth mage was coming this way... and I was right in their path.

Once again, a solid wall of soil slammed into me, bringing *two* mages along with it. Cal swore as I flew out of the hole in the wall and crashed on top of him. Miles ran in to meet the two newcomers, while I rolled to my feet and flung a paralysing cantrip at one of the mages before he could disappear into the ground again. The narrow space made it hard to fight effectively, while the shaking walls and floor didn't help in the slightest.

"If he keeps this up, the whole tunnel is gonna come crashing down." I spat out a mouthful of soil, looking for the box of cantrips, but it'd disappeared in a shower of earth.

"Nah, it's sturdier than that," said Cal. "Earth mages built this city, in fact."

"Better hope it holds up." I sank my fist into one of the mages' jaws. "Or else it'll become a mass grave."

The mage grinned, soil between his teeth. "You're all dead."

The ground trembled again, and movement came from near the stairs. Then a gust of wind blasted through the tunnel, knocking all of us off our feet at the same time. I crashed on top of one of the mages in a confusion of limbs, dizzy and bruised. As I raised my head, two figures emerged from the staircase nearby. Ryan and Trix.

"Oh, hello," said Trix. "What're you doing down here?"

"Getting attacked by earth mages." I pulled myself to my feet, treading on the mage's face in the process.

Cal surfaced, too, covered in dirt. "Took you long enough to show up."

"You're welcome," Ryan said, blasting air magic

through the tunnel again and knocking down a fleeing mage. Trix, meanwhile, ran towards the dazed-looking mages and threw a punch at one of them when he tried to rise. I didn't know why it surprised me that he could fight. Despite their mild temperament, elves were resilient and tougher than they looked, and most spells just bounced off them. Handy to have around in a crisis.

With Trix and Ryan on our team, we made short work of the earth mages and had them piled up on the floor of the tunnel in seconds. Cal, meanwhile, widened the hole in the wall so I could dive in and retrieve the box of cantrips. Breathless and covered in dirt, I displayed my haul for the others to see. Dozens of golden cantrips filled the box, each bearing an all-too familiar mark.

"We should bury them," said Ryan.

"No," Cal said. "Any earth mage would be able to dig them up again unless we hid them somewhere which was magic-proofed."

"Let me see." Miles strode over, his face dirt-smeared and a growing bruise above his eye. "I'd offer to hide them in the Spirit Agents' base, but you're better off handing them over to the authorities."

"Meaning the vampires?" said Ryan. "They haven't exactly stepped up to help us."

"Did none of them come to help at the Withered Oak?" I asked Miles.

"No," he said. "Their security human said they were asleep and to come back at dusk. Told us to pile up the mages' bodies on their doorstep."

"No surprise there," Ryan said. "We usually can't count on the vamps to show their faces unless there's a direct threat to them."

"If those cantrips had got out into the city, they'd have had a real problem on their hands," I pointed out. "Tell you what, I think we should give them to Devon. She'll be able to figure out what they're designed for. Maybe track where they came from, too."

"And we'll get the vampires to lock up these dickheads." Ryan nudged one of the earth mages with their foot. "Doubt that's their only haul of illegal cantrips, but at least we shut down their operation in the Withered Oak."

"More like burned it down." I grimaced. "I hope the owners had fire insurance."

Cal scowled at the unconscious mages. "We ought to report them to the Houses. They'll sort them out."

"I wouldn't count on that," I said. "Haven't you heard?"

"What?" he said.

"The House of Earth is under the control of the Family," I said. "Or some of them are. These aren't the only earth mages I've seen carrying illegal cantrips around."

His expression shuttered. "So that's why they aren't answering the Death King's requests for an audience."

"Does he not tell you anything?" At least it wasn't just me he refused to share pertinent information with.

"I haven't had contact with the House in years," Cal said. "Not since the Death King bought out my sentence, like he did with Davies. He's no friend of the Houses, but I rather hoped they'd see the error of their ways."

He was imprisoned in the House of Earth? And Davies was in the House of Fire? It surprised me a little, though perhaps it shouldn't have. I hoped for all our sakes that Cal didn't plan to betray the Death King as well.

"I know," I said. "He sent me to speak to the House of Fire and it was a disaster. That's how I found out about those cantrips—someone used one to kill the jailor. Except the jailor himself was allegedly working with the enemy, and I'm pretty sure there's traitors within all four Houses now."

Cal gave me an assessing look. "Where are these cantrips coming from, then?"

"I have no idea."

"You're lying." The Earth Element faced me. "I know you used to be imprisoned in the House of Fire, too, and I'm not entirely convinced you shouldn't have stayed there."

"Cal," Ryan said in a warning tone. "Get these bastards aboveground. Someone fetch the vampires, too."

"It's a waste of time if there's still cantrips being passed around behind the scenes," said Cal. "And Bria knows where they're being made."

"I really don't." But there was one place we hadn't checked. Somewhere I hadn't considered as an option... yet I was all out of better ideas.

Cal scoffed, grabbing one of the fallen mages by the scruff of his neck. "Right. I'm going to fetch the vampires and get them to deal with these scumbags."

As he dragged the mage's limp body up the narrow staircase to the surface, Miles shuffled closer to my side. "Want me to punch him?"

I shook my head. "He's right... there *is* one place I know of where the cantrips might be coming from. It's a long shot, but I can't think of anywhere else."

"Where?" Miles asked.

Cold slid through to my bones. I swallowed hard. "I think it's time to pay a visit to my family's old house."

12

Within the hour, the vampires had sent their human assistants to haul the captured mages away, while Ryan and Cal dropped the cantrips off with Devon in the Death King's castle. I, meanwhile, joined the spirit mages and headed back to Elysium. If I was really going to risk going back to the place where I'd grown up, I'd better get it over with before I lost my nerve altogether.

Miles offered to come with me. I was glad to have company, at least at first, but the second thoughts rushed in when we left the Spirit Agents' base on foot. More than fear of the earth mages lurking beneath the city stalked my steps. I didn't want him seeing the place where I'd grown up, even if it'd lain in ruins the last time I'd set eyes on it. But I was all out of better ideas.

"Whereabouts is your family's home?" Miles asked.

"The middle of nowhere—literally," I said. "Way north of Elysium. There's also not many nodes nearby, so we'll have to walk it from Elysium's north side and hope we don't run into anything nasty on the way."

"Well, shit," he said. "You can walk really fast, right? I saw you."

"I can," I admitted. "But it'll take a regular person a lot longer, and I'm not sure we have all day."

"I can astral project," he said. "I can still use magic that way, but I can move faster."

Maybe that's the best option. "Just don't vanish on me."

"Of course I won't," he said. "I'll catch you up."

If Miles astral projected, it'd be a buffer of safety if we did run into the Family out there. Not that I was less of a walking target myself, but at least there was no danger of them hurting him. I didn't like to think how Lex and Roth would react if they learned of my growing attachment to the leader of the Spirit Agents. In their eyes, it'd be just another weakness for them to use against me.

I used the nodes to travel to the northernmost point of the city and found Miles waiting on the other side, transparent and hovering above the ground.

"No trouble?" I said.

"Shelley is going to drag me back to my body if I stay out there too long," he said. "Fair warning."

"Better than both of us getting stuck." I bloody well hoped we wouldn't end up falling into one of the Family's traps, but it was impossible to be certain what we'd run into. I wouldn't have thought they'd go back to the house after their escape, given the state I'd left it in, but I was through waiting for them to come to me. Time to hunt them down myself instead.

We headed north. I walked at super speed while Miles

floated alongside me, ghostlike and insubstantial enough for me to wonder if his abilities were in any way dampened while he was in that form. Part of me wanted to ask if he was sure what he was getting into, while another part of me was reluctant to rock the boat. Not until we reached the house, anyway.

When we passed by the Houses' facility in the north of the city, I found my steps faltering. The grey stone construction looked grim and imposing, but I could only imagine what it looked like on the inside.

"I never found out how they escaped," I murmured. "I imagine Adair used his mind-control when the guards got careless and tricked his way out, but nobody in the House of Fire will give me the details. Even their files say nothing."

He shot me a sideways look. "Would it make you feel any better if you knew?"

"Probably not, no," I admitted. "Your family…"

"Yeah, they're still in there," he said, his voice soft. "Best place for them, really. Lot of people who piss off the Houses don't get that lucky."

"Which House did it?"

"Doesn't matter." Despite his casual air, his tone was laced with a pain I recognised all too well.

"Guess not," I said. "I was going to offer to give the person responsible a kick for you on the way back."

His brows rose. "Already tried that. Didn't really work out. Reckon I'd be in a cell of my own if I hadn't been a minor at the time."

"No wonder they aren't your biggest fans." He was lucky he'd walked away with his limbs still attached, but even the Houses had some old superstitions around spirit mages. With good reason. While he might play the fool on a not-infrequent basis, I couldn't forget that he'd brought Harper back to the dead and fought off an army. Yet would that be enough to keep him alive if we ran into the Family?

"Are you sure you want to come?" I said, as we reached the next stretch of the city's outskirts. "Last chance to back out."

"Us outcast mages have to stick together," he said.

His words caught me off guard, especially after what had happened between him and Shawn. I supposed he'd spent years giving his fellow spirit mages a fair shot, even if it backfired on him sometimes. This was also the guy who'd recaptured a bunch of vampire chickens after their escape had landed me in hot water with my ex-boss, for reasons I still hadn't entirely worked out.

While it was undoubtedly dangerous that he might breach the boundary of mistrust surrounding my past, I had to admit it was kind of nice to have company while I walked up north. We didn't exactly have an attacking force at the ready, but maybe it was best not to run in with all guns blazing. Not until we knew what we were up against, anyway.

"Do you really think the Family is back in their old house?" he said.

"No idea," I said. "I destroyed the entire estate, but maybe they got their earth mage allies to build a new house."

"Why do they never show up in person?" he asked. "Aside from your brother, I mean?"

"They have this thing about maintaining secrecy," I said. "The Houses didn't actually know their identities until they caught me."

He shot me a sideways look. "They caught you? I thought you turned them in."

"I did," I said, "but I also let the House's guards catch me first. It was the only way I could think of to ensure the consequences didn't come back to bite me if they failed to get the Family behind bars. I left them unconscious and tied up when I destroyed their estate, but I couldn't bring all three of them with me single-handedly."

"So you let the Houses catch you first." A note of sympathy came into his voice, which might have bothered me if it'd come from anyone else.

"Yeah," I said. "It was easier than I anticipated, but the Family never saw it coming. They didn't expect anyone to best them."

Especially one of their own creations.

"I bet," he said. "But how did they recruit people to join them if they never came into the city in person?"

"They used to send recruiters on their behalf, mostly," I said. "They hired humans, practitioners usually, equipped with some of their experimental cantrips. Might be doing the same again, for all I know. We saw some of those assassins in the attack the other week, so they're definitely still up to their old tricks."

Which made them more likely to be at the old base, but I would have thought the Houses would have at least sent someone to check up on their old address after their escape.

"And your brother?" he said. "Adair? *He* showed his face in public."

"He wanted revenge on me," I replied. "That's why he got openly involved with Shawn and the other spirit mages. The others don't like getting their hands dirty. Not directly."

"You'd think someone would have searched their house, though."

"Yeah," I said quietly. "You would think so."

We walked on through the outskirts of the city, until the buildings gave way to wasteland broken by the occasional crumbled ruin of an old house. The wasteland had once been fields, the buildings comprising towns or villages or farms. Most of the Parallel looked the same these days. The Death King controlled only one small portion of the wasteland compared to how far it actually stretched, though there were large areas which were inaccessible thanks to the aftereffects of the war. This one wasn't, but I still watched my step, in case I trod on the magical equivalent of a landmine. Even with my speed, it took half an hour before I started to see familiar sights. A forest of twisted trees. Ruined buildings. Broken pieces of metal fence. And then…

I halted in front of a gate which had been ripped up from its roots, around a burned stretch of earth. "Here we are."

"Nice decor." Miles floated up to my side.

The house itself lay in a heap of charred ruins, but the ground around it was turbulent, as though churned up by giant hands. Or earth mages. *This place is still in operation, all right.* Worse, they seemed to have brought in new staff.

Miles caught sight of the piles of upturned soil, too. "Is that what I think it is? Are there earth mages down there?"

"There were always tunnels under the estate," I whispered. "I thought they collapsed. But I guess they started recruiting from the House of Earth for a reason."

I'd been too wrapped up in looking for their new hideout to even consider that they might not have abandoned the old one, regardless of the fact that the Houses knew where it was now. But then, why wouldn't they, if they planned to take over the Houses from within? I should've known better.

Miles sucked in a breath. "What... what *is* that?"

I followed his gaze to the side of a cliff which formed the far boundary of the grounds. Without the house blocking the way, the golden sheen of the metal forming the cliffside was starkly obvious now.

"That," I said, "is why they built the tunnels. I guess they reopened the mine."

Truth be told, I'd expected someone else to swoop in and claim it first, but the few who'd known the Family lived here might have been too frightened of their potential return to risk breaking onto their property.

"The mine," he echoed. "So—they're making cantrips out of that stuff?"

"Nah, they don't have the finesse," I said. "If I had to guess, they're having someone else dig it up and then handing it over to practitioners. That's what they did before."

Question was, where were the practitioners? I wouldn't have thought the Family would let them live *on* the property, but no other buildings or landmarks were within sight. The Family had picked this place to build their estate for a reason other than its remoteness: the metal, infused with magic, was the material used to make cantrips, and I hadn't been able to make a dent in it even after I'd razed the place to the ground.

"I suppose we could close off the tunnels and slow them down," I said to Miles. "That ought to put a dent in their smuggling operation."

"Where are the rest of the Family, though?" he asked. "Are they underground, do you think?"

"I honestly have no idea." I scanned the ground for a tunnel opening and felt the distant rumble of movement below the earth as I walked a little further until I came to a tunnel which was large enough for a person to walk into. While part of me wanted to check for any potential stragglers before I caved it in, a bigger part of me whispered that it was their own damn fault if the place collapsed on them.

Movement stirred within the tunnel opening, revealing something coiled, and... shaped like a snake. A giant house-sized snake. *Oh, fuck the Elements.*

"You've gotta be kidding me." Miles drifted behind me. "I wish I'd brought one of those mind-control cantrips with me, but I left them at home. With my body."

"Shit."

To my horror, the wyrm stirred, its eyes opening to slits. Its head moved sinuously, half asleep, before its gaze fixed on me.

"Uh." I raised my hands. "Hey, there. Don't mind us. We're just leaving."

Miles was transparent, less of a target, but me? I was a tasty snack. The wyrm's eyes opened fully and then it reared up, its head towering over the ruins. Wings sprouted from its back, while I broke into a sprint, putting on enough speed that the world turned into a dark blur. The beast snarled, its head waving around as though confused as to where I'd disappeared to. Then its huge body shifted, triggering a tremor below my feet. Even my speed couldn't get me out of the way in time as its tail flicked up, sending me flying into the air. I landed on my feet by sheer instinct, skidding to a halt in the mud.

Miles's hands glowed, blasting spirit magic at the wyrm before it could hit me again. The air flickered in front of me as I caught my balance, and I glimpsed the golden sheen of a cantrip at my feet. *Uh-oh.*

The air flickered and then resolved into an image of a smaller house standing among the ruins. *An illusion spell.* A good one, too. So they *had* rebuilt part of the house, and then hidden it behind an illusion. Yet I hadn't seen any living people around. So who was here?

As though conjured up by my thoughts, the smell of flowery perfume caught in my nostrils, and my heart leapt into my throat.

"Miles," I said. "Go back."

"What?" he said. "I won't leave you here alone."

"Believe me, you're better off running," I said out of the corner of my mouth. "I can catch you up. Go back to Elysium. Please."

"No way," said Miles. "You're the one who's vulnerable here."

"I'm not." He didn't know what these people were capable of. "I just need to check something out, then I'll be right behind you. Promise."

His features twisted in indecision, but something in

my expression must have convinced him, because he vanished without arguing further.

I took one more step, and the ground exploded. The beast's tail flung me into the air, and I landed hard, breathless, on my back. The perfumed smell intensified, and I opened my eyes and looked up into a nightmare with a stunning face, a waterfall of dark hair, and pale elven features. Lex still didn't look a day over twenty-five, though she'd been around since long before the war.

The woman who'd raised me bared her teeth in a crooked smile. "How nice of you to drop in, Bria."

I groaned. "Why booby-trap your own house?"

"Couldn't have anyone sniffing around, could we?" Lex's smile widened. "Don't worry, the beast is quite tame. For me, that is."

"Why come back here?" I said. "Everyone knows where your estate is now. It's not a secret any longer."

"Everyone?" she said. "No, only the Houses of the Elements knows our location, and they aren't long for this world."

My blood chilled. "What did you do?"

"Why, nothing," she said. "Yet."

My hopes of the Houses somehow thwarting them had already been low, but not only did the Family walk free, they'd ensnared at least one House in their grip already. Maybe more.

I shifted into an upright position, silently calculating my escape route. "Is Roth around?"

At least Adair was out of the picture for now, but Lex was far worse. She hadn't changed an inch in the five years she'd been imprisoned. Even her clothes were flawless, as though she'd raided a vampire's wardrobe. Her lacy red dress was positively indecent for a woman who was old enough to be my grandmother, while her deceptively delicate hands belied the terrifying power at her disposal. Yet Roth put both her *and* Adair to shame. If both of them were here, I was doomed.

"Not at the moment," she replied.

"What about Adair, then?" I said. "Why'd you leave him in jail? You could have rescued him at any time, right?"

"For one thing, it was his own fault for getting caught," she said. "I thought it would be more fun if you were the one who set him free."

"No chance." I'd about had it with the mind games. "Where are the people you have carving cantrips for you? I know you aren't doing it yourselves."

I was stalling, I knew it, but if she used her magic on me, it was game over. I needed to get the hell out of here before Miles came after me in person and ended up ensnared, too.

"The cantrips?" she said. "I wouldn't bother your mind about them. There's nothing you can do."

A likely story. The cantrips might be powerful, but they had to be carved by hand. By practitioners. Which meant this operation covered far more than just the three of them.

"I beg to differ," I said. "There's plenty I can do, if you haven't forgotten how I stopped your schemes five years ago."

"You put our plans on hold," she corrected. "You never stamped them out for good. With the Parallel in chaos, it'll be our time to shine, and the second war will be even more bounteous than the first."

The war. I hadn't been born back then, but after the

war thirty years ago, the Family had first risen to power. Before then, the Council of the Elements had been the ruling force in the Parallel, but when they'd been all but wiped out during the fall of the spirit mages, the Houses had sprung up in their place. The Houses had done their utmost best to stamp out any trace of illegal magic in the Parallel, but some mages slipped their notice. People who didn't fit into the usual categories.

People like the Family.

I didn't want to think what they might achieve if another war broke out, without the Houses or even the Order to keep them in check.

"How do you know the war won't end with people like you being prosecuted?" I said.

"Because we support the winning team," she said. "The spirit mages will rise again, and our soldiers will aid their army on the path to victory."

My heart lurched. "I didn't think warfare was your thing."

"Oh, it isn't," she said. "However, war breeds chaos like maggots festering in a corpse, and you and Adair were created for such a scenario. The pair of you will help us take over the Parallel once we've cleared the way for you. After we've burned the city of Elysium to the ground."

"And you think I'm going to stand back and let you do it?" I called my fire magic, and twin flames sprang to my hands.

"Oh, I'm sure you'll *try* to fight back," she said. "That'll make it all the more entertaining."

She made a brief gesture with one hand, and my body froze, my heart stuttering in my chest. While Adair's power gave him influence over anyone who looked him in the eyes, Lex's magical ability involved full-body manipulation. She could stop my heartbeat with a snap of her fingers if she wanted to—or worse, force me to watch as she hurt my friends.

There was a good reason I'd told Miles to leave.

Her hand moved down, and I felt my heartbeat slow. Shit. She wasn't actually going to kill me this time, was she?

"I could leave you like this all day," she purred.

Sweat beaded on my forehead. I was acutely conscious of the cantrips inside the pendant around my neck, cantrips I couldn't reach. Not while I was frozen like this. Her wide smile told me she knew perfectly well I had no way out.

"If you do," I bit out, "I'll hardly be able to help your son escape, will I? Did you know it's the King of the Dead who has him captive now?"

"Him?" Her grip on me lessened slightly. "How inconvenient."

"I'm the Death King's Fire Element," I added. "He'll send people looking for me if I don't come back soon. Sure you can take on an army of liches? Your abilities have no effect on the dead, do they?"

A scowl twisted her lips. "The Death King has my son, does he? Interesting. I suppose I'll have to pay him a visit."

Her words struck a horrifying chord inside me, but as I managed to move my hand, inch by inch, I gave a final lurch and grabbed the pendant around my neck.

My fingers found a cantrip and fumbled a button, which blasted a paralysing wave at her. Then I ran like hell.

She didn't stop me. Not even as I ran through the

collapsed gates, sprinted across the open wasteland and north, away from the house's ruins and towards the pillar of light indicating a node. Closer, closer—

I ran into the node, turned on the transporter spell, and then I was gone.

13

Pain squeezed my entire body as I emerged from the Death King's private node. Night had fallen without my noticing, and it felt like several decades had passed since the fight at the Withered Oak. Though I knew even she couldn't move faster than a transporter spell, I half expected to find Lex had already sent someone to break Adair out of prison while I was gone.

Instead, when I picked myself up off the ground, I found myself face to face with Miles. Judging by his transparent state, he must have astral projected up to the castle. "Bria, I thought you were coming back to Elysium. What the hell happened back there?"

"Sorry." My voice sounded leaden, hollow. "I have to warn the Death King… my family survived. They're using their old base after all, and now they know Adair is here."

Part of me wanted to march straight into the jail and demand for him to tell me what Lex was playing at, but that wouldn't do anything but convince him that I'd let her words get to me. She knew how to get under my skin almost as effectively as Adair himself did. They had that much in common.

His arms folded across his chest. "You're shitting me."

"Nope." I ran a weary hand through my hair. "She didn't kill me. That's not her plan. She wants to do worse."

His expression stiffened. "That's not reassuring, Bria."

"I thought you knew what you were getting into." *Quiet, Bria.* I knew I was being unfair, but well, I *had* warned him, and seeing Lex again had reminded me of the fragile nature of the new life I'd built.

One card would fall, and the entire house would collapse.

Miles's brow furrowed. "I can't help you if you won't tell me what's going on, Bria."

I looked away. "This isn't something I want anyone else wrapped up in."

"I thought you wanted to join me," he said. "And the Spirit Agents."

I shook my head. "Not against the Family. It isn't the same… they're not even human."

"Some say spirit mages aren't either." He floated closer to me until we were inches apart, and tension simmered between us. "Whatever you've been called, I've heard it all before, I guarantee it."

My eyes stung and I blinked hard. "It's not about what I've been called, it's what I was made to be. I wasn't born like this by happenstance. Lex and Roth saw themselves as gods who moulded me into the image of who they wanted me to be."

"But you're not that person." The intensity in his voice

surprised me. "You do whatever you like. That's one of the things I admire the most about you."

Unexpected heat seared my face. "It makes no sense to me."

"Did I say it had to make sense?" he said. "I've heard every possible kind of story from spirit mages who went through hell with the Houses. This Family of yours can't be worse."

"I wouldn't speak too soon," I told him. "The people who raised me didn't care about anyone but themselves. They still don't, not even my brother and me. We were supposed to be their soldiers, nothing more. Now they want to take over the Houses of the Elements, and I'm not so sure we can stop them."

"You got them to admit it?" he said. "That they're after the Houses?"

"More or less," I said. "Though Lex wouldn't tell me *where* those cantrips are being created. She did more or less admit she has practitioners doing her bidding."

"We can go back to Dawson's place and trace them from there," he said. "Not a perfect idea, but it's better than nothing."

"Might be our only choice now," I allowed. "But you know… the Family isn't beatable. Not by normal means. They're functionally immortal and have a nasty habit of running away."

I'd inherited that trait, but I'd have to find a new way to thwart them again, no matter how impossible it seemed. And there was no room for anyone else in that struggle. I knew that much.

"Hey." Miles floated closer to me again. "It's okay. You

beat them alone last time, right? This time you have backup."

"You're deluded."

He grinned. "Maybe. But you're forgetting I once learned spirit magic alongside the Death King."

"I did forget that," I allowed. "The Death King, though, he's not exactly—"

"I wouldn't finish that sentence." He jerked his head at a spot over my shoulder.

Unseen in the darkness, the Death King himself approached both of us, looking as menacing as ever. "Bria, go back to the castle and join the other Elemental Soldiers."

I faced the Death King. "I have something I need to tell—"

"Later," he said. "Miles, I need to talk to you. Bria, go on."

"What—" I broke off, sensing that now was not the time to admit I'd gone and given away the location of our new prisoner to the one person who might be able to slip past his security. Besides, Miles's revelation was a reminder that I wasn't alone. Hell if I knew what I'd done to deserve that level of loyalty, but I wasn't complaining.

I went inside the castle via the back doors, leaving a trail of mud behind me. I didn't have time to change into clean clothes, but since nobody said I shouldn't, I took the opportunity to wash the mud off my face in the bathroom and then went to find the others Elemental Soldiers. All three of them were in the break room, strapping on weapons and slipping cantrips into the pockets of their coats.

"There you are, Bria," Ryan said. "Where have you been?"

"Dealing with a bit of family drama," I said. "What's going on here?"

"Liv," Cal said. "As usual. She wants us to go on an absurd rescue mission."

"What for?" I asked.

"Hawker was keeping and torturing a bunch of elemental sprites inside one of the citadels," explained Ryan. "She wants us to get them out of there while Hawker is gone."

"*Sprites?*" I echoed. "What's he doing with those?"

"Sounds like he was using the sprites as a battery to keep the transporter running," said Ryan. "I'm not all that keen on the idea of walking right into a trap, but I'm more than happy to shut down his little experiment."

Experiment. Using sprites as a battery to power the transporter linking the citadels? Was that how they'd been kept running for so long? It sounded like the kind of twisted idea the Family would come up with, which, after my narrow escape from Lex, made my gut clench in dread.

"I can come, but..." Dammit. The Death King might not be willing to listen to me, but maybe I'd have more luck with the other Elemental Soldiers. "But I found out where those illegal cantrips are coming from. Where'd you put the ones we got from those earth mages in Arcadia?"

"Here." Ryan indicated a muddy box behind the sofa. "Devon isn't around, but we'll give them to her later. You know where they're being made?"

The others watched me, and the words stuck in my

throat. "I'm not exactly certain where they're being manufactured, but I found out where those mages were going when they went underground in Arcadia, and why the Family recruited them."

Quickly, I summed up what I'd discovered at the Family's old estate. I left out most of my confrontation with Lex, but I did tell them about the cantrip's source.

"They're not going to come back to get them, are they?" said Felicity, eyeing the box of cantrips.

"Nah, probably not," I said. "I'm guessing Liv hasn't seen them yet, if she's been planning rescue missions. How'd she get that close to Hawker, anyway?"

"He tried to recruit her," said Ryan.

My jaw dropped. "He thought *Liv* would join him?"

"Apparently," said Felicity. "Didn't work. She escaped him, but there were issues, and she had to leave the sprites behind."

I studied the box of cantrips. "You sure it's safe to leave them unattended?"

"Safer than anywhere else," said Ryan. "I'm confident that nobody within these walls will betray us. Only the liches are an uncertain bet, and they can't pick up cantrips."

"Might be an inferno or two we can use." I crouched down and peered into the box, picking up one of the cantrips. The topmost stack were all infernos, but beneath, the other cantrips bore unfamiliar marks. "Nobody touch any of these."

"Why?" asked Felicity.

"In case they're laced with that magical virus," I said, thinking of Lex's warning. "Liv couldn't have picked a better time for this, could she?"

"No," said Ryan. "We'd better go before she comes back here and drags us outside in person."

"All right," I said. "Adair hasn't made any trouble, has he? Because the Family knows he's here."

"His cell will be under close guard," Ryan said. "We'll make sure of it."

"Okay." That would have to do. Lex's abilities didn't work on liches, so she wouldn't get past the gates, and the only humans living in the castle would be with me on Liv's ill-advised rescue mission. As long as we didn't run into Roth out there… but if Liv had seen him, she would never have made it back here to tell the tale.

I slipped a couple of the inferno cantrips out of the box and into the pendant around my neck before leaving the break room with the others. Outside the castle, I found the shadowy form of a lich waiting for me.

"Hey," said Harper.

"Hey," I said. "Where have you been?"

"Around," she said. "Miles came here looking for you. How'd you get split up?"

"I went looking for my family," I said. "Let's just say I got more than I bargained for."

In truth, I had no idea what to do with the new revelation that they'd fixed up their old base, let alone Lex's proclamation that she intended to step in to take advantage of a war which looked more and more inevitable by the day. The Family had always thrived on chaos. Even before they'd started outright interfering among the Houses, they'd sent in spies and assassins to sow paranoia in the city. That was one reason nobody had been sorry to see them locked up, yet they'd escaped anyway. Had the House of Fire's jailor helped free them? Tay had acted against him, which ought to prove she wasn't supporting the Family any longer, but I couldn't help wondering if she'd known their location all along.

"I want to come with you to free the sprites," said Harper. "I can help."

I turned to her. "You want to come to the citadel?"

She drifted closer to me. "Yes. If Hawker has any cantrips which can bring me back to life, they've got to be there."

"Are you sure he'd have left them lying around?"

"It's worth a shot," Harper said. "I can't deal with this crap any longer. I hate being dead."

Sympathy squeezed my chest. "I'm not saying you don't have good reason to, but experimental cantrips… they can have downsides. Big ones. I can check with Liv, if you like. She might know if there's a chance of finding them there."

"Thanks, Bria," said Harper. "I appreciate it."

I turned away from the castle and saw Miles and several other spirit mages gathering in the ground, while Liv herself stood further off. If she'd been the one who'd brought the warning, she'd know if Hawker was likely to have a cure for the liches hidden in the citadel, so I made my way over to her.

When Liv caught sight of me, I said, "Harper wanted me to ask if you found the cure yet."

"You mean for being dead?" said Liv. "Yeah, there's a cantrip which technically returns someone to life, but there's a major downside. Also, Hawker stole it anyway. He's only using those fake ones."

"Fake ones?" I said.

"They bring you back to life but make you rot from the

inside out and fall to bits," she said. "Trust me, Harper doesn't want that."

"Guess not." I reached into my pocket and held up one of the inferno cantrips. "You want a way to destroy the machinery? This shit works. I already blew up one of them."

She eyed the cantrip. "Is that one of those inferno cantrips which amplifies fire magic?"

"You've got it," I said. "If I tell you to move, then I'd get outta the way."

"I'll take your word for it on that." She sounded like her usual grumpy self, and I wondered what had possessed her to go and hear Hawker out when he'd tried to recruit her. On the other hand, I'd rather not tell her what *I'd* been doing for the last hour, so I returned to Harper's side.

"Liv said Hawker's using fake cantrips which bring you back to life and make you rot from the inside out," I told her.

"Oh, ugh," she said. "You know what, I prefer being a lich, thanks."

"Exactly my thinking."

I'll find a way to help her. On top of the other shit going on, it seemed a tall order, but who knew, maybe the enemy *had* left a clue lying around which would enable me to help her return to life. It was no more outlandish a notion than the idea of capturing the Family again, after all.

Dex flew over to me. "Ready to stage a rescue mission?"

"You're coming to save the sprites?" I said.

"Yes," he said. "Wouldn't miss it. Where've you been all day?"

A shadow fell over us as the Death King descended the stone staircase at the front of the castle, sparing me from having to reply. The King of the Dead wore a human face which looked younger than I'd expected, though it must be an illusion. A convincing one, too.

"Come with me," he told our group. "We will go in through Arcadia's citadel. Expect an ambush—and expect them to be armed."

Yeah, I figured that much.

The Death King swept out of the gates, towards the node. Liv walked to catch him up, while I kept both eyes open for potential intruders lurking in the swamp.

Miles caught my arm. "You're jumpy. Sure you're up for this?"

"I'm sure." *I think.* "Someone's gotta do it."

I walked with him towards the node, keeping my fingers and toes crossed that no members of the Family waited on the other side.

14

None did. We landed in Arcadia's dark street, where the Death King led the way across the town square to the citadel. I'd assumed the way in was still barred, but he reached out and did something to the door, which slid open as though pulled by a mechanism from inside. Neat trick. I'd have asked him how he did it, but several liches waited on the other side of the door, and not the friendly type. They moved in a tide of shadow, and our allies stepped up to meet them.

I'd never duelled a lich before, but a flame from my hand took care of two of them, burning them to ashes. They'd regenerate, but hopefully somewhere far away. Ryan's air magic had a similar effect, blasting the liches into the air like a curtain swept up in a breeze and sending them into the path of my flames. Between us, we cleared the way into the lower room of the citadel.

The inside of the citadel looked the same as ever, dominated by a long spiralling staircase leading to the upper floor. Liches gathered at all levels of the stairs, waiting for us. Easy pickings. Raising a hand, I shot a fireball and incinerated several liches in one go. Ryan's air magic took care of another, while Miles and his fellow Spirit Agents duelled with the ones on ground level. Cal and Felicity took up positions outside the doors, no doubt to stop anyone else from getting in. Or possibly to stop the liches from getting out.

A lich barred my path to the stairs, but Miles's hand shot straight through it and it crumpled into nothingness on the spot. Liv ran past and hopped onto the lowest stair, calling over her shoulder, "The transporter links up to wherever they're keeping the sprites. Not sure which citadel it is, but it definitely isn't Elysium."

Then where? I'd never been anywhere outside of Elysium and Arcadia. That meant treading on unfamiliar territory, but it was too late to turn back now.

Liv reached the top of the stairs first, opening the door and disappearing into the room above, while Ryan followed on her heels. Dex flew overhead, showering sparks onto the remaining liches. I sent a fireball at another, then I ran for the stairs with Miles on my heels.

Part of me expected to find the Family waiting on the other side of the door, but by the time we reached the top, Liv and the others had taken care of the liches and left the path to the transporter clear. The bank of machinery covering the back wall looked as pristine as ever, though it was Elysium's transporter that I'd blown to pieces a few weeks ago.

Liv hopped onto the platform, while Miles and I moved in to join her. The surface looked silvery in the light, but up close, it was pale gold. The image of the huge chunk of golden metal at the Family's mine appeared in my head, sending a shiver through my bones. Then light flared up, carrying us away to another near-identical room.

More liches met us on the other side, and I gladly unleashed my flames on them. Why hadn't anyone stronger come here to block our path? It seemed suspicious to me, but I wasn't one to let a stroke of luck go by without taking advantage. I shot a ball of fire across the room and turned two of the liches to ashes at once. Dex and his fellow sprites from the castle surrounded another, Ryan's air magic pushing the flames into the liches like a wildfire fanned by a breeze.

Despite the fire ripping through the room, the machinery remained untouched, pristine. Only an inferno cantrip could destroy them, but I'd have to wait until the path was clear to use mine.

The light of the transporter spun across the gleaming grey walls as Liv cut a path through to a door at the back, the only part of the room which differentiated it from the other citadels. She kicked the door open, revealing a smaller room dominated by a large cage. Wires passed through a series of holes in the wall, connecting the cage to the machine on the other side... and inside the cage were countless sprites.

The sprites' transparent bodies were pressed against one another, their eyes looking piteously up at us. Fire and water, earth and air, trapped in a cage barred from the outside. One look at the complex mechanism told me no unlocking spell would work on it.

I pulled an inferno cantrip out, at the ready. "Okay. I'm gonna blow the doors off that thing. Stand back!"

"Hang on!" Liv backed through the door into the main

room, and I heard the transporter light up again. I waited to make sure the others were out of range, then I took aim and hit the switch on the inferno cantrip.

Miles grabbed my arm and we ran out of the back room, an instant before the inferno cantrip exploded. We slammed the door on the roar of noise, and its metal surface trembled under the impact of the blast. As we reached the transporter's light, the door shuddered open, revealing orange flames filling the room and the lights of a thousand triumphant sprites as they flew away to freedom.

That was when I realised my mistake. In destroying the cage, I'd wiped out the transporter in the process. The machinery resembled a pile of lifeless metal, its lights extinguished. Smoke poured out from the platform in the room's centre.

"Oops. Might've overdone it."

"You think?" said Miles, with an eye-roll.

"Dammit," Liv said, glaring at me.

Only five of us had been left behind: Miles, Shelley, Ryan, Liv… and me. Even the Death King had been left on the other side.

"The Death King's going to kill me for this, isn't he?" I murmured to Miles.

"Probably," he said. "On the plus side, the sprites might come to your defence."

The sprites themselves had almost dispersed by now, a flood of bright colour fleeing the back room. I walked to the doorway and saw the cage was in ruins, without a single sprite left inside it. Wires hung loose, sending sparks dancing across the floor. How on earth had Hawker and his allies captured so many sprites?

That was a question for another day, because if the Family found us here, we'd left most of our army behind. Though from the expression on Liv's face, she was more likely to kill me than the alternative. I still had my own transporter spell concealed in my pendant, but if a node lay at the heart of the citadel, I couldn't sense it now.

I'd blown up our only way out.

15

I half expected Liv to punch me in the face. Instead, she said, "Let's have a look outside. Might as well see what we're up against."

"Did you go over this plan with the Death King first?" Ryan asked. "Because he'll be pissed with you if you gave him no warning before stranding us in the middle of Elements-know-where."

I wasn't a hundred percent sure whether they were talking to me or to Liv, to be honest. After all, if not for Liv, we never would have been here in the first place.

"Keep your hair on," I said. "I bet we're close to the city. The spirit mages didn't build their citadels in the middle of nowhere."

"And you'd know?" Ryan said.

"Okay, there's no need for the attitude," I said. "You *told* me to blow the bloody thing up. Not my fault we were on the wrong side of the transporter."

Miles grinned. Shelley poked him in the arm. Hard. "This isn't funny."

"Absolutely not," Miles said in solemn tones. "Terrible mistake coming here. Terrible."

"Shut the fuck up, Miles," said Shelley. "Where *are* we?"

I looked for Liv, only to find she'd disappeared through the door leading out of the room. I walked over, confirming another staircase led down into the lower level, the same as the other citadels. The grey walls and floor were covered with faint runes, dimly lit by the dawn light filtering through from somewhere outside.

I descended the stairs and found Liv had opened the front door, revealing an expanse of wasteland that extended in all directions. A wasteland that looked awfully familiar. We couldn't be near the Family's house, could we? There were no visible signs of life within sight, and the five of us spread out, surveying our odd surroundings.

"What're the odds that we run into Hawker's evil lair out here?" said Liv. "Actually, it kinda looks like the other end of the Court of the Dead, but his territory goes on for miles."

"I can look for signs of civilisation," I said. "I'm probably the fastest, unless any of you are up for astral projecting."

In truth, I'd quite like to get away from their accusing stares, but if we *were* within sight of the Family's house, I needed to track down a node, asap. I'd worry about the consequences of showing off my super-speed in front of witnesses later, so I walked across the barren ground and picked up speed, leaving the others in the dust.

"How are you doing that?" Liv called after me.

"Bria has skills," I heard Miles say to her. "I could technically astral project, but I don't quite trust you not to murder me while I'm standing here unprotected."

"*Me?*" Liv said. "If I'm pissed off, it's because I literally have less than a day to live. I don't have time for a goddamned sleepover in the arse-end of nowhere."

Less than a day to live? No wonder Liv had dragged us on a rescue mission straight after her confrontation with Hawker. I'd need to ask her about that later, once we'd reached safety. I scanned the wasteland, seeing no signs of anyone living among the carcasses of wrecked buildings, shattered piles of stone and brick and metal. Maybe it'd been a town once, but the sole landmark was the citadel, its dark spire piercing the otherwise unbroken horizon.

A sudden flare of white light flashed behind me. I spun around on the spot, seeing the Death King appear out of thin air next to the citadel. He then walked up to Liv, and the pair of them vanished in a second flash of light.

"Did he just ditch us?" Miles said incredulously.

Looked that way to me. I continued on through the ruins of the town. The horizon was low enough that I would have been able to see any nearby nodes, but I didn't see a single bright torrent of energy in sight. The ground between the ruins was trampled earth, with shards of glass and metal sticking out at intervals. The flat horizon revealed no sign of the cliffs behind the Family's house.

They aren't here. It's safe. Or as safe as an abandoned wasteland in the Parallel, at any rate. I strode back to the citadel, where Ryan and Shelley both watched me with their eyes wide.

"Are you secretly an air mage?" asked Shelley.

"No," Ryan and I said at the same time.

"Hey, I'm not trying to steal your spotlight," I said to Ryan. "There's nothing or nobody alive out there."

Miles caught my eye, and I wondered if he knew I was implying that we weren't near the Family's house. The slight problem was that I didn't know *where* we were, and it didn't look like the Death King had the slightest intention of coming back for the rest of us.

"I have a portable transporter spell but no way to use it without a node," I admitted. "Also, it only works on one person at a time."

"What use is that, then?" Shelley grumbled. "If we all get eaten by phantoms, I'm blaming you, Miles."

"Hey!" he said indignantly. "It wasn't my idea. Pretty sure it was Liv's."

"You opted to go along with it," she said. "More because of Bria than anyone, but still."

I cleared my throat before they started arguing. "What was Liv talking about then when she said she had a day to live?"

"A cursed cantrip, apparently," Miles said, glancing at Ryan.

"Don't look at me," said the Air Element. "Hawker used it against her when she refused to join him. That's why she had to run."

"Wait, there are cantrips in there?" I walked towards the tower again. I hadn't looked, but it was worth seeing if Hawker had left anything behind. Like a way of fixing the transporter and getting the hell out of here.

Only Miles followed me into the tower, our feet echoing on the polished floor.

"Am I in trouble with your second-in-command?" I

asked. "Or is there a chance the Death King might swoop in to save the rest of us?"

"No." He walked behind me as we climbed the spiralling staircase to the upper floor. "He took Liv back because she'd have died otherwise. The rest of us are cannon fodder."

"It's nice to be appreciated." I opened the door to the upper room and skirted the inert platform towards the bank of machinery.

"I appreciate you," he said from behind my shoulder. His words brought a shiver to my skin, but a moment later, a tell-tale glint caught my eye.

I crouched down. Sure enough, a handful of blank cantrips lay beneath the machine's hunk of ruined metal. I gingerly turned one over with my foot, but no mark covered the back. *Not the Family's...*

Miles picked up one of the cantrips. "Not sure we'll find any kind of transporter which'll work without a node, to tell you the truth."

"That's not what I'm looking for," I said. "These aren't the Family's. I thought for a moment we might be near their house, but there's nothing out there. Hell of a weird place to build a citadel."

I picked up another cantrip, then it hit me that I should probably take my own advice and leave them alone in case they turned out to be laced with the virus. I gave the machine another scan instead, eyeing a cantrip-shaped slot in the side. "What's that?"

Miles's expression darkened. "That's how the transporter works. A portable transporter cantrip was inside the machine itself. All you need is a battery. Like those sprites."

"Living batteries." I tasted bile at the back of my throat. "Wait, could you put a different cantrip in there and use it the same way?"

"I'd wager that's exactly what it's intended for," Miles said. "As for why they picked somewhere so remote, this is probably why."

"It didn't used to be." The town had once been intact, and the sight of it stirred a sense of familiarity within me despite my best efforts. "The transporter is out for the count. I can run, but I'd have to carry you if I wanted to get us both out of there at once."

He raised a brow. "You, carry me?"

"Why not?" I said. "I'm stronger than I look."

"Uh-huh." He gave a knowing smile. "Want to demonstrate?"

"You asked for it." I grabbed him around the middle and lifted him into the air. Unfortunately, I hadn't accounted for the wires underfoot, and when I tripped against the machine's side, I overbalanced and crash-landed on top of him. The breath fled my lungs as he looked up into my eyes, my knees on either side of his waist.

"Gotcha," he said softly. "Now I have you where I want you."

A voice in the back of my head told me to get up and stop screwing around. Flirting was one thing, but heavy contact was a no-go in my line of work. I couldn't even remember the last time I'd let anyone get that close. What was I doing?

His fingers caught my wrist, tugged gently. "Hey. Let me into your thoughts."

My thoughts were a whirling dervish, flitting past like hummingbirds. In the end, all I said was, "Are you sure my weird elf powers don't freak you out?"

"Are you kidding me?" His fingers teased my wrist, and warmth pooled inside me. "I've seen weirder."

"So complimentary." Ah, fuck it. I leaned over and kissed him on the mouth. He lifted his head in response, his lips soft on mine, his hands releasing my wrists and cupping my head to pull me onto him.

Footsteps hammered on the stairs. I jerked back and hit my knee hard on the floor. A series of curses escaped me. "Owww."

Behind us, the door slammed against the wall. Shelley walked in and gave us both a look of utter disgust. "I swear, if you two start boning next, I'm leaving you in here."

Miles grinned. "That wouldn't be comfortable, would it?"

"Gotta love that apocalyptic decor." I pushed to my feet, wincing. "Ouch. Yeah. Bad choice of make-out spot."

"Not the worst." His words were a murmur in my ear as we walked to the door.

Shelley shook her head at us when we caught her up at the foot of the stairs. "I can see something over there that might be a node. Find anything in the tower?"

"Just a few abandoned cantrips," I told her. "Nothing useful."

Shelley pushed open the door. Darkness shrouded the ruins as the sun's rays withdrew beyond the horizon. It'd been a hell of a long day, and it seemed we'd have a longer night ahead if we didn't find civilisation soon. All kinds of beasts came out at night, and while vampires wouldn't be seen dead in a place like this—relatively speaking—phantoms and revenants would have no shortage of hiding places.

I absently rubbed my sore knee, fighting the sinking feeling in my chest as I looked at the ruined city. Glass crunched underfoot, and shadows stretched spidery fingers towards us.

Ryan strode back into view. "Finished slacking off?"

"We weren't slacking off," I protested. "We figured out the machinery in there can be used as a battery to power up any cantrip, not just transporters."

"Looks like you were more interested in finding alternative uses for the floor," Shelley said.

"Seriously, though," Miles said, "the sprites have gone, but something linked up the citadel with the others, didn't it? I'm not sure the sprites were the only battery source."

"Does that mean there are power sources... *living* ones... in every citadel?" said Shelley.

"I didn't see any cages in Elysium, did you?" I reminded them both.

"Liv implied that this was the place where they brought the liches back to life," Ryan said. "They hooked up a cantrip to the machine and used it to turn a lich into a living mage again. I reckon they needed a stronger power source to pull that off."

My throat went dry. "You're joking."

"I probably should have asked her to confirm it before she took off," said Ryan. "I'm starting to think she and the Death King ran into trouble."

"Nah, they ditched us," said Miles. "They ran off, and we should do the same before we get eaten."

"I agree," said Shelley. "Pity we can't apply an inferno cantrip to the whole tower."

"Nah, it's impervious to damage," I said. "What's it made out of?"

"No clue," said Miles. "The spirit mages who founded the place would know, but they're dead."

Yeah. They were, and yet the citadel alone had survived whatever disaster had destroyed the rest of the town. "The spirit mages built the tower, but I guess they left it here when they abandoned the place."

Had the spirit mages ever had dealings with the Family? I'd thought not, but they seemed to believe they supported the winning side despite the fact that the spirit mages had been the undisputed losers of the last war.

"Look," Shelley said, pointing. "I see a node over there."

I squinted at the horizon, where the sun's rays dazzle the eyes. "Are you sure it's a node?"

"Either that or a really big bonfire," said Miles.

Shelley shook her head at him. "It's a node. Trust me."

"Better get there before we find out who really lives here," Miles said. "Remember the incident with the ogre's nest."

"*Miles!*"

The pair of them launched into an argument, while I strode ahead and scanned the route ahead in search of hidden enemies. Lex's words rang through my head, much as I tried to shut them out. She was right in that I hadn't always been part of the Family. I'd been born else-where... somewhere which didn't exist any longer. Some-where she assumed I didn't remember. And I didn't, not really, but sometimes when I closed my eyes at night, I saw the town in my dreams. A town dominated by a pillar-like structure, obsidian in colour, the only land-mark which wasn't burning in magical fire.

It was nothing but a memory too old for me to recall in any detail. For all I knew, my subconscious had made it up. Yet the sense of familiarity grew worse the further we walked. The town was a wreck, as though something far more devastating than a war had taken it to pieces. Elysium might have taken a hell of a beating, but enough of it had survived that it remained inhabited. Arcadia, too. The war had left most of the major cities standing, but on a local level, it was hit and miss, and this place had clearly taken the brunt of a major magical assault. A targeted one.

The white glow grew brighter in the distance, then split into two blots of blurred light.

Miles halted behind me. "Shelley, that isn't a node."

"What?" Shelley peered ahead of us. "Oh…*fuck.*"

The glowing mass had begun to move towards us. Nodes didn't move, nor did they fly, with transparent arms outstretched and glowing from within.

Phantoms: the Parallel's version of ghosts. I conjured fire to my hands in warning. "Go away."

They ignored me and closed in around our group, emitting moaning noises and seemingly unafraid of my fire.

"I think they want us to leave," Miles said. "Too bad, mate—we don't have anywhere else to go. Mind moving out of the way?"

"They can't understand you," said Shelley, conjuring spirit magic to her hands.

As cold hands reached for me, I fired off a ball of flames into the mass of phantoms, causing them to scatter. Their group reformed a second later, sweeping towards us and emitting a low moaning noise that sounded like half-formed words.

"Go away!" Shelley blasted them with spirit magic at the same time as I threw another fireball. Miles did likewise, his hands blazing with light. Our combined magic broke through their mass, sending them scattering in all directions. This time, they got the message and pulled back out of range, leaving the path clear. The so-called 'node' had vanished from sight, leaving nothing but wasteland behind.

Teeth bared in frustration, I marched ahead. An image kept intruding, the vivid picture of a burning town with a sentinel-like tower in the centre. I did my level best to push the image away. Getting out of here was more important than finding out what this place had once been... and who'd once lived here.

It took several minutes before I became aware of a scuffling sound among the ruins of a nearby building. Too loud to belong to a phantom. A hairless head popped up from the shadows. Then another. *Revenants.*

"Shit," said Miles. "I think we attracted the locals."

"The good news?" I said, conjuring up a flame. "There must be a node nearby. They feed on the nodes, right?"

"Best news I've heard all day." Miles blasted the revenant with a handful of spirit magic, sending it recoiling. Shelley intercepted another, while I hurled a fireball, lighting up the gloom ahead.

We rounded a corner, spotting the welcome sight of a pillar of light. It wasn't until we got closer that I saw the dark shapes moving within it. Revenants surrounded the node, feeding on its magic.

"No other way out," I said. "Ready to run?"

"You bet." Ryan conjured a handful of air magic, drawing the revenants' attention. They abandoned the node and flocked towards us in a swarm.

A fireball grew in my hand, and I flung it at the revenants. Two of them burst into a torrent of flame in an impressive display which caught the others in its orbit, fuelled by Ryan's fire. Bits of burning revenant scattered all over the swampland, and Miles whistled approval.

"Thanks, Bria," said Miles. "You found our node *and* took out the dickheads guarding it."

"It's her fault we got stuck there," Shelley reminded him.

"Actually, it's more the Death King's fault that he rescued Liv and left the rest of us behind," I put in.

Ryan snorted.

I glanced at them. "Tell me I'm wrong."

"She isn't wrong," Miles supplied. "He *did* ditch us. I'm insulted."

"Liv probably got injured again," said Ryan.

"She did say she had a day to live," said Miles. "Anyway, don't blame Bria for the mess. Blame the dickheads who locked up those sprites."

"He has a point," I said to the others. "How'd they catch so many of them?"

"You think I know?" asked Ryan. "I can only assume they used magic to do it."

"Never mind them," said Shelley. "We're going back to Elysium. The others will be worried. They might even have sent a search party after us by now."

Miles gave her a nod, then he turned back to me. "Will you be okay?"

"Sure." I fixed on a smile. "Nothing wrong with me that a long nap can't fix."

"Come on," said Ryan. "We have to report back to the Death King."

I grimaced. "I can't wait to see what's gone to shit in the Court of the Dead while we've been gone."

16

Nothing, as it turned out. The grounds were quiet, the castle undisturbed. I made my way back to my room and more or less collapsed on the bed. I woke a few hours later with a blazing headache and checked the time. I'd slept half the day, to no surprise given how long it'd been since I'd last had a proper rest. I went to shower and dress, then grabbed some food from the break room. Nobody else was around, including the Death King. I had yet to update him on my discoveries of the previous day, but it was his own damn fault for leaving us alone in the middle of nowhere and expecting us to walk back to the castle on foot.

It was pure luck that had spared us from running into the Family again, and while I wanted to tell him they'd reclaimed their own hideout, the Houses needed to know more urgently. Someone ought to clue them in about the incident at the Withered Oak, for that matter, but I doubted Harris would give a shit that a group of rogue mages had got themselves locked up by Arcadia's vampires. I hadn't checked up on Tay for a while, come to that, but if anyone else in the House was working with the Family, then it was only a matter of time before they picked up where Zade had left off.

Since nobody seemed inclined to give me orders, I left the castle for the node and travelled to the centre of Elysium. The first thing I noticed was that the lock had been removed from the door to the House of Fire. Had they got over their brief spell of paranoia? Or had they somehow learned I'd broken in? I doubted that was the case, so I knocked on the door.

Harris answered, along with another half-dozen guards who spilled out and surrounded me on all sides.

"Hey, there," I said. "What's going on?"

"Bria Kent," said Harris. "You're under arrest."

For a brief moment, I considered running, but I figured it was best to humour them until we cleared up whatever they'd got themselves worked up over this time. *They can't possibly know I broke into Zade's office, right?*

I raised my hands in surrender. "Hey, I just got here. What am I being arrested for?"

"Conspiring against the Houses of the Elements," he answered.

"What does that mean?" I said. "Seriously, I haven't been anywhere near the Houses in the last day."

"We saw you go to your family's estate," Harris said.

Oh, *shit.* I should have known they'd be watching me—from a safe distance, of course. "I wanted to see if they'd left any clues behind. It turns out they're hiring earth mages—"

The guards shunted me through the doors to the building and down the staircase off the corridor. *Shit.*

They're seriously taking me to the jail? To my horror, someone grabbed the pendant from around my neck and pulled it free, then more hands dug into my pockets and took my spare cantrips.

"You met with the Family," said Harris. "Don't deny it."

"I didn't expect to find anyone there," I protested. "How was I supposed to know you let them move back into their old property after their escape without even trying to stop them?"

There was more I wanted to say, but I couldn't reference Zade's files without admitting I'd broken into his office. Not that anyone was inclined to listen, either way. The guards herded me downstairs, then led me to a cell and pushed me into it. Tay's cell, in fact... but she was no longer inside it.

"Where's Tay?" I asked.

The door slammed on me, and Harris leered at me from the other side of the bars. "You'll be staying here this time. No escaping."

"Where's Tay?" I called after him as he retreated. "Seriously, this isn't a joke. Where did you take her?

Nobody replied. I stared into the darkness in disbelief for a long moment. Had Tay made a break for it? That was the best-case scenario. Because if she hadn't escaped... if they'd killed her...

I shut down that line of thinking hard, instead examining the door for a possible way out. Of course, it was magic-proofed, too, so after trying every angle, I sat down on the bench and waited for someone to come back.

The minutes dragged. It felt like a million years before anyone came downstairs, and I was beginning to doze off when Harris walked into view again.

"Where is Tay?" I demanded. "If you had her killed, I swear to the Elements, I will rip out your throat."

"Your friend Tay gave us the slip last night," said Harris. "Tell me where she is."

"What?" I said. "You think I helped her escape?"

She's free? It didn't surprise me that she'd run, and I wouldn't deny it was a relief that she'd got out before they'd decided to punish her for Zade's death. Question was, where had she gone?

"Was that a confession?" he said.

"Look, if I'd helped her escape, I wouldn't have come back here, would I?" I said. "Ask the Spirit Agents who were with me yesterday evening. Or ask the Air Element. We spent a fun night stranded in the middle of nowhere after staging a rescue mission on the Death King's orders."

"Your allies are no more reliable than you are," he said. "You were seen heading to the Family's house several hours before her escape—"

"Look, I don't even know when the Family got back to their estate, *or* how they rebuilt it," I said. "Since nobody told me how they escaped from prison *or* that they went right back to their old haunts. It's not like you didn't have the resources to have them followed."

He moved closer to the bars. "You—"

A sudden crash came from upstairs. Behind him, a body came flying down the staircase, head over heels, wearing the guard uniform of a member of the House of Fire.

"What the—" Harris spun around. "Who's up there?"

The guard lifted his head, groaning. "The—earth mages."

Oh, damn. It seemed the House of Earth had finally made their move.

Without looking back, Harris ran for the stairs. I tried to get the door open again, but of course they'd taken my unlocking cantrips. My fire wouldn't help, either.

'Hey!" I said to the fallen guard. "Help me out of here."

He crawled upright with a groan. "Are you serious?"

"Look, I didn't do anything wrong, but if it's the House of Earth who's attacking you, they were compromised a long time ago," I told him. "They're buying cantrips on the black market, nasty ones. The same cantrips killed Zade."

"I heard your friend was the one that killed Zade," he said uncertainly. He was young for a guard, with light brown skin and dark hair matted with blood.

"Clearly, she isn't the threat at the moment," I said. "I can help you fight those earth mages. Trust me, you want me on your side, not against it. Harris arrested me on false pretences."

"Harris is a dick." With a nervous look over his shoulder, he ran over to my cell and unlocked the door. "Don't tell anyone I let you out."

"Cheers." I climbed out of the cell, halting when footsteps sounded on the stairs. A lithe figure descended into view, dirt smearing his pale face. *Earth mage.*

I tackled him, knocking him off his feet and running past him up the stairs. He hadn't been prepared for my speed, and he toppled straight into the guard's fist. I left him behind and continued running up the stairs to the surface.

When I reached the main hallway, chaos greeted me. The front door stood open, while the bodies of several guards littered the hallway. I vaulted over the bodies and ran into the room where I knew they'd stashed the cantrips they'd confiscated from me during my arrest. Nobody tried to stop me, but I made a point of knocking down as many earth mages as possible on my way through. Once I had my pendant back, cantrips and all, I was out the door before anyone could get their hands on me.

Outside, more confused fighting littered the streets. While some of the attackers were earth mages, others fought with knives. I only needed to see the uniform of a masked assassin to know who'd sent them. The Family had made their move against the House of Fire, and possibly the other Houses, too. The streets were awash in confusion, bolts of magic flying through the air.

I broke into a sprint around the corner behind the House of Fire, eyes open for the nearest node. An assassin blocked my path, a cantrip gleaming around his neck. His fist shot out, but I ducked, glad that despite the enhancements the Family gave their assassins, my own speed still outranked theirs. A knife flew from his hand, grazing my shoulder, and a fireball sprang to my palms.

"What're you playing at?" I said. "I thought the Family wanted me alive."

No response came. The fireball left my hands and blasted him sideways into another assassin, and I ran on, following the route which circled the four Houses of the Elements from behind. The House of Earth was up next, and I skidded to a halt at the street's end. The entire route was blocked by a tall barrier made of packed earth, which definitely hadn't been there before. The barrier entirely covered the street's end, leaving only one path open.

I took that route and ran on, but it became clear that

every street entrance I passed was blocked by the same barriers the earth mages had conjured up. The routes to the citadel and the town's centre were still open, but they would take me directly into the middle of the fighting. Which was no doubt the intention. The mages had blocked off the centre of the city, turning it into a cage. With the Houses warring from within and nobody able to get in or out, it'd be a bloodbath. Gusts of air rippled past, water and fire extinguished one another, while the ground trembled beneath my feet and assassins leapt across the rooftops flinging knives into the melee.

To get out, I'd need to find a way to vault over one of the barriers caging the centre of the city, find somewhere to hide inside one of the few empty buildings—or go to the one node near the square and expose myself in the process. Not good odds.

The assassins made up my mind for me. Two jumped off the nearest roof to bar my path. A fireball flew from my palms, and they ran to the side to avoid being incinerated. I skirted the corner and nearly tripped over the body of a fallen mage. His body was covered in blisters.

Those cantrips again. If anything, they were a more deadly method of killing than using elemental magic, especially if the earth mages had been spreading them around the Houses.

The two assassins rose to their feet again with jerky motions like puppets on strings. I darted to the side, avoiding another knife, and Miles and Shelley ran over to join me, hands blazing with spirit magic. The assassins backed off, sensing they were outnumbered, and our combined attacks took them down.

"How'd you get in here?" I asked the two spirit mages.

"Through the node," said Miles. "We were on the brink of coming to bust you out of there."

"I had it covered," I said. "But—why are they blocking off this part of the city? Did they not remember people could just use the nodes to get in and out instead of moving around on foot?"

"I don't know, but the Death King called us to meet with him," he said. "When he heard you were missing, he told us to go to Elysium. I think he figured out you'd gone to the House of Fire."

"And there I thought he'd forgotten I existed." I picked up the pace when the node came within sight. "Tay escaped, too. The House of Fire tried to blame me for helping her out of her cell. That's why they locked me up."

"Your friend is working with the enemy again?" said Shelley.

"I don't know." Her absence was an ache in my chest, but what if she'd been involved in the enemy's attack? I couldn't go looking for her either way, not when I had zero clue where she'd gone. Besides, we had bigger problems on our hands.

We ran down the narrow street, blasting down any assassins who got in our way. The closed-off streets gave me claustrophobia, but I made it to the node without being cornered. "The Death King had better be able to spare some people to help us."

"That'd be welcome," said Shelley, catching me up, "considering we helped *him,* and he repaid us by abandoning us in the middle of nowhere."

"C'mon," said Miles. "Coast's clear."

Our group hopped through the node and landed in the swampland. The quietness disturbed me, as though part of me had expected to find the Court of the Dead under attack as well. Instead, outside the gates, the Death King stood nose to nose with a vampire. They appeared to be engaged in a heated argument, but when I tried to enter the grounds, Liv barred my path.

"Where have you been?" she said.

"Elysium," I replied. "I take it you know the Houses of the Elements are under attack?"

"The *Houses?*" Her brow furrowed, and she turned to the vampire who stood arguing with the Death King at the gates. "You didn't say the Houses of the Elements were under attack. That's a world away from a handful of mages stirring up trouble."

"I'm terribly sorry my report wasn't accurate enough for you," said the vampire.

Liv's eyes narrowed. "Look—you do realise Elysium overlaps with London, aka the site of the next Order meeting?"

"The Order?" I said. "What's going on with the Order?"

Liv turned to me. "The Order is under the control of the enemy and we've just found out that Hawker and his allies have access to a major gathering in London. We think he might be planning to seize power by unleashing a massacre."

The Order? They're attacking the Order as well as the Houses? For all I knew, their real target was the ordinary world on the other side of the nodes, but knowing the Family, it might well be both at once.

"Holy shit," I said. "Why would he do that?"

"The Order is the centre of the magical community on Earth," Liv replied. "Plus it's an easy way to cover up a coup. Hawker and his allies already did it once."

Behind me, Miles gave a low whistle. "Scumbags. The other Spirit Agents are on their way here."

"Good," said Liv.

With her no longer blocking my path, I slipped through the gates, followed by Miles and Shelley. I could feel the Death King watching me from behind, but he continued to argue with the vampire, no doubt trying to convince him to lend a hand. I'd have to tell him about my experience in the House of Fire later... not to mention Tay's escape.

"Not sure the other Spirit Agents will want to help in London," said Shelley. "They know what they do to spirit mages over there."

"Not sure they'd be keen on me, either." The Order, though, wasn't my priority. The assassins had blocked off the entire centre of Elysium, including the citadel. I knew the Family must be involved, but in order to figure out the extent of it, I needed to talk to my brother first.

"Bria." Ryan walked across the grounds towards me, dressed in full armour. "Where have you been?"

"Locked up in the House of Fire," I said. "Didn't the Death King tell you?"

"He sent Shelley and me after her, but he didn't know she was locked up," said Miles. "That, or he didn't trust the other Elemental Soldiers not to leave her there to rot."

"That—" Ryan broke off. "Look, Liv didn't even wake up from the coma she fell into after returning from the citadel until an hour ago, and then she casually dropped the bombshell on us that the Order is hosting a meeting tonight. Which would explain why Hawker left his citadel unattended. He has his eye on bigger things."

"It isn't him who's attacking Elysium," Miles put in. "The House of Earth is, along with those weird assassins."

"The Family's assassins," I clarified. "Not practitioners, but they're carrying cantrips which boost their strength and speed. If *they're* going to London, no way are the ordinary people prepared to face that shit. Even the Order won't have seen them before."

"So they don't use magic at all?" said Ryan.

"They use cantrips, that's enough," I said. "Nasty ones, too."

Like the ones that killed the jailor and the other guard.

"Sounds familiar," said Ryan. "At the last event they attacked, they used inferno cantrips to kill and injure Order members when they were off duty. While everyone was distracted, they swooped in and took over Birmingham's branch of the Order. They're probably doing the same in London. The only difference is that we're forewarned this time."

"Assuming Liv is right," I added. "Hawker must be sure he has enough people on his side to take on the Houses as well as attacking London at the same time."

"It's not just him," said Ryan. "There are traitors within the Order itself."

And then there's the Family, too. No doubt they were waiting in the wings to scoop up whatever was left behind after the dust settled.

Felicity and Cal walked up to join Ryan, also dressed in full armour and armed to the teeth.

"That family of yours is involved in the attacks?" said Cal.

I ignored the jab. "They're more likely to be watching Elysium. They've never shown much interest in Earth."

"They're the creators of the inferno cantrips," said Ryan. "I'm taking a wild guess that they're interested in seeing how much damage they can cause with them."

They probably weren't wrong. The idea of the deadly cantrips being unleashed on unsuspecting humans filled me with revulsion, but I didn't relish the idea of the Houses being razed to the ground either.

A few more spirit mages entered the grounds, followed by the Death King, and Miles went to talk to them. The vampire, it seemed, had left, and I had words to say to His Deathly Highness before he sneaked off again. I marched over and planted my feet in front of him.

"Thanks for checking up on me after you abandoned us in the wilderness." Sarcasm dripped from my voice.

"You seem to have made it back in one piece," he said. "I did send the Spirit Agents to get you away from the House of Fire."

"Did you expect me to end up getting locked in a cell while a battle broke out among the Houses?" I queried. "Because it would have been nice to have some warning."

"Unfortunately, I am incapable of being in seven places at once," he said. "After Olivia was injured upon her return from the abandoned citadel, I had to take care of some trouble here in the castle. I trusted yourself, Ryan and the Spirit Agents to make it back here successfully, and I was right."

"You trusted us," I repeated. "Do you trust me, though? You let me run around and do whatever I like, yet it seems like nobody except you ever knows what the hell is going on at any given time."

"Welcome to my world." Liv walked over, fighting a smile, for some inexplicable reason.

The Death King addressed Liv. "Can you tell your friend Devon what's going on? We might be in need of her help."

Liv returned to the castle, and the Death King faced me again. "I take it you mean to explain exactly *how* you got yourself arrested by the House of Fire?"

"They blamed me because Tay escaped from jail," I said. "They assumed I helped her escape, but I didn't, and frankly, I have no idea where she went. They also accused me of conspiring with the Family against them. Then they were attacked, and I took the opportunity to run."

"Attacked by whom?"

I had an inkling he already knew, but maybe he'd be able to help me make heads or tails of this mess. "The House of Earth, along with assassins belonging to the Family. They've cut off the entire centre of Elysium so nobody can enter on foot. Now Liv tells me they're after the Order in London, too."

"I suspect Hawker and his allies decided to attack on multiple fronts," he said.

"It might not be him who's behind the attack in Elysium." I drew in a breath. "The Family... I know where they're based. They're hiding in the ruins of their old estate north of Elysium. They tend to like to watch the chaos from a distance, so they probably won't show up in person unless we hunt them down. But I'm no match for them alone."

The Death King's countenance radiated disapproval. "When did you plan to mention this to me?"

"When you showed your face!" I said, exasperated. "As soon as I got back here after finding out, you wanted me and the Spirit Agents to help Liv rescue those sprites and then we wound up stuck in the tower. Maybe I'd have been able to tell you if you hadn't vanished with Liv and left us behind, but instead you let us fight our way back alone."

Lex had all but warned me of her plans, but I hadn't had the chance to pass on her warning to anyone else. I was exhausted, like a candle flame burned down to the base, and I wanted to lie down and sleep, not face off against my depraved family for the second time in the space of a day.

"And that friend of yours… is *she* with the Family?" he said.

"I don't know," I admitted. "I think she killed the jailor because *he* was conspiring with the enemy, based on a letter I found in his office which referenced the Withered Oak and illegal cantrips. But the House of Fire refused to listen to me up until the last possible moment. It doesn't matter now, anyway. All the Houses are in trouble if the assassins are running around armed with the same cantrips which killed two people while hardly leaving a mark on them… and we know for a fact they have at least one box of them from the supplier."

"Yeah, slight problem," Miles said from behind me. "One of my people just got back to me and says the node isn't working."

"Which node?" said the Death King.

Tate walked over to join Miles. "We can't get through to the centre of Elysium anymore. Someone turned off the nodes."

17

I stared at the two spirit mages for a moment. "Seriously?"

"Seriously," said Tate. "The whole place is blocked off. I can get through to the edges of Elysium, but we'll either have to walk to the centre on foot or find another way in. Which would be easy enough if someone hadn't decided to put barriers on all the streets."

"Wonderful," said Shelley. "That's us screwed then, isn't it?"

Behind her, the other Elemental Soldiers approached us in a group, facing Miles and the other Spirit Agents.

"Change of plans," Ryan said to Miles. "The Death King wants you to come to London."

"What?" said Miles. "He does know the Order has total freedom to arrest us for simply *existing* over there, doesn't he? They think spirit mages are the scum of the earth."

"The liches can't survive away from the nodes," said Ryan. "It has to be living people who goes on the mission, and he has exactly four of us at his disposal."

"That blows," said Miles. "Not that I'm against a trip to a fancy gathering in London, but I have zero desire to get blown up by an inferno cantrip either."

"Nor me." I looked for Liv and spotted her talking to Dex outside the castle, next to Harper. To my surprise, Harper wore an illusion of her old face, which was convincing enough that for a heartbeat, I wondered if she'd managed to get hold of a cantrip which returned her to life after all.

"Hey, Bria," she said, when I approached her.

"Hey," I said. "Nice illusion."

"Thanks," she said, with a smile which almost looked real. "I've been practising. I thought it'd be enough to help me get to London with the others, but apparently wearing an illusion won't be enough to stop me from falling to pieces if I go too far from the nodes."

"Why would you want to go to London?" I asked.

"I'm not staying alone in the castle this time," she said. "I'm sick of being afraid of those bastards."

"Being wary of falling to pieces is a pretty valid thing to be concerned about," I reminded her. "There's no way around that, is there?"

She shook her head. "No, but I just have a bad feeling about everyone leaving the castle at once."

"Why?" I asked.

"Hawker wants the Death King's power," she said. "That's his aim. This crap he's doing in London is just a distraction."

"You sure?" I hadn't thought of the possibility of the castle being a target, too, but Hawker's goal was to take the Death King's soul amulet and his territory along with it. If the Death King insisted on going to London himself, that would leave the path to the castle wide open.

The Death King himself spoke, addressing all of us. "My Elemental Soldiers will stay here at the castle," he said. "Yes, that includes you, too, Ryan. I know for a fact Hawker wants my soul amulet and I won't leave it unattended. Bria will go with the Spirit Agents."

I stared at him for a moment. *He wants me to go to London?*

"But—" Ryan began.

Liv cut in. "Stay here. Hawker wants the Death King's power. And even if he doesn't show up here, Cobb wants the same, and that dude is being suspiciously quiet lately. Trust me, it's for the best."

"Fine," the Air Element ground out. "But I expect you to return promptly or else I'll be there to collect you in person."

"And me?" I said. "Whatever happened to us going to Elysium to help the Houses?"

"The nodes in Elysium's centre have been switched off," said the Death King. "Or so I am told. London is the enemy's target. Keep your distance from the gathering, and make sure nobody sees you."

"The Order will be checking IDs at the door," said Liv. "Only the Death King and I have invitations. The rest of you will have to wait outside."

"We're not signing up to get arrested, trust me," said Miles.

"Any sign of trouble and we're out of there," I added.

Liv and the Death King went through the node first, vanishing in a flash of light. Then the others followed in groups. I joined Miles and the others, and we stepped into the node's path.

We landed on London's street, which appeared strange and bright to my eyes even with the sun already sinking in the sky. Exhaustion dragged at my limbs, but I couldn't rest now. Not with both realms in danger and the people who'd raised me at the heart of it all.

While Liv and the Death King headed towards a fancy hotel which was the designated place for the Order's gathering, I joined the Spirit Agents and we positioned ourselves next to the node, watching out for trouble. We all had invisibility cantrips at the ready, which eased my fears that the Order would arrest us. Considering the shit storm in Elysium right now, the Order was frankly the least of my concerns.

"How'd they block off the nodes?" I watched the current of light beside us, impatience burning beneath my skin.

"No idea, but they zapped out the nodes in the whole centre of Elysium," Miles responded. "Using cantrips. No doubt ones they got from our friends at Dawson's."

I swore under my breath, recalling how Liv had used a similar cantrip to cut off my escape from the Death King's castle when she'd thought I was working against him. The only way in or out of the centre of Elysium was to climb over the walls… or tunnel underneath them. Convenient, considering the Family had a group of earth mages on their side.

Damn, we're in trouble.

I glanced down the darkened street. "Does the Death King know how bad things are in Elysium?"

"I don't think he cares," said Miles. "I'm not sure what

he's doing meeting with the Order, either. Personally, I think he just wants to take out Hawker himself."

"He's welcome to handle the bastard," said Shelley. "I don't give a shit about this Hawker dude. I'm more concerned with whoever locked off half our city."

"No kidding." My gaze followed the smartly dressed people heading into the hotel, who looked as though they belonged to another world to the rest of us. Which they did, due in no small part to the Parallel taking the brunt of the backlash of the last war. The Order had sprung up precisely to stop a repeat performance, yet I didn't know how many among their number were aware that another war stood on the horizon, looming closer by the day.

Two dark-clad figures emerged from a nearby street, hidden amongst the long shadows cast by the streetlamps. *Those aren't guests.*

"Guys," I whispered. "We have company."

The sight of the gleaming golden cantrips in the assassins' hands made my heart sink. Looked like my hunch had been right, and the Family's assassins had found their way to Earth. Despite the nagging worry about the Order's penchant for targeting mages who stepped out of line, innocent people were here who didn't deserve to die at the hands of the Family's assassins. We had to intervene.

"Get rid of those cantrips first," Miles said. "Don't touch them."

Spirit magic blasted from his palms, knocking a cantrip out of the nearest assassin's hands. The second ran at me, but I threw a fireball at him, causing him to drop the cantrip before it went off. I ran up to the assassin and kicked him in the kneecap before he could rise to his feet again.

"Why are you attacking people on Earth?" I demanded. "What did they ever do to you?"

He reached for his cantrip, and I kicked it away from him. Blood dripped from his mouth, and a chill raced through me as his body shuddered, eyes rolling back in his skull. His hand fell limp to the ground, and my gaze landed on the cantrip inches from his hand. That wasn't an inferno cantrip. It was a copy of the one which had killed the jailor.

Don't touch it, Devon had said. Until it wiped itself clean, it was contagious.

"Don't touch the cantrips!" I called to the others. "They're laced with a magical virus."

The Spirit Agents had brought down three more assassins, all of whom lay on the pavement, inert, their faces flecked with blood.

I ran over to Miles. "Any of them still alive?"

"Doesn't look that way," he remarked. "Were they told to take their own lives rather than surrender?"

"That's usually the instruction they're given," I said. "The Family doesn't tolerate failure."

"That family of yours is messed up," Shelley remarked.

"You think I don't know that?" I said. "But seriously—we need to get rid of those cantrips. Don't touch them. They're contagious as hell. The assassins were probably told to drop them here on purpose."

All eyes went to one of the Spirit Agents, who held a cantrip in his hand. At once, he let it fall from his grip, but the damage was already done. The mage fell to his knees, his face blistering, his body spasming. Horror coursed through me as the others ran over to him, unable to help —and I spotted a lone figure standing near the node.

Tay.

Miles caught my eye, and I gave him a look telling him to stay back. The spirit mage who'd picked up the cantrip had fallen limp, no longer moving. *Zade died the same way.*

If Tay had come to fight alongside the assassins… but I didn't think that was why she was here. Still, I kept an eye out for the traps as I walked over to the node and halted in front of her.

"You fell for the ruse," she said.

"What?" I said, uncomprehending. "What are you talking about?"

"You know you're being set up to take the fall, don't you?" she said. "When I escaped, I hoped you'd come chasing after me instead of coming here with the others. The enemy knows you're here. They're counting on it."

I took a step towards Tay. "Where else was I supposed to go? The House of Fire locked me up in your place. They blamed me for your escape."

"I knew that as soon as you inevitably found the Family's location, they'd come for you again," she said, not acknowledging my comment about the House. "They would have taken the House of Fire much sooner if I hadn't stopped them."

So I'd had it right. She'd killed Zade in order to stall the Family's plan, but in the end, it hadn't been enough to keep them out of the Houses.

"Are you on their side or not?" I could see Miles signalling to me from beside the bodies of the assassins. We had to get them out of here before we drew too much attention, but something was wrong with Tay. Her eyes were wide, as though she was trying to signal something she couldn't say aloud.

"Just believe me when I say there's nothing I can do to help you," she said. "Except warn you to stay out of Elysium. You have no idea what they're doing over there."

"Nothing you can do?" I echoed. "Why can't you tell me?"

"Because—" An explosion drowned out her words. The fiery blast of an inferno cantrip ripped through the hotel's entryway, engulfing the front of the building in flames.

Shit. The enemy was in there all along.

A second blast came from the direction of the hotel, echoing through the night. Tay cringed, backing away towards the node. Her words were muffled by the ringing aftermath of the blast. "Get rid of that cantrip. Kick it through the node, bury it if you have to, but *don't touch it.*"

"Wait!" But she was gone, vanishing into the torrent of light.

Miles ran to my side. "Did she do that?"

"No, she was trying to warn me." I backed up to the node. "The Family, they still have a hold over her somehow. We need to run before we're blamed for that blast— and get those cantrips out of here. The bodies, too."

"Guys, we have to get those bodies out of here!" Miles ran to help the others pick up the fallen assassins and haul them through the node.

When the last body of a fallen assassin disappeared through the node, I kicked one of the cantrips after him. "Don't touch those things. We need to get them out of here, too."

"On it." Miles pulled on a pair of gloves, and picked up

two of the cantrips, tossing them through the node to the other side. Panic had erupted around the hotel, and the sound of sirens interspersed with the panicking, fleeing guests. The possibility hit me that Liv and the Death King had been caught in the blast, too, but there was nothing any of us could do. Besides, the infernos weren't the only threat. Who knew how many of those lethal cantrips were already loose in the city?

"Done." Miles ran back to my side. "Let's move."

We stepped through the node and landed on the outskirts of Elysium, down the road from the Spirit Agents' base. A barrier of earth still cut off the centre of the city, while our lack of allies couldn't be more obvious. *What if the Death King* was *caught in the blast?* What if our small group was all that remained of the forces standing against the might of the rogue spirit mages and the Family?

Miles and the Spirit Agents set about kicking mud over the cantrips and burying them beside the bodies of the fallen assassins. Not ideal, but it was that or carry them with us and risk falling victim to their lethal magic. Shelley carried the body of the Spirit Agent who'd touched the cantrip, a bleak expression on her face. "Who the fuck created a cantrip which can kill at a touch?"

"Same person who created the infernos." I scanned the rooftops, spotting movement above. "The assassins in London came from here. We need to find shelter before more of them come back."

The ground trembled underfoot, and a sudden piercing pillar of light appeared in the corner of my eye. I rotated on my heel and saw the citadel light up from top to bottom as though plugged into a live wire.

"What the hell is that?" I said.

"Let's find out." Miles took a step closer, shielding his eyes. From here, the citadel looked like a giant node in its own right, the obsidian exterior smothered in vibrant whiteness. *That's new.*

"I think," I said, "the enemy just announced where they're hiding."

With the nodes switched off and barriers blocking the middle of the city, we had no way in. Except... "If we used one of the other transporters, we might be able to get into the citadel."

"Why would you *want* to get in?" Shelley said.

"Because I bet that's where the enemy is hiding," I said. "And I don't know about you, but I'm not so sure the Death King will be coming to help us."

The Family, though? They were gleefully watching from afar as their cantrips wrought havoc in two cities, and the Houses fought to the death. Someone had to bring them crashing down.

"The other Elemental Soldiers are back at the castle, right?" said Miles.

"Yeah, good point." I backed up to the node again, which looked like a pale imitation of the giant pillar of light emanating from the citadel. "I bet if we go into Arcadia's citadel, their transporter will still be working. We can get in that way."

"Right." Miles eyed the others. "Anyone coming with us?"

"Shit, why not," said Shelley. "If the Houses are falling to bits, it's only a matter of time before the fight reaches our base."

"Precisely my thinking." I didn't see Tay anywhere, but

she must have transported herself elsewhere. She didn't seem to have any intention of helping, but she hadn't stopped us either. At this point, that was the best we'd get.

"We'll take the body back to our base," Tate told his sister, indicating the dead Spirit Agent. "The Death King…"

"He was in the hotel when the blast went off," said Shelley. "I don't know about you, but I think we're on our own."

"He's pretty much indestructible, though, right?" said Tate.

"Let's hope so," Miles said. "Come on."

A small group of us made for the node, where we stepped into its light and reappeared in the swampland. There, we found Ryan pacing in front of the castle gates. They zeroed in on me immediately. "Problems?"

"You might say that," I said. "The Family's assassins attacked the meeting in London, and we had to run back to Elysium before we were blamed."

"Where's the Death King?"

"Presumably still in London," said Miles, rightly thinking that now was not the time to insinuate that the King of the Dead had perished in the blast. Besides, he had a few remaining tricks up his sleeve, I had no doubt. "Elysium is fucked, though. I think the enemy is using the citadel as a base and they turned on the transporter again."

"While the middle of the city is cut off and the Houses are warring with one another," I added. "Oh, and those contagious cantrips are everywhere. If you want to come with us, we're going to Arcadia's citadel. If their transporter is still working, then we can get into Elysium that way and find out what the hell is going on over there."

If I blew up their transporter again, it would at least slow them down, but that wouldn't take care of the fact that the enemy had staged an open attack on Earth of all places. Not to mention the fact that they'd shut down half of Elysium's nodes and turned the middle of the city into a death trap. I might not live there anymore, but Elysium had been the first home I'd had after leaving the Family's house. I wasn't about to let them trample it flat.

"All right," said Ryan. "I'll come with you to Arcadia, but we might have a hard time getting into the citadel without the Death King."

"I can help." Harper glided over to us, still wearing her human face. "I can get us into the citadel, no problem."

"Thanks," I said, relief sweeping over me. "Okay, let's move."

Miles led the way through the node, and this time we landed in the street near Arcadia's citadel. The city was deceptively quiet, but tension sat heavy on my shoulders, along with the memory of the chaos we'd left behind.

Harper approached the citadel first, and the door opened at her touch. The room within was empty, the spiralling staircase bare of any foes. Harper glided into the lead up the stairs, and we followed close behind her. In the upstairs room, the machinery was as pristine as ever, not at all as though I'd blown it up a few weeks prior.

"Careful," I murmured to the others. "We don't know what we'll find on the other side."

"Bring it," said Ryan.

Harper floated over to the machinery and its buttons

lit up in response to her spirit magic, while the rest of us climbed onto the platform in the room's centre. I hadn't known Harper had become so comfortable with the machinery, but she didn't need to be able to touch it for her spirit magic to activate the transporter.

Lights spun around us as we vanished and reappeared in a room nearly identical to the one which we'd just left, containing a bank of metal and buttons hooked up to the wall and another platform in the centre. The machinery was *almost* the same, but with one key difference. A cage stood at its side, connected to the machinery by wires, but instead of sprites, it contained a dead body. The man lay sprawled on the floor of the cage. I didn't know who he was, thankfully, but the living man standing in front of us could only be Hawker, the elusive traitor lich.

Or rather, a lich no longer. His hair hung to shoulder length, his face was faintly lined with wrinkles, and he showed zero signs of ever having been dead.

Facing off against him were the Death King and Liv.

18

I *knew they survived.* How Liv and the Death King had got here from London, I had no idea, but relief crossed Liv's face when she set eyes on our group.

Hawker turned his gaze on us. "You weren't supposed to be able to get in."

"You didn't account for all of the Death King's spies," said Harper. "Some of us figured out how to operate the transporter."

"Damn right," I said.

Hawker scanned our group. "I have to admit, I hoped to minimise casualties."

Liv stepped in, her hands igniting with spirit magic. "You massacred a roomful of people, you sick bastard. You deserve everything you get."

Magic blasted from her palms. Hawker dodged her attack, but Ryan's air magic sent him crashing into the bank of machinery. Recovering, Hawker slammed a button and the transporter ignited.

The platform spun with light, carrying a new group of

strangers into the room. Humans, hands aglow with the same white light as the transporter itself. *Spirit mages.* Ryan ran to help the Death King intercept the new arrivals, Liv on their heels.

"I thought you were supposed to be back at the castle," she said.

"Like I'd leave you two to deal with this alone," Ryan responded. "What happened in here?"

"A new node links this place directly to London," Liv explained. "Not only that, it also links to all the other citadels with a working transporter, and anyone who uses it can get out onto Earth. We have to shut it off."

Shit. It links directly to London?

I threw a fireball at the spirit mages, which hit one of them in the back. Liv moved to fight alongside the Death King, while the rest of us jumped into the fray. Lights flew back and forth and mingled with the brightness around the edges of the room, a reminder of the pillar of light surrounding the citadel from the outside. *Can people on Earth see this, too?* The ordinary people, unaware of the magical world, might well think the apocalypse was nigh.

The only way to turn off a transporter, as far as I was aware, was to use an inferno cantrip, but there was no way I'd risk it in a crowded room like this.

"We need to shut that thing off." I caught up to Miles, fighting spirit mages off with fireballs as I did so. "Can we do it from Arcadia?"

"We can try." He shoved his fist into a spirit mage's chest, and the mage collapsed into a heap. Vaulting the body, he made for the platform, while I threw fireballs left and right to clear our path.

Reaching the platform, Miles caught my arm, pulling

me up alongside him. Then the pair of us vanished in a flash of light and reappeared in the near-empty room of Arcadia's citadel.

"Where's the power source in here?" I looked around the room. "There's no sprites…"

"There doesn't need to be." Miles hopped off the platform. "The machine has its own battery inside it already. Hawker was trying to do something specific in the other citadel, Liv said, something he needed a shit-ton of energy for. The sprites were there to give it a boost."

"That's sick." The humming machine seemed downright quiet compared to the chaos we'd left behind, but my heart continued to pound with nerves. "Was he trying to turn the citadel into a node, like he did in Elysium? He was using… using the sprites' life force as a battery, right?"

"Yeah." He looked pale. "Thing is, it didn't have to be sprites. Those cantrips he used… the infernos… when he killed those people in London, he used their life force to fuel the node linking it up to Elysium."

Nausea flooded me. "There's gotta be a way to turn it off."

But if he'd used those people's *lives* like a giant battery and the spirit energy was still flowing back and forth between the two realms… I was in way over my head here. I was no spirit mage. Yet from the disgusted look on Miles's face, he would never have considered the possibility of using spirit magic in such a way before.

The transporter lit up, lights spinning across its surface. I tensed, conjuring fire to my hands as a lich appeared on the platform.

"It's only me," Harper said. "We're in trouble. Hawker

grabbed Liv and took her through the transporter some-where else."

"What?" I said. "Why would he take her?"

"Because he wants her to help him," said Harper. "The Death King went after them, but Hawker used some kind of spell to paralyse everyone else in the room. It didn't affect me, so I had to run. There was no other way out except the transporter."

"Because they turned off the other nodes in Elysium," I said. "Shame we can't do the same to the transporter."

Or... could we?

Miles caught my gaze. "What is it? You look like you just had an idea."

"It's a long shot," I admitted, "but didn't Liv have a cantrip which can turn off a node? If the citadel in Elysium is basically a giant node, too, wouldn't it work on that one as well?"

"You mean the same way they shut down the nodes in Elysium?" Miles said. "Might be something there."

"What would happen if we put one of those cantrips inside the transporter, then?" I jerked my head towards the machine. "Didn't you say that thing's like a giant battery? If we put the cantrip into the machine in Elysium, would we be able to cut off the link to Earth?"

His eyes widened. "Crap. You're right. That might just work."

"But Liv and the Death King are gone," said Harper. "I don't know where you'd find another of those cantrips... unless Devon has one."

"She's our resident cantrip expert," I said. "We have to go back to the castle and find her."

Miles nodded, and we ran down the stairs and out into

the streets of Arcadia. From there, we ran to the node off the square, vanished in a flash of light, and reappeared outside the castle. I hit the ground running towards the gates—until Tay blocked my path. Her expression was bleak, yet her countenance was resolute.

"Not the time, Tay," I warned. "Might've escaped your attention, but we're dealing with a serious shit storm here."

"I told you to leave," she said. "Not go back to Elysium."

"I'm trying to get into the castle, Tay. It's my home, technically. Let me through."

"Nowhere is safe, not even here," she insisted. "Those cantrips… they'll spread outside Elysium before long."

Crap. What with the chaos in the citadels, I'd pushed the Family to the back of my mind, but they could spread the infected cantrips a lot quicker with a huge node which linked the city of Elysium to London on the other side.

"Then we have to shut off their transporter, and to do that, we need to get into the castle." I tried to walk past her, but she barred my path again. Her eyes were wide, her movements stiff and reluctant… and then it hit me. "You're still under Adair's control, aren't you?"

She nodded, biting her lip. "I can resist up to a point, but… I can't let you into the castle."

"Can't let *me* in, or the others?" I stepped aside, seeing Harper's shadowy form moving closer, followed by Miles. "You're not disobeying orders if you stay here, are you?"

She shook her head lightly, and the pair of us moved to the left of the gates, leaving the path open for my allies to get inside. Adair's powers might be unyielding, but there was always a gap if you thought hard enough. I had to trust the others would be able to find the right cantrip to stop that transporter, because Tay wasn't budging an inch.

"I can speak to my brother," I said to her. "I'll convince him to let you go."

"That won't work," she said. "He'll order me to kill you just to watch us fight it out."

Ugh. He would, too. Anything to stop me from standing in the Family's way. But they were the ones who'd unleashed the cantrips on the city, and they alone knew how to stop them.

"All right." I gave no warning before I leapt forward and tackled Tay around the middle. We crashed into a heap on the muddy ground, and her expression turned to shock before she fired magic at me. Electricity numbed my arms and I bit back a scream, fighting through the pain as I wrestled Tay's hands behind her back. Once I had her secure, I sprang to my feet and shoved her in front of me towards the gates. Two liches moved to intercept me, but I didn't stop walking.

"I'm taking her to the jail," I told them. "She's under Adair's hypnosis. I'm gonna convince him to let her go."

"Not alone." One of the liches broke away and insisted on flanking us all the way to the jail, but even the persistent chill didn't stop Tay from fighting me with every step.

Once we reached the jail, I wrestled Tay through the doors and shoved her into an empty cell. Then I slammed the door on her. "Sorry. I'll let you out when I can."

Adair watched me through the bars of his own cell. "Had a falling-out with your friend, did you?"

I caught my breath. "Release her from your control, Adair."

He snorted. "No chance."

"You're only exerting control over her because the others want nothing to do with you," I said. "I noticed they started their plan without you."

He snickered. "Doesn't matter. They'll do their part and I'll do mine."

"Dammit, Adair!" I said. "What do the Family have to accomplish by supporting Hawker in his attempt to link Elysium and London of all places?"

"Sounds like he already succeeded," he said. "The Order is obsolete. They deserve to fall, to pave the way for something new."

"Innocent people died, Adair," I said. "Those infected cantrips—where the fuck are they coming from?"

"The only way to get rid of them is to set me free," he said. "I'm immune to their effects, like you are. Anyone else who touches one of those cantrips dies. No exceptions."

"I'm not falling for that."

Adair laughed under his breath. "Would you stake your friend's life on it? Do you think the Death King will spare her when he gets back—*if* he gets back?"

"He'll be back, but you'll wish he'd killed you when I'm finished with you." I was done with using Tay's life as a bargaining chip. "As for Tay, she can do whatever she likes as long as *you* aren't around."

"Tay, use your magic," he said. "Get her over here."

A heartbeat passed. Then Tay was on her feet a moment later, electricity shooting from her hands and through the bars of her cell. Pain rattled my teeth in my skull, and my legs gave way. *Dammit... I should have known Tay wouldn't let herself be locked up again.*

Tay leaned out of the cell door, and the coldness of a cantrip pressed into my hands.

"Guess what?" Adair said softly. "I lied. Those cantrips *can* kill us… just not permanently."

At once, an unbearable itching sensation spread across my palms, while tingles spread up and down my arms. Tay caught my face in her hands, her mouth twisted with emotion, but she couldn't stop her own hands from turning me around until my gaze connected with Adair's.

"Get me out of here," he said.

My hands moved to obey even as my mind screamed at me to stop. I could no more have resisted than I could have stopped breathing. As his cell door opened, Adair shoved his way out, joining Tay, whose expression brimmed with remorse. I tried to speak, but my mouth felt as though it was superglued shut.

Adair grinned, gesturing at the two liches who guarded the jail doors. "Burn them."

Flames leapt from my hands, as though of their own accord, reducing both liches to twin piles of ashes. Adair then seized my arm and dragged me out into the light. Tay walked along behind us, not speaking, as the node beside the jail came into view.

"You can't go through there," I ground out through clenched teeth. "That's the Death King's personal node. Nobody living can use it."

Adair reached for the pendant around my neck. "You have a way around that, don't you? You go first."

Shit. I did. The transporter spell. He grabbed the pendant and pulled me one-handedly into the node. The transporter spell flashed, and unbearable pain speared my body from within.

I landed on my knees on hard ground, the crumbled remains of the Family's estate nearby. My head hit the earth, my vision fading until nothing remained but darkness.

———

I woke up in a cell. Or something like it. The small empty room looked more like a cave, but I saw enough to know I was back in the Family's home.

I slumped back into a sitting position. I was screwed. I'd already lost my chance to save Tay from Adair's influence and stop the Family unleashing their cantrips on the city, and to add insult to injury, it turned out the infected cantrips could hurt me after all. By now though, sensation had come back into my limbs, and the rash had vanished from sight. The others who'd picked them up wouldn't be so lucky.

Lex walked into view, a smile on her mouth. "I have to say, you look much better than you did when Adair sent you here."

"Was this the 'chaos' you were talking about?" I spat. "Sending your assassins into London and unleashing inferno cantrips on innocent people? Setting the Houses against one another and spreading lethal cantrips through Elysium's capital after cutting off the nodes so nobody could get out? That doesn't look like staying out of the magical world's business to me."

"Oh, most of that wasn't our doing," she said. "I heard

you did your level best to intervene, regardless, but it's pointless."

Who needed a war when they'd already killed countless people without laying a finger on them? Worse, a node linked the two realms more closely than ever before, the Order *and* the Houses were in disarray, and the Family would have free rein to run amok in both realms if we weren't careful. Unless Devon had a cantrip to hand to turn off the node in Elysium's citadel… but my friends would have to handle that alone. I wouldn't be getting out of this cell anytime soon.

I fixed a glare on my face to cover my panic. "Yeah, it's always my pleasure to screw things up for you."

"I have to say, I was surprised your friend was the one who finally convinced you to help Adair escape," she added. "Loyalty is hard to find, isn't it?"

Damn her. Tay had been fighting Adair's control all along. That she'd managed to delay for any length of time at all had been a small miracle.

"Bet that pissed you off," I said. "How she stopped you from taking over the House of Fire by killing the jailor you sent to infiltrate their ranks, I mean."

"Clever of her," said Lex. "Very clever, given the limited options at her disposal. If I'd known how good she was, I might have recruited her sooner."

"You ruined her life," I said. "As much as you ruined mine. You must have known giving magical enhancements to a child would end in tragedy."

"Her family were fully complicit," she said. "They're more to blame than I am. They wanted a rare mage whose skills they could exploit. I suppose she never told you that. She was ashamed, I imagine."

"You haven't the right to play with people's lives like that," I said to her. "Not you, and not Roth either. Where's *he* hiding, anyway?"

"Roth is watching the action," she said. "Chaos is easy to unleash but harder to manipulate, and we don't want the whole system to collapse just yet."

"So that's the plan." Bitterness laced my words. "You want the Houses of the Elements totally under your control, not awash in total anarchy."

"Of course we do," she said. "We almost had them once already, before *you* stopped us."

"I'm not going to apologise for it," I said. "I saved lives by burning this shithole to the ground. I forced you to stop your plans in their tracks."

But they'd resumed their strategy the instant they'd escaped and found their way back here. Of course they had. They were resourceful and cunning, traits they'd passed onto me, and which I'd need to employ if I wanted to get the hell out of here.

"Yes, you did." She glanced behind her. "It's awfully quiet out here, isn't it? That's one thing I always noticed after the war… the silence."

"You lived through the war thirty years ago," I said. "You took advantage back then, too."

"Of course we did," she said. "When the mage council had their falling-out, someone had to be there to pick up the pieces."

"What makes you so sure the spirit mages will win this time?" I said. "Last time, they lost. Everyone else did, too."

"Exactly," she said. "They have the same advantages as before, but without the tyranny of the Council of the Elements to contend with."

"Didn't they *kill* the Council of the Elements?" The spirit mages had done a fair job of wiping each other out, too, but I couldn't forget they were the ones who'd built the citadels. And, presumably, the transporters, too.

"Did you know this territory used to belong to the elves?" she said. "Before the mages forced them to leave, that is. We're hardly the first to take the Parallel's resources for ourselves."

I frowned at the change of subject. "The mages drove out the elves?"

"Why is that hard for you to believe?" she queried.

"It isn't," I said. "I'm surprised you care."

"You need to understand why the mages' attempts to take power will always end in failure," she said. "They're a poison. Killing one another off was the best thing they could have done. This new war will have a similar result, except it will be the Houses that fall. The Houses, the Order... they're all fatally flawed."

"Speak for yourself." The Family's motto was to let everyone else kill each other and then rise from the ashes. Yet they'd hardly stood on the side-lines in this case, considering they'd provided the enemy with the tools to wreak havoc on two worlds. "You want to take their place, do you? I thought you hated the spotlight. Unless you want to spend the rest of your miserable existence watching people die for your own amusement."

She smiled. "I can guarantee you'd have been much happier if you'd just stayed put and hadn't intervened. You should have stopped asking questions. Then we wouldn't have had to find a way to destroy you, too."

"That's funny, because it was asking questions which

made me realise what scumbags you were," I said. "That you never cared for me at all."

As if I could ever forget what she and the others had done to me. To everyone. Even Adair was a victim of their lies, even if he'd embraced them wholeheartedly. He'd been brainwashed from the moment he could walk.

"Then I'll let you stay here for a while and think on your mistakes." She took a step back from the door to my cell. "I imagine Elysium's mages will be desperate by now. Desperate enough to accept help from anyone... even such abominations as we are."

She walked away, leaving me alone in my cell. Several long minutes passed before I heard footsteps. I rose to my feet, ready to face the last remaining member of my family.

Instead, someone else altogether walked into view. I rose to my feet and leaned up against the cage bars. "Tay?"

Tay edged up to the cell door and whispered, "I had to let them think I'm still completely under their control. Adair didn't tell me not to come back here, so I found my way to a node as soon as he looked the other way."

"Damn," I said. "Thanks for taking the risk."

"Also, I have help," she added.

The outline of a fiery humanoid figure appeared above her head. "At your service."

"Where'd you come from?" I asked Dex.

"I saw that dickhead of a brother of yours haul you out of the Death King's jail," he said. "I tried to intercept him, but he moves fast, doesn't he?"

"He does." Relief washed over me. "Can you get me out of here?"

Tay strode up to the door, an unlocking spell at the

ready. She flicked the switch on the side of the cantrip and the door sprang open. Then she pressed the pendant into my hand. With a mouthed *thank you,* I slid it open and found my cantrips were still inside it. I retrieved two invisibility cantrips, but when I passed one to her, she shook her head. "I'm still under Adair's control. I can't risk it."

"I'll come back for you." I flicked on my own cantrip, vanishing from sight. I was free, but it wouldn't be long before they realised Tay was in here.

I walked towards the exit, but I hadn't gone ten steps before Lex reappeared, seeing the empty cell... and Tay. *"You."*

Tay's hands crackled with magic, blasting Lex off her feet. Lex sprang upright with her teeth bared in a snarl, and I took the opportunity to sprint out into the corridor. Freedom beckoned, and I pelted for the door. Dex swooped out ahead of me into the night, while I followed, my heart torn in two. I didn't want to leave Tay behind, but if I didn't run now, I'd never make it back to Elysium in time to make sure my allies weren't caught up in the chaos destroying the Houses.

I'll come back, Lex. And this time I won't let you cage me again.

19

Dex and I ran over the collapsed gates to the Family's estate and out into the wasteland, where I pinpointed the glowing shape of the node. "That way."

While the fire sprite flew above my head, I put on a burst of speed and left the remains of the Family's house in the dust.

"Evil fuckers," said Dex. "This place is a dump, isn't it?"

"I bet Elysium is in a worse state," I said. "Those infected cantrips kill anyone who touches them. Except me, and that's if I trust what Adair told me."

"If you're going to explode, give me some warning first."

"Ha ha." I ran on towards the node. "We never did find where they were manufacturing those cantrips, either."

"Not much out here." Dex zipped past me. "Your spirit mage friends are waiting on the other side. In Elysium. They thought that's where you'd been taken."

"Shit."

We vanished into the node's light, then reappeared in an alleyway. A pillar of light shone above the rooftops, indicating the citadel. My feet caught on something on the ground, a golden disc engraved with a now-familiar pattern of runes. Someone had left a cursed cantrip by the node, so that anyone unlucky enough to land on top of it would fall victim to its magic.

"What sick bastard would put that there?" I muttered to Dex.

Similar cantrips littered the ground like discarded coins. Valuable, if not in the monetary sense. Yet anyone who touched them would be dead within minutes.

"Someone left them lying around on purpose," said Dex.

"Exactly my thinking." I kicked dirt over the nearest cantrip, smearing it into the mud.

Behind me, the node ignited as a figure appeared within it. I conjured fire to my palms, extinguishing it as Tay approached us.

"How'd you shake them off?" I backed up a step, in case Lex leapt out behind her.

"Adair wasn't there," she said breathlessly. "Lex, though… she'll be back."

"What's this in aid of?" I indicated the cantrips on the ground. "Someone's been busy."

"We're too late," whispered Tay. "The assassins already spread them all over the city. That was always the plan. Nobody will know how lethal they are until it's too late."

"You're joking." She wasn't. There were a half-dozen cantrips on this street alone, let alone throughout the rest of Elysium.

Tay drew in a breath. "We have to get back to the House of Fire. It's the only—"

Blurred movement came from the rooftop as she spoke, and her words cut off in a choked noise. Then Tay fell across me, a knife buried in her back.

"Tay!" I lowered her to the ground, scanning the roof for her attacker—but he was gone, as though he'd never been there, leaving nothing behind but the knife jutting from Tay's back. Her heartbeat fluttered against my fingertips as I held her, numb disbelief seeping through me.

Blood beaded her mouth when she whispered, "The House… get to the House."

"Tay… no." The words stuck in my throat like broken glass. "Tay. Stay with me."

Movement stirred on the rooftop nearby, and I sprang to my feet. Fire leapt to my palms, coalescing into a whirl-wind which I sent straight at the assassin above me. He crumpled to the ground, rolling over in an attempt to put out the fire, and Dex flew at him in a shower of sparks.

I crouched beside Tay, the assassin's death throes becoming distant as everything aside from Tay's stifled breaths faded to white noise. "Tay. Hang on. I'm sure I can get a healing cantrip—"

She cut me off by gripping my hand in hers, blood peppering her lips. A rattling groan escaped her, and she half pulled me down so she could whisper in my ear.

"You're better than they are," she said to me. "You always were."

Then she breathed her last.

Tears burned my eyes. I bowed my head over her body for a long moment, my throat raw, my vision blurred. Part of me knew I needed to get away from here in case Lex followed her out of the node, but I couldn't bring myself to let go of her. It wasn't until a shadow fell over me that I looked up. Miles approached, and his arms enfolded me. "Bria. Thank the Elements."

I held him for an instant and then got to my feet, swallowing hot tears. "She's dead."

"She's the one who took you to the Family, right?" He squeezed me tighter and I held on right back.

"No," I mumbled into his chest. "No... Adair did. He was controlling her using his powers, but she fought against him until the end. She helped me escape. Risked her life in the process."

Miles released me, scanning the alleyway. "Is that the guy who did it?"

My gaze went to Dex, who hovered above the limp body of the assassin. "Yeah. Did you manage to get one of Devon's cantrips to take to the citadel and turn off the node?"

"Ryan's taking care of it," he said. "As soon as I realised you were gone, I came back here to look for you."

I looked down at Tay's body, my heart clenching. "Tay... with her last words, she told me to go back to the House of Fire."

"The House of Fire?" he said. "Why?"

"I don't know, but she said it was the only way to stop them from spreading those cantrips around the city." I glanced at the golden disc on the ground. "They're everywhere. It's how they're distributing the virus, and they cut off the nodes to ensure nobody can get out."

Anyone who picked them up would unknowingly get

infected. How were we even supposed to fight against an invisible force most people weren't even aware of?

Dex flew up to me. "When your friend was on her way to rescue you, she was talking about the House, too. And… she mentioned a cure for the virus."

I clapped my hands to my mouth. "Is that what she wanted me to go back for?"

Did the House have the cure, or had she hidden it herself while she'd been imprisoned? It wasn't like we could get near the House of Fire either way, unless we got past the earthen barriers surrounding the middle of the city and then fought our way through the chaos. Not good odds.

"You're sure she didn't want you to get arrested again?" said Miles. "Just saying, a cell is safer than being outside at the moment."

"Not while the city is in this state," I said. "I doubt there's anyone left in the House to arrest me at all."

A bright light dazzled my eyes as the glow around the citadel intensified, forcing me to turn my head away from the vibrant light. We still needed to shut down that transporter, but Tay had died to give me a fighting chance to stop the cantrips spreading the virus around the Houses. If we didn't stop it, the transporter wouldn't matter. Everyone in all four Houses would be dead.

"All right," said Miles. "If you're sure it's in the House of Fire, I'll hold the fort out here, and you take Dex with you."

I opened my mouth to argue and then closed it again. "Okay, but if things get too rough out here, run. I don't want you touching one of those cantrips and getting infected."

"I know, don't worry. We've lost too many people already."

Tears threatened, but I blinked them away. I couldn't afford to get sentimental, not when I had a job to do, and one chance to stop the virus before more lives were lost.

The fire sprite swooped ahead of me, peering over the nearest wall of earth. "Nobody's on the other side, but unless you've learned to fly, you're not getting in.'

"I'll go via the rooftops, then."

I did a running jump and leapt onto the windowsill of the nearest house, pulling myself up onto the roof with my fingertips.

"Whoa." Miles gave me an admiring stare. "Watch out for those assassins, okay?"

"Way ahead of you." I scanned the rooftops, picking out a likely route to the middle of the city. Then I broke into a sprint and leapt to the next roof.

As kids, Adair and I had held endless competitions where we raced one another over the rooftops of the Family's estate. While I didn't generally come out the victor—Adair had always hated to lose—I'd retained my excellent balance skills and knack for picking out the best climbing routes, both of which came in handy when dodging assassins and duelling mages while navigating my way to the middle of Elysium. The citadel's glowing light guided me over the rooftops, until I dropped to the ground behind the House of Fire. Amazingly, the building was still standing, but someone had barricaded the doors once again and more golden cantrips littered the ground outside.

I flicked on an invisibility cantrip first, then strode towards the back door. While a spell opened it easily enough, the guards nearby zeroed in on Dex and me immediately. And of course one of them was Harris.

"Who's there?" he demanded.

Ignoring him, I walked into the corridor, while he kept staring at the same spot. "Who's there? Show yourself."

"Up yours, motherfucker," said Dex, and spat fiery sparks into his face.

Harris recoiled with a yelp, tripping over his own feet. While he shouted for backup, I ducked between the guards into the main corridor. Dex continued to throw sparks among them, causing enough of a distraction for me to remain undetected. Where would Tay have hidden a cure? I'd have to start with her cell, so I went downstairs, leaving Dex to keep the guards busy.

Once I reached the lowest level, I made my way to Tay's cell and peered inside. The cell, however, was empty, the door ajar. Had someone already removed the cure, or had I guessed wrong?

Footsteps sounded behind me, and I rotated, still unseen. Harris stood there, blocking my path back to the stairs. "I know you're there, Bria. I might not be able to see you, but I know it's you."

Dammit. I didn't have time for this. "Get out the way."

"Why did you come back? Did you think we had that friend of yours again?"

Anger clenched inside me at the memory of Tay's body lying there on the ground. She'd died to give me a fighting chance to stop the Family's deadly cantrip, and I wouldn't let this dickhead get in my way.

"Where is it?" I asked. "Tay had the cure for those lethal cantrips. Did you take it off her?"

"What?" he said. "What are you talking about?"

"The cure," I said. "You know those cantrips killing all your guards? There's a cure, and Tay had it. What did you confiscate from her when you imprisoned her?"

He stumbled back a step. "What? There was no cure."

"She wouldn't have *told* you she had a cure in case you destroyed it out of spite," I said. "Come on. Tell me."

"We confiscated some cantrips off her when we first brought them in, but Zade put them in his office."

Dex flew downstairs, and a blast of fire hit Harris in the back. "Need a hand?"

"Someone must have stolen the cure," I said, as Harris spun and swiped at the sprite, unable to touch him. "I didn't see it in Zade's office, so I bet they took it straight back to the Family."

"Dammit." He threw another shower of sparks, forcing Harris to duck, and I ran for the stairs and sprinted back up to the surface. I hadn't seen anything in Zade's office that might have resembled a cure, but someone had cleared out the place. Not Tay, either.

The Family must have had it all along.

On the way out, the guards tried to grab me, but I dodged, kicked and when all else failed, threw fireballs into the air until they left the path free for me to run to the exit and out into the street.

The world flew by as I sprinted down the street and took the closest route onto the rooftops, where I climbed up and retraced my steps to the barrier cutting off the middle of the city. Over the barrier, I spotted Miles and ran towards him, leaping down to land at his side.

"No luck?" he said.

I shook my head. "Zade confiscated everything from Tay when he took her in, and someone cleared out his office ages ago. If the cure was in there, they'd have taken it straight back to the Family."

"Damn," said Miles. "I had a thought, though. The people spreading those cantrips throughout the city can't use the nodes to get around, so they must be moving on foot."

"They're earth mages." I indicated the earthen wall behind us. "What're the odds that they're under our feet right now?"

"Pretty high," he said. "But only an earth mage can track them, right?"

"Not necessarily." I pushed against the earthen wall with my palms, but it was totally solid. Elysium wasn't like Arcadia, with a wide network of underground paths, but the earth mages could easily create one of their own.

"There are only two of us," said Miles. "We can't take on the entire House of Earth. I mean, I can give it a shot, but Shelley will be pissed off if I die and leave her to run the Spirit Agents alone."

"I can bring backup," said Dex. "The others are back at the citadel or on the Death King's territory. I'm sure there are some liches who'd be willing to lend a hand."

"I'd rather not take even more people away from the Death King's security." It was bad enough that the man himself was absent. "I doubt the entire House of Earth is involved, but I reckon collapsing their tunnels will slow them down. If they're leaving the cantrips through the city, they must have left a trail behind we can use to track them down."

I backed out of the street, my eyes on the rooftops in case any more assassins appeared. It wasn't until we'd walked for nearly ten minutes that I found an upturned heap of earth concealing an opening to a tunnel.

An earth mage was here.

Miles hissed out a warning when I kicked the earth away, exposing the hole until it grew large enough to accommodate a person. Below, a proper tunnel had been carved out through the middle of the street. In true earth mage style, they'd created tunnels which looked like they'd been there for years. I'd bet the rest of the centre of Elysium contained similar tunnels to enable them to spread their cursed cantrips throughout the city.

"Sure you wanna go down there?" he said.

"No, but we need to stop those bastards." I dropped into the tunnel, while Dex flew down and lit up the way through the gloom.

"Incoming!" Dex warned.

Two mages flew through the tunnel, crashing in front of me. I tensed, ready to attack, only to see they were both unconscious. A lithe figure with pointed ears followed.

"Trix?" I stared at the elf in disbelief. "What in the world are you doing here?"

"I heard Liv was in trouble, but I can't get into the citadel," he said.

"So you decided to go underground instead?" I said. "The Elemental Soldiers are still in the citadel, as far as I know."

Trix leaned down to pick up one of the cantrips the mages had dropped.

"Don't touch that!" I said sharply. "It's infected with a magical plague. Hang on. I can get rid of it."

I kicked a pile of soil on top of the cantrip. Not perfect, but it'd have to do for now. In the meantime, I climbed aboveground to join Miles, who regarded the elf with an expression of confusion. "You came here alone? Did you know the House of Earth has been taken over by the Family?"

"Is that why they're all underground?" asked Trix.

"Wait, you saw them?" I said. "Which way did you come into the city? Through a node?"

"Yes," he said. "I came as close as possible to the barrier around the citadel and started looking for ways in, but most of the tunnels lead to dead ends."

"Did you run into anyone else?" I asked. "Because we're looking for someone carrying a cure."

"There's a cure?" said Trix.

"Maybe," I said. "If not, then we're screwed."

But Tay seemed to think there was. We needed one, badly, and despite everything she'd done, I wanted to honour her last wish.

20

Dex led the way as we descended into the tunnel again. Trix had left a trail of unconscious guards along the way, and it was a good job he hadn't picked up one of those cantrips. Though it might not have as much of an effect on an elf. They were immune to most diseases which affected humans, which was why it had always surprised me that so many of them had died in the war or been driven out. After Lex's revelation, though, I couldn't help thinking there was more to their fate than any of us knew.

I did my best to bury every cantrip I found below our feet, but all it'd take was one more earth mage to dig them up again, and without a cure, we had no way to stop their effects.

"This must be why they took over the House of Earth first," I remarked. "They needed the tunnels to get around, and an earth mage can move much faster belowground than a regular person. It's easy to hide a cantrip smuggling operation if nobody can follow you. They dug a bunch of tunnels on the Family's estate, too, probably for the same reason."

Trix's face screwed up in confusion. "What family? Yours?"

"No, *the* Family," I said. "They experiment on mages and create illegal cantrips for their own amusement. They're behind this whole operation."

Trix stopped walking. "They created the cantrips? The infernos, too?"

"Yes… why?"

"Because," he said, "it was something similar which wiped out the elves' communities years ago, around the time of the war."

My spine stiffened, while Miles turned to look at the elf, too. "Seriously?"

The elf gave a solemn nod. "Yes. Few people remember, but it's true."

My throat went dry. "I didn't know."

But it made a horrible kind of sense. Lex had hinted that she and Roth had used the war to do much more than take advantage of the chaos the warring mages had unleashed on the Parallel, and it would have been easy to hide any crimes in the confusion which had followed.

Trix's head drooped with sadness. "The elves tend to be forgotten because the war affected the whole Parallel, but we were driven out of our strongholds long before the war reached the humans' cities."

I swallowed hard. "They didn't wipe out all the elves, did they? Some of you survived."

"We did," he said. "I was born after the war, but I don't remember my family. They were killed when my town burned down when I was a child."

"I'm sorry," I said. "Um—you should know, I'm half elf, and I don't remember my family either. My real family, not the ones who raised me."

He was silent for a moment. "*They* raised you? The same humans who are killing people in this city?"

"Did I mention I had a messed-up upbringing?" I picked up the pace, hearing movement aboveground. "I'm pretty sure they helped the spirit mages destroy one another in the last war, too. And now they're trying to do the same again."

We passed beneath another opening leading aboveground, while the tunnel came to an abrupt halt against a dead end. Trix climbed up through the opening first, and there came the sounds of a scuffle from above our heads. Two mages fell unconscious in his wake, and we stepped around their bodies and surfaced into the light. At once, I recognised the area as the northern part of the city. Not far from the facility where the Family had once been imprisoned… and near the path that eventually led to their home.

Last time I'd tried to take Lex on alone, and I'd lost badly. I was under no illusions that I could beat her *and* Adair in a fair fight, but to get the cure, I'd have to find a way to get past them. Otherwise, it was only a matter of time before all my allies succumbed to the virus, too.

"Hey." I leaned over one of the fallen mages, who was still conscious. "Where is Lex? Where's Adair?"

Laughter rippled from his throat. "It's too late… for all of you."

The ground exploded, and the wyrm shot out of the earth, tail lashing, leathery wings beating.

"Shit." I dropped the guy and backed away from the

wyrm. "Miles, please say you have another of those mind control cantrips."

"No, I'm all out." His hands glowed. "We'll have to use force."

"No need for that," Trix said blithely, approaching the creature. Its tail lashed, its teeth dripping drool onto the ground.

"Trix, don't go any closer," I warned. "That thing is lethal."

"Not at all." He waved up at the wyrm. "It's just confused, isn't it?"

"So am I," Miles said. "But I'd rather not watch you get eaten. Get away from it."

Trix whistled, and the creature descended, landing in front of Trix with its head bowed as if in submission. Miles and I both gawped at the improbable sight of the giant monster greeting the elf like a loyal dog and not a giant fanged beast.

"What the hell is going on?" I said.

Trix glided forward and petted the wyrm on the head. "The elves have always had an affinity with animals. Even creatures like this are easy to get along with if you know how to tame them."

Nonplussed, I watched him stroke the beast until it made a contented noise, as though it hadn't tried to kill us all—several times.

"This is the weirdest day of my life," said Miles. "And yes, I include the vampire chicken incident."

"Tell me about it," I muttered. "All right. Trix, would you be able to set that wyrm loose on the Family?"

"What?" he said. "No. Creatures like this one are calm under normal circumstances."

"I wouldn't call this 'normal circumstances'," Miles remarked.

"Not to mention the Family is hoarding the cure," I added. "If we don't get it from them, the Houses are screwed. Their house is north of the city, somewhere in the wasteland over there."

"Excellent," said Trix. "The wyrm can take us there. I'm sure he'll be willing to lend a hand. Or wing."

Miles and I exchanged baffled looks. "Help? How could that creature possibly help us?"

"Wait and see."

Ten minutes later, I was riding on the back of a giant wyrm, over the city and into the wasteland to the north. Miles sat behind me while Trix sat in front, whispering instructions to make the wyrm fly according to his directions. I had absolutely no idea whatsoever how he pulled it off, but at this point all I could do was sit back and enjoy the ride. Okay, 'enjoy' was a relative term, but it was better than being eaten alive.

The citadel was the only obvious landmark from up here, a giant obsidian pillar glowing against our backs. Ahead of us, I could make out the shape of another similar pillar, further in the wasteland. Elysium was closer to the place where we'd ended up stranded than I'd thought... and so was the Family's estate.

"Where is the house?" Trix asked.

"It's north of Elysium." I pointed. "Somewhere up there. The estate is totally flattened, but it's where the wyrm came from so it should know the way back."

Trix muttered something to the creature and we veered away up north. How could he possibly be communicating with it? If he could teach me that skill, it'd come in handy, that was for sure. I'd be able to get control over Neddie the zombie horse, for instance—but that was a lesson for another day. Before long, the wind picked up until I could no longer hear anything except for the sound of the creature's wings beating below us. Then I recognised the shape of the rugged cliffs bordering the Family's estate, the golden glow of the mines near-invisible from above.

"There." I pointed down, and Trix murmured instructions told the wyrm to fly low enough for us to see the pile of upturned earth and metal. The illusion must still be in place over the rebuilt house, but I didn't see Lex... or Adair, either.

"Looks abandoned," said Trix.

"There's a house down there covered with an illusion spell." I indicated the spot below the chunk of metal sticking out of the ruined ground. "And there's the mine where they get the material for their cantrips."

A few miles west of the estate, I spotted an odd flickering across the air. Not a node, though it looked similar... and suspicious.

"What's that?" asked Trix, pointing directly at the flickering lights playing across the air.

"An illusion spell, I think," I said. "Let's see what they're hiding down there."

We flew closer, past the node and towards the darkened pillar of the citadel among the ruined town. I couldn't help thinking of the people who'd lived there, before the war. Before the Family had killed them.

A crack appeared in the illusion spell, and I glimpsed a large structure below, shaped like one of Arcadia's warehouses.

I leaned forward. "I think we've found where they're manufacturing those cantrips."

"Bastards," said Miles. "Wanna blow that place sky-high?"

I nodded to Trix. "Can you fly us lower?"

As we dropped in the air, something heavy slammed into the wyrm, which screeched in pain. I clung on tight as we spun out of control. A bolt of light shone over the wasteland, and my stomach dropped as I realised the citadel was *glowing,* like the one in Elysium. The wyrm cringed away from the light, tilting sideways in the air.

I clung to its back, but my grip slipped, and I tumbled into empty air as we plummeted towards the earth.

21

I slammed into the ground, hard. I lay there for a moment, dazed, my head spinning. From the splintering pain in my chest, I'd cracked a few ribs, but I'd have to deal with the pain later.

"Miles?" I struggled upright, but the others were nowhere in sight. The wyrm must have crash-landed somewhere, too, because I didn't see its sinuous shape in the sky. All I could see was the flickering outline of the warehouse… and ruined houses on either side of me.

I pushed to my feet, biting pack a gasp of pain, and bone crunched beneath my feet. I recoiled, realising I'd landed on a skeleton buried in the remains of a collapsed house. Elf or human, I didn't know. Tears burned my eyes. I blinked them away and walked on towards the flickering light. If the warehouse contained the cure, I'd snag it. Even if it didn't, it was past time I stopped the Family's new operation in its tracks. This must be where they were manufacturing the instruments of death they'd unleashed on Elysium.

I slowed my pace as I neared the warehouse, yet I didn't see anyone guarding the doors. I reached the entrance and peered inside.

Horror struck me like the force of a blow. Inside the warehouse, a large number of bodies littered the ground, all wearing the same drab grey clothing. Golden cantrips lay among them, each of them blank.

I pressed a hand to my mouth. The people who'd been carving the cantrips were *dead.* And from the look of things, they'd been killed by their own cantrips. I looked around, for any signs of a living person who might offer an explanation, and movement pinged on my vision.

One person stood among the dead, unmistakably alive. I approached him, my throat closing up. "You."

Shawn the spirit mage approached me, his eyes alight with malice. "I wondered if I'd run into you or Miles first."

"You got out of jail," I said.

"The vampires let their security slip," he said. "They aren't the only ones, either. I'm here to deliver you to your family."

"Did you kill all those people?" Anger rose inside me like a tidal wave. "Did you use the cantrips against them?"

"They'd outlived their usefulness," he said. "Problem with most people is that they're only too willing to work for you as long as you give them what they want. But there's always a small number who insist on asking for more than we're willing to give. So it was simpler to take them down. They've fulfilled their purpose, after all."

"You're one sick bastard," I said.

I was almost certain he'd been fed that line by Adair… which meant the odds were high that my brother was somewhere nearby, too.

"I'm on the winning team," he said. "Like that family of yours. You know, they're still willing to give you another chance, even after everything you did. Can you believe it?"

"So you broke out of jail to come back to the Family?" I raised an eyebrow. "Didn't know you cared that much for them. I thought you'd be fighting alongside Hawker at the citadel with the other spirit mages. Or did you miss your chance to get in there before they locked the doors?"

"I was more interested in finding your friend Miles," he commented. "I knew the two of you would be together, and that you'd be looking for a way to stop the virus from spreading. So I came here to wait."

"It'd have been awkward if I'd never showed up, wouldn't it?" The guy seemed to be operating according to his own agenda, but there was no way he'd reached this place without running into at least one of the Family. He wouldn't have killed their people without their say-so, as much as he seemed to enjoy pretending to be acting alone.

I heard a rustling sound behind him, and trod forward, trying to see who else might be there. *Adair?*

In a blur of movement, Trix appeared, leaping at Shawn from behind. He startled, tipping over, as the elf slammed his head into the floor.

"You killed them!" he said. "You killed the elves."

My mouth fell open, and I looked more closely at the bodies on the warehouse floor. Some of them *were* elves, as well as humans. Where had he captured them from?

Shawn's hands lit up with spirit magic and he pushed Trix off him. I ran up to help him, the best I could with the broken ribs, and shot a fireball at him. He deflected with a blast of spirit magic, and the two attacks rattled the walls of the warehouse. The place wouldn't stay standing for long, but it'd already served its purpose in the Family's eyes.

Just like the people inside it.

Anger clenched my hands and I fired off another ball of flame, pivoting behind Shawn. The next fireball caught him in the small of his back, while Trix gave him an uppercut to the jaw which sent him sprawling onto the ground.

"Good punch," I said to the elf. "Where's the wyrm?"

"I think it crash-landed," he said. "It'll be dazed, but it should recover soon."

"How did you control it like that?" I asked, unable to help myself.

"Haven't you ever learned how to use elf magic?" he said.

"No," I said. "It's not like I ever had much contact with other elves."

"Oh," he said. "That's a shame. I can teach you, if you like."

The offer took me off guard. I'd always *looked* like an elf, but I'd assumed my mage powers were all I'd had. Yet my resistance to death hadn't come from nowhere.

"I'd like that," I said. "Once we're out of here. Have you seen Miles?"

"No," said Trix. "This place... it gives me a bad feeling."

"Yeah, me too," I said. "I think Adair might have the cure. It's not in the warehouse, but someone came here and ordered everyone to die, and I don't think it was Shawn."

Unless they'd been operating on a previously given instruction, it would have been Adair's persuasive magic which had forced them to end their lives. The Family were one step ahead of me, as per usual.

"Who's Adair?" asked Trix.

"My brother... well, not by blood," I clarified. "Adair... he's half elf, like me, except not nice in the slightest."

That was putting it mildly.

"Oh, that's sad," he said. "I don't have any family left."

My heart clenched. "I'm sorry."

"Why are you apologising?"

Because my family might have killed yours. But I didn't know for sure, and now wasn't the time for that conversation. Sudden movement came from behind us, and we both turned around as Shawn rose to his feet, his gaze strangely blank.

"What the—?"

That's when the other fallen bodies in the warehouse climbed upright as though propelled by an invisible force. In unison, every single one of them turned in our direction.

"Oh, *shit*," I said.

I backed up. So did Trix. While both of us had the advantage of enhanced speed, Miles didn't, and he might be anywhere down here, vulnerable to getting trampled. Or worse, in the hands of the person who was controlling them.

Lex. Her power afforded her control over the dead as well as the living. I hadn't seen her use it for a long time, but nobody else could be responsible.

The Family had already taken one friend from me. I wouldn't let them take another. Especially Miles.

"Run," I told Trix. "Go ahead. Keep an eye out for Miles. I'll take care of Shawn."

He wasn't dead, and for all I knew, he'd regain consciousness any second now. I'd rather put him down permanently first. Not that that would stop Lex's army of zombies, but even an elf would have trouble handling her, with or without Adair fighting at her side.

"I won't run," he said. "I'm going to call the wyrm back, but it might be a little loud. Should I?"

"I'm all out of better ideas," I said. "All right."

He let out a whistle, loud and shrill. I all but jumped out of my skin, not expecting the sudden noise, yet no wyrm appeared.

"Trix, I don't think the wyrm's listening to you."

"Huh." His brow wrinkled. "That should have worked."

The bodies began to walk again, feet dragging on the battered ground. "You know what, let's use my idea and run instead."

As we did so, I shot a fireball over my shoulder to slow some of them down. We cleared the rise of a small hill—and stopped abruptly at the sight of Adair standing in the shadow of a large coiled shape, wearing a lazy smile. The wyrm curled up at his back, its jaws closed around Miles from behind.

22

I faced my brother. "Let him go."

The wyrm kept a firm grip on Miles, while Trix halted, staring up at him.

"Stop," Adair said, and Shawn's unconscious body skidded to a halt behind us. The others, however, kept on moving, zombie-style. Lex was somewhere nearby, all right, but had declined to show her face. Shawn and Adair were quite enough to deal with on their own, though. Not to mention the wyrm.

"What do you want from me?" I demanded. "Where's Lex?"

"She has important business to deal with in Elysium."

"She isn't here?" It didn't take a genius to figure out that she'd gone after the Houses. Or what was left of them.

Miles, meanwhile, remained stuck in the monster's mouth, unable to move. I kept one eye on him as I approached my brother. "So she left you here alone. Again."

"This time you won't beat me," he said. "You'll see there's no other option but to join me."

"Someday you'll take a hint," I replied. "I wouldn't join you if you paid me."

"But would you if it meant saving your friend?" he said.

Dammit. "Let him go. He's not part of the deal."

"We don't have a deal," he said. "And since that other traitorous little friend of yours is dead—"

Fire punched from my fist, right at his face. He barely got a yelp out before he fell flat on his back. The wyrm growled, keeping its jaws locked around Miles's body, but its movements were slow, reluctant. Maybe Trix had had it right. The beast didn't want to hurt him.

Adair climbed to his feet, spitting out curses. "Attacking me won't help you. Your friend is doomed and so are those spirit mage allies of yours back in Elysium."

Miles stiffened, but he was still unable to move without ending up impaled on the wyrm's teeth. "Is that what Lex is doing? Or is that a lie she told you to get you out of the way?"

"She has the cure," he said, with a grin. "And she's taking it to Elysium right now to offer to the Houses in exchange for their cooperation."

Oh, Elements. So that was their plan—bribe the Houses into taking their side. It might well work, too, with no other cure within sight and the Order on the side of the enemy. Meanwhile, our own side was looking pretty damn sparse. In fact, I couldn't even see Trix anywhere. I wouldn't expect him to run off, but I didn't blame him if he had, considering the army of zombies drawing closer to us by the second.

Behind Adair, the air shimmered with an odd light. *Is that another illusion?*

It hadn't been there before, so it wasn't a cantrip, surely. A gasp lodged in my throat as I made out the shapes of a dozen tiny humanoid faces among the lights. The sprites we'd freed from the citadel. Trix popped up behind them, unseen by my brother. *Thanks, Trix.*

Adair tilted his head. "Well? Going to agree to join me?"

"I'd rather eat dirt." I gave a slight nod to Trix, a signal to attack.

At once, the sprites moved in and swarmed over Adair, and he yelped as a conflagration of elemental magic hit him at once: earth, air, fire, water. Even the wyrm cringed out of the way, its maw opening wide enough for Miles to lunge for freedom. Meanwhile, Trix ran over to join us.

"Thanks," I said to the elf. "Where on earth did you find all those sprites?"

"They were hiding among the ruins," he said. "They said you helped free them."

"We did." I watched with satisfaction for a moment as Adair struggled to swat them away, then my gaze found the approaching zombies. "We should go before those guys catch up."

"Agreed." Miles eyed the wyrm, while Trix approached it from the side.

"You okay?" I asked Miles.

"I'm covered in slobber, but I'll live." He tensed when the wyrm moved, but it didn't attack.

At Trix's instructions, the beast lowered its head, and we climbed onto its back.

"Get back here!" Adair snapped, but even he couldn't

mind-control an entire flock of sprites and a wyrm all at once.

The wyrm took to the sky, just as a bolt of light shot up behind us. I twisted around, seeing the citadel in the wasteland igniting.

"What's going on over there?" I said. "That place can't still be active now the sprites are free."

"Unless Hawker got in there and fixed the transporter," added Miles. "Or Shawn. Dickhead's been out here for a while."

Not to mention Adair. The wyrm flew more slowly than before, and if Adair got away from those sprites, he'd catch up to us, no problem. We needed to get to Elysium and find Lex and the cure before it was too late. If she'd manipulated the Houses into pledging their loyalty to her in exchange for ridding the city of those cantrips, the Family would have more power than they'd ever had before.

"Speaking of Shawn, didn't you want to finish him off?" I said.

"Nah, he's not worth the effort," Miles said. "Why'd they kill off the people in the warehouse?"

"Because they already fulfilled their purpose." A lump grew in my throat. "They created those cantrips to spread the virus around the city, and now the Family has the only cure."

We flew low over the rooftops of Elysium, where I spotted a flash of red moving among the houses. Lex. I'd know that bright dress of hers anywhere. It might've surprised me to see her moving on foot, but she had no need to fear an attack. Nothing could touch her.

"That's her?" said Miles, leaning over my shoulder.

"I have to face her alone," I said. "If you can bring backup, though, it'd be appreciated."

"Bria, you can't go down there alone."

"I won't watch you die." Watching the wyrm bite into him had been bad enough. I wouldn't lose anyone else today. "Besides, she won't kill me. She can't."

"She can still make you into her puppet."

"Not as effectively as Adair," I said. "Also, she doesn't know we have a few hundred sprites on our side. If you can find a way to get them to come and help, I can stall her until then. The important part is getting the cure. I can hold out until then."

"I hope you're right," said Miles.

"Okay… we're going down." Trix steered the wyrm lower, and I leaned over the edge until Lex looked up and saw me. I gave a little wave, to be rewarded by her expression of incredulity.

Without taking my eyes off her, I jumped down from the wyrm's back and landed in front of her. "So you have the cure, do you?"

"Bria," she said. "I'm glad you came to see me. I was afraid you were going to run again."

"You're messed up," I said. "Where is the cure, then?"

"Roth has it," she replied. "When he delivers it to the Houses, he and I will be heroes."

"You're the one who unleashed the viral cantrips to begin with!" I said, my heart sinking hard. *He has it. He's way ahead of us.* "You can't rewrite history."

"Can't we?" she said softly.

A spasm of anger shook me. They could do exactly that. They'd even rewritten *my* history, erasing all traces of where I'd truly come from before they'd got their claws in my life.

"I know about what you did to the elves," I said. "You can't call yourselves heroes after you burned down their homes and helped the mages destroy what was left of them."

"What does it matter?" she said. "They're ancient history."

"No, they aren't," I said. "Not as long as I'm here."

"You're no elf," she said. "You don't even remember where you came from."

"I do remember." My voice rose. "That town over there. By the citadel. That's where you captured me from. It's true, isn't it?"

She studied me. "I thought you were too young to remember."

"That's what you'd like to think." I swallowed down the scalding tears threatening to rise to the surface. "You didn't care either way, did you? You killed them for no good reason at all."

I'd always known on an instinctual level that the Family had never been the loving parents they'd pretended to be for most of my childhood, but not that they'd done anything as grotesque as to massacre my birth family along with everyone else who'd lived in their town. As if that wasn't enough, they'd then taken me captive, erased my history, and made me believe that I'd only ever been what they'd made me to be.

"I wouldn't worry your head about it," she said. "The elves are gone."

"Then where did you get the ones at the warehouse from?" I demanded. "Where did you capture them?"

She tilted her head. "Why the sudden interest? It's hardly relevant to your current dilemma."

It is. I might still fear what she could do to me, but my rage and disgust outweighed my wariness, and knowing what she'd done to my former home set a fire burning in my veins.

I would take great pleasure from crushing the life out of her with my bare hands.

"Tell me where Roth is, and I might let you walk away in one piece this time."

She gave a laugh. "You thwarted me by chance last time, nothing more. Besides, those cantrips have already spread throughout the city. The Houses are desperate enough to sign a deal with anyone in exchange for a cure. You've already lost."

I took a step towards her, and a piercing light shone from the distant shape of Elysium's citadel.

"It looks like the battle is over," she said. "I wonder if any of your friends survived?"

Shit. The battle was over? I couldn't tell the victor from this far away, but if the transporter remained active, it didn't look good. I needed to finish this fast.

While her attention was on the citadel, I conjured fire to my hands once more. Lex studied, no longer laughing. "So you really want to do this, Bria? To the person who raised you?"

"You *stole* me from my real family." An inferno coalesced in my hands, searing the ground below our feet. "I'm through playing games with you."

23

"Very well," she said, dismissing the flames I threw at her with a wave of her hand. "We'll settle this once and for all."

She made a twisting motion with her hand. At once, my own hand moved in unison with hers, until the bone strained. Pain ripped up my arm and I bit back a scream, determined not to cry out. I just had to hang on until backup arrived, or until I found a way to get through her defences. My head swam with dizziness, and I gritted my teeth to keep from passing out from the pain.

My feet swayed, reminding me the ground beneath us was still unsteady from the earth mages' tunnelling. *Maybe I can work with that.* I clenched my teeth against another sharp stab of pain, then I used my free hand to throw a fireball at the ground.

Flames burned the soil away and shook the earth below our feet, forcing Lex to brace her hand on the wall to steady herself. The moment the pain lifted, my next fireball hit her in the face. She yelled in shock and pain as it burned through her flesh straight to the bone.

She'd recover, quicker than I'd like, but I had to find the man who'd raised me and get that cure from him before it was too late for the entire city. I'd worry about Lex and Adair later.

I took off at a run, the ground flying away beneath my feet. Roth would be somewhere near the Houses, I was sure, but hardly anyone was out on the street at all. They must have run for shelter when shit had hit the fan. Sensible, given the golden cantrips lying in the streets.

At the first opportunity, I clambered up onto the rooftops and then leapt from one sloped roof to the next until the world became nothing but a breathless blur. When I spotted a familiar landmark, I landed on my feet on bare ground littered with bodies. The area surrounding the Houses was eerily silent, and the citadel's light had died down enough that I knew the battle was over. The assassins must have withdrawn, leaving the deadly cantrips to do their work. As I approached the citadel, it lit up again, in a single blink. A signal. An invitation to enter.

I walked up to the door, which opened at my touch. The room within was littered with bodies, too, yet silence prevailed. I climbed the staircase, my heart beating fast.

When I opened the door to the upper room, one lone man stood alone next to the transporter. Like Lex, Roth hadn't aged a day. His features suggested elven heritage, his hair was glossy black, his suit impeccable enough that he might've walked into that gathering in London and not stood out in the slightest.

It's true. They've won.

But I didn't see Liv's body among the dead, nor the Elemental Soldiers. Roth tilted his head, a smile playing on his mouth.

"There you are," he said. "I thought you'd recognise my signal."

"Give me the cure," I warned.

"I have something more important," he said. "I found a friend of yours."

Someone stepped into view. Tay, her hands limp, her eyes blank. Still dead… yet Lex's final act had been to reanimate her. Zombie-Tay walked over to me, her face blank, and halted in front of me. There was no life left in her, I knew, but part of me balked at the idea of striking her down all the same.

"I wonder why she gave her life for you," Roth said softly. "She had so much to give us, yet she threw it all away."

"Stop talking." I walked past her, conjuring a fireball to my hand. "I know she's dead. She can't feel pain. But you can."

We circled one another, and he held up a cantrip with a smile. "This is the cure. Want it? All you have to do is agree to work for me."

I could see where this was going. "You're manipulating me. You have zero intention of following through."

"I plan to keep my word," he said. "I don't want to argue with you, Bria. Despite the way you've shunned your upbringing and brought disaster upon us, you aren't our enemy. You're our ally, and I hope you'll choose to fight by our side before the choice is made for you."

"You mean before you force me to 'choose' to help

you." My hands clenched. "Yeah, no thanks. You can get stuffed."

"Shame," he said. "I think you need an incentive. You see this machine here? You know what it does?"

"Amplifies any cantrip inside it," I said. "Not news to me."

"Any cantrip." He indicated a slot on the side, in which a cantrip had already been placed. "Know what this one does?"

I couldn't see all the markings on its surface, but I saw enough to make ice flood my veins. "The virus..."

"Exactly," he said. "This handy device amplifies the effects of any cantrip, including ones of our own creation. If, say, there was a cure for the magical virus currently flooding the city, then it would be possible to spread its effects so that nobody else would die if they touched one. On the other hand, if you were to refuse to cooperate with me..."

The virus. It was lethal enough on its own. How much worse would it be if it was amplified via the same machine which linked the citadels together?

On the other hand, if I agreed to join him, I'd once again give him and Lex total domination over my life. I'd be knowingly letting them turn me into a weapon to use against anyone... including my allies.

My gaze fell on the machine, and the absence of glowing lights on its surface caught my attention. "Did Liv and the others drain the batteries out of that thing? Looks pretty dead to me."

"Oh, that doesn't matter," he said. "When the life force of any living creature might be used as a battery, our source is limitless."

Nausea flooded me. "Like those sprites… and humans, too."

"Life energy," he said softly. "The same source spirit mages use. We're not so unalike."

I recalled the sprites trapped in that cage and fought back the urge to vomit. "I don't see anyone living in here aside from the two of us."

Ryan and the others were supposed to be getting hold of a cantrip to turn the machine off, but it already looked dormant. The dim light of the transporter told me I wouldn't be able to use it to hop through and find the others, either, but the viral cantrip inside it would activate the instant he turned it on.

Roth smiled. "I know what you're thinking. I'd advise you not to challenge me. If your friends are on their way to help you, they're within range of this lethal cantrip, too."

"It's no use to you without a battery."

"I wouldn't speak too soon," he said. "I could make you turn it on yourself."

He wasn't even kidding. Adair could influence your actions and decisions. Lex could influence your body. Roth? His power was even more sinister, if possible. Not one I had the ability to resist. But turning my back on him now was out of the question.

Out of the corner of my eye, I saw a shadow stir, and I readied myself. "Try it."

At once, a wave of sadness hit me, pushing me to my knees. Tears blurred my vision, and the sight of Tay's lifeless body nearby only poured fuel on my grief. Gasps shook my body as the impact of everything I'd lost hit me like a train, combined with the remorseless pain Roth's power inflicted on me.

Roth's talent brought him absolute control over my emotions, but I hadn't counted on my own buried pain aiding him in bringing me down. I could hardly move, my body trembling all over. *Dammit. I won't be brought down by this.*

I raised my tear-streaked face and saw a shadow detach itself from the wall and fall over Roth from behind. The dark form of a lich moved closer, and when he turned around, shock momentarily flickered through his features.

Bet you didn't count on one of my allies already being here, did you?

I still had people left to protect. People counting on me. People like Harper.

The unbearable flood of sadness lifted enough for me to raise my hand and fire a blast of magic into him. Roth staggered, the flames eating away at his fancy clothes and scorching the skin off his bones. He let out a horrible laugh, the skin peeling back from his teeth and making him look even more grotesque than usual.

Then he slammed a palm into a button on the machine. At once, light spun across its surface. My heart gave a lurch when the cantrip in the slot on its side ignited, too.

"I lied," he said softly. "There was already enough power left inside it to set off the virus."

"You bastard," I said.

"If anything, I did you a favour," he responded. "As long as you remain in here, you'll be unaffected. Even if you leave, the virus will never result in a permanent death for you. The others, however, won't be so lucky."

Roth gave a triumphant smile laced with pain, and then he hopped through the transporter and vanished.

Harper floated over to me, the illusion of her face flickering into view. "Shit. Did he set off the virus?"

"Yes… and he took the cure with him." The horror of what he'd unleashed sank in as I stared at the spot where he'd vanished. Then my head snapped up when Zombie-Tay walked over to me again. Impossibly, she was still standing, though no alertness shone in her eyes.

"I'm sorry," I said to her. "I guess we'll all be joining you soon. I mean, I can stay in here forever while everyone else dies, but I'm not all that keen on the idea, to tell you the truth."

Tay made no move to attack me. She wasn't under anyone's control, not anymore, but she wasn't alive, either. She'd keep standing only until the remnants of Lex's magic faded.

"I'm sorry," I said to her. "I know you tried to warn me. You tried…"

"What's that in her hand?" said Harper.

I looked down, catching sight of a gleam in the palm of Tay's right hand. I reached for it, and her arm jerked forward, pressing the cantrip into my palm. I looked at its marked surface, disbelief flickering through me. She'd had the cure with her all along. "Thanks, Tay."

I knew she couldn't hear me, not really, but she might just have saved us after all.

Harper moved in behind me. "Bria…"

The transporter lit up again, and several people appeared on the platform. Ryan and Trix, followed by

Miles and several of the sprites we'd saved from the trap in the other citadel.

"There you are!" said Miles. "We've been flying all over the city looking for you."

"Don't move," I warned. "Roth… he put the virus into the machine."

"Doesn't look like it's switched on," Ryan remarked. "This place burned up in the fight."

"He said there was enough power left in there to activate it." I held up the cantrip in my hand. "I have the cure. I thought you lost the battle. This place was empty…"

"Hawker fled," Ryan said. "Along with what was left of his army."

"So did Roth," I said. "He hopped through the transporter. Lex was in a bad way, but she's probably run back to the house by now."

"Adair did the same," Miles said. "Once the sprites had finished picking at him, anyway. We'd have gone after him, but I was worried when I couldn't find you. I ran into Ryan…"

"I was on my way from the Death King's castle," Ryan said, holding up a cantrip. "Got this from Devon."

"It's a magical neutraliser which will block the node," Miles said in explanation. "It should be enough to cut off the link with London."

"Damn, nice going," I said. "So—r"

"Ah, shit." Miles looked down at his hand, which had begun to break out in blisters.

"Dammit." I grabbed for the cantrip in the slot on the machine, tugging it out with my fingers, but the damage was already done. Ryan's face had begun to blister, too. They'd already been exposed to the virus.

With frantic movements, I turned to the cantrip Tay had given me and flicked the switch on the side of it. When I thrust it into Miles's hands, the marks began to fade immediately. I then grabbed Ryan's hand and did the same, releasing a relieved sigh when the rash vanished from their palms.

"Thanks," said the Air Element. "Damn. I didn't see anyone outside, but if they were out while that cantrip was active…"

"I know," I said, with a grimace. "But even if not, anyone who picks up any of those cantrips in the streets is liable to fall under the same effects. I'll do it."

I shoved the cure cantrip into the side of the machine, but the light was dead. It *had* powered down. Worse, the blisters were creeping onto my own hand. I slammed my palm onto the button which turned on the machine, but to no avail.

"It's dead?" said Ryan.

I swore. "I can't turn on the machine without a power source, and Roth… he hinted that it's powered by life energy. Human or sprites. But there's nobody here but us."

"Did you say sprites?" Dex flew up to me. "There's a few of us here."

I shook my head. "I wouldn't ask you to do that."

"You sure?" Miles said. "I don't think they have to be trapped in a cage to power the transporter."

Not like I had anything to lose by asking. "Okay, Dex. Can you check with the others?"

He flitted over to another transparent figure hovering in the corner, and a glowing water sprite zipped over to join us. "You want us to power the machine?"

"Only if you don't mind," I added. "I need a power source to activate the cure for the virus. It won't help the people who've already died, but it'll stop anyone else getting hurt and give them time to get those cantrips off the streets. Can any of you lend a hand? I promise I won't hurt you."

"Don't worry," Dex told the sprites, several of whom had gathered to listen. "We can trust her."

The group of sprites grew larger, gathering above the glowing machinery. Magic spun around them, forming a kind of shield which ignited the buttons on the machine almost immediately. Bolstered, I hit the button again. The instant I did so, the air ignited with magic.

The blisters faded from my hand. As the cantrip's effects spread, I noticed Tay had fallen to the ground, the effects of Lex's magic finally giving out. It was too late to save her, but with her final moments, she'd saved countless lives.

Now we had to make her sacrifice count.

"We have to get the rest of those cantrips off the streets," I said. "Once we do, we'll bury them where they can't be found. Then we'll put in that neutraliser spell of yours, all right?"

"I'll hang onto it," Ryan offered. "Once we put it in here, we'll have to leave it there in case Hawker's people come back."

So they'd survived. "It's not over, then."

"No, it isn't over, but you still saved everyone," said Miles.

My eyes burned with tears as I looked at Tay's body. "She's the one who gave me the cure. She saved us all, in the end."

24

Upon our eventual return to the Spirit Agents' base, we burned Tay's body along with the others whose lives had been lost in the battle. I knew she would have preferred it that way. She'd hated the idea of being buried, and it seemed fitting to scatter her ashes in the city where the two of us had made our home.

The other Elemental Soldiers didn't kick up a fuss about me staying behind for her cremation rather than joining them back at the Death King's castle after we'd finished helping with the clean-up in Elysium, which I appreciated. While we'd helped to clear every infected cantrip we found off the streets, the Houses of the Elements remained in a state of shock and would do for a long while yet.

Upon my return to the castle, I half-expected the Death King to call me in to berate me for failing to stop the Family's plot. Instead, he didn't ask to speak to me at all. The following day, Miles showed up at the castle with the news that the node linking the citadel with London had been officially turned off.

"The Order's not happy, though," he commented. "They're trying to pin the blame for the attacks on *us*. The Spirit Agents."

"They what?" I said. "How'd they figure that one out? Didn't anyone see Hawker was the person who massacred everyone?"

"There were few surviving witnesses," said Miles. "The Order hates spirit mages. I know they're under the control of the enemy at the moment, but blaming us for everything has always worked for them before. Keeps everyone's attention off the real issues."

"Bastards," I said. "They should be more worried about what happens if Hawker and *his* band of spirit mages try to start another war."

"There is that," Miles said. "For the record, I have zero intention of joining them. In case it wasn't obvious already. I didn't even know it was possible to do what that sick fucker Hawker did in the citadel. Trapping sprites in cages."

"And unleashing a deadly virus on the city." I grimaced. "Though that was more likely the Family's idea. They got away, too."

"We'll get them next time, Bria."

I'd expected such a response from him, but his confidence didn't dispel my unease. Opening up to him would put more at risk than I'd been willing to admit. And then there was Adair to consider. He'd held Tay under his command, and I didn't trust him not to try the same with Miles, too.

I drew in a breath. "I can't guarantee they won't target you to get at me, like they did with Tay."

"They're welcome to try," he said. "We beat them before. You did it twice, even."

"Barely." I broke my gaze from his. "They're worse than I ever knew. I'm pretty sure they helped wipe out the elves, then captured their children and created people like me to assist them in their scheme to take over the Parallel. That's the legacy they're trying to hand over to me. And if you get involved with me... that's what you'll get drawn into."

He tilted his head on one side at the words *if you get involved with me.* Because while a large part of me wanted to warn him to run for the hills, he'd had ample time to do exactly that. Yet after everything, he was still here.

As though he'd sensed my thoughts, he said, "I'm already involved in this, Bria. Ever since Shawn started his bullshit scheme to have me killed, I've been in on this. And the best part of the whole fiasco is that it brought me face to face with you."

My face burned. "You've met my family. Doesn't it bother you at all, knowing I'm linked so closely to people like that?"

"You what?" he said. "They might have raised you, but you aren't like them in the slightest."

"By some miracle." I'd be lying if I said I hadn't had a screwed-up childhood, even if the true extent of the Family's depravity hadn't hit me until way into adulthood. "I can credit Tay with most of that. When we met in the House of Fire, she helped me see the impact of what the Family's cantrips were doing to the people they were used on. Tay wasn't the only one, but it was her story which taught me that not everyone grew up like I did."

When I'd met her, part of me had still been Lex's shadow. I'd been riven with guilt over what I'd done to her and Roth, and I'd been unable to see past the blinders they'd put on me even after I'd set their estate ablaze and left their corpses in the ruin. The impact of the lives they'd ruined hadn't sunk in until the House of Fire had locked me up, and in the process, I'd met Tay. She'd been the one constant in my life since my escape from the Family, and now I was going to have to learn to live without her.

Miles's eyes shone with sympathy. "I'm still impressed. You were a kid, yet you managed to break away from all that."

"Not completely." I looked away. "They still want to recruit me. I'm not sure they'll ever give up on that. Now they're walking free, and the Houses… they're in no shape to stand up to another attack."

The enemy might be in retreat, for now, but the infected cantrips wouldn't be the end of their attempts to gain domination over the city of Elysium. I had little doubt about that.

"The Houses aren't your problem," Miles told me. "As for the Family…"

"Nobody can beat them," I said. "Not permanently. They're functionally immortal. I should have guessed they stole that ability from the elves along with everything else they took."

His jaw tightened. "There's always a way. Even liches can die. And spirit mages. You just need to find their weaknesses. Your elf friend might know."

"Who, Trix?" I said. "I guess he did promise me lessons in elf magic."

The elves weren't as extinct as they'd appeared, even with their strongholds destroyed… and if I wanted to find a permanent way to be rid of the Family, I might have to look in unlikely places.

"It's worth a try," said Miles. "I have to get back to the others. See you soon, okay?"

"Sure." I leaned in as he wrapped me in a firm hug and kissed me, temporarily dispelling my lingering grief and guilt over the horrors of the previous day.

While he left the castle grounds, I spotted Trix and Ryan near the gates. The former gave me a wave from the back of a zombie horse, while the Air Element looked altogether more relaxed than they usually did.

"Hey." I walked over to them. "Made friends with Neddie?"

The zombie horse, upon seeing me, tipped Trix off its back, and he landed with a thump in the mud. "Ow."

"Sorry," I said. "He doesn't like me."

"Maybe it's elves he has a problem with," Ryan said. "You're back, then?"

"I never left," I said. "Besides, I thought His Deathly Highness wasn't giving orders. He wasn't injured in the battle, was he?"

"No," said Ryan. "I haven't spoken to him, either, but I've been running back and forth from Elysium since the battle. Checking up on the citadels, you know. Oh, there's Liv."

I turned to see her descending the steps at the front of the castle, talking to Devon, and walked over to meet them. "Devon's nullifying cantrip saved us back there."

"It did," Liv said, "but it's only a temporary measure. Those citadels are built to last and so are their machines."

"Hey, Bria." Dex flew over our heads. "Liv wanted to ask you to join our D&D group."

"I—what?" Liv spluttered. "I didn't say that."

"I did," said Dex. "Right, Devon?"

"We're open to anyone, technically," said Devon. "Unless you object, Liv. Ryan plays with us. We're still working on convincing Cal and Felicity."

"Uh-huh," I said, baffled by this turn of events. "I'll join in if someone can explain to me how to play."

Liv still looked disgruntled, but before she could say another word, the castle door opened and a lich floated out. "The Death King wants to speak to you, Bria."

"Me?" I frowned.

"Alone?" said Liv, her own expression a mirror of mine.

"Yes," said the lich.

All right, then. I walked into the castle and approached the dais at the back of the hall. The Death King wore an illusion of his human face, which made him look a little less sinister than usual. Or maybe it was me. After all, I'd faced my Family again—all three of them—and escaped intact. Even the King of the Dead would have a hard time scaring me after that.

"Hey, Death King," I said. "Um, sorry I never got the Houses to cooperate with you."

"I believe you dealt with the difficult situation the best you could," he said. "The Houses have a lot of rebuilding to do, if they survive, and I believe they need to rethink their relationship with the Order."

"Does the Order even still exist anymore?"

"For now," he said. "As for the Houses, I believe that they can be persuaded to join my side, given enough time."

"Let me guess… you want *me* to convince them they're better off teaming up with you."

"Only after they've had time to rebuild," he said. "First, however, we might need the assistance of the elves."

That, I hadn't seen coming. "Which elves? I don't even know where most of them live."

"I think we'll find ourselves in need of their help," he said. "And I think you have the skills you need to find them."

My mouth fell open. Okay, if Trix had survived, others had, too, but I was way in over my head when it came to tracking down the others. I hadn't known the Death King had even been considering them as potential allies. Did he know what the Family had done to them?

As he continued to watch me, expecting an answer, I said, "I can promise to try, that's all."

The fight with the Family wasn't over. All three members walked free, while they had the skills to amass an army if they had their way. All I had was a ragtag group of allies, living and dead, a heritage I'd barely begun to uncover… and so much more to lose than before.

This was war… and I'd take it to the Family on my own terms this time.

ABOUT THE AUTHOR

Emma is the New York Times and USA Today Bestselling author of the Changeling Chronicles urban fantasy series.

Emma spent her childhood creating imaginary worlds to compensate for a disappointingly average reality, so it was probably inevitable that she ended up writing fantasy novels. When she's not immersed in her own fictional universes, Emma can be found with her head in a book or wandering around the world in search of adventure.

Find out more about Emma's books at www.emmaladams.com.

www.ingramcontent.com/pod-product-compliance
Lightning Source LLC
Chambersburg PA
CBHW020746190726
48285CB00006B/1898